The
Accidental Father

The
Accidental Father
GREG WILLIAMS

First published in Great Britain in 2009 by Orion Books,
an imprint of The Orion Publishing Group Ltd
Orion House, 5 Upper Saint Martin's Lane
London WC2H 9EA

An Hachette UK Company

1 3 5 7 9 10 8 6 4 2

A CIP catalogue record for this book is
available from the British Library.

ISBN (Hardback) 978 0 7528 7430 2
ISBN (Trade Paperback) 978 0 7528 9201 6

Typeset by Deltatype Ltd, Birkenhead, Merseyside

Printed and bound in the UK by CPI Mackays, Chatham ME5 8TD

The Orion Publishing Group's policy is to use papers that are natural,
renewable and recyclable products and made from wood grown in sustainable
forests. The logging and manufacturing processes are expected to
conform to the environmental regulations of the country of origin.

All efforts have been made to trace the copyright holder of the
song lyrics to 'Studda Step' by Biz Markie as reproduced.
The publisher will be pleased to correct any omissions.

For my family.

Acknowledgements

As ever, I'm indebted to my peerless agent, Jonny Geller, and the other fine people at Curtis Brown, including Kate Cooper, Tally Garner and Alice Lutyens. I'm also very fortunate to work alongside the accomplished folk at Orion, amongst them the ever-enthusiastic Jon Wood, Jade Chandler and Gaby Young. And, of course, my wonderful family who, every day, give me good reason to laugh and to love.

Prologue

I had no idea what time it was when I got to the high street. I guessed that it was around eight thirty. The schools had yet to open their doors, but there was plenty of traffic on the roads; mums en route to drop off their precious offspring, I expected. Stumbling along the drenched pavement in a daze, my legs shaky and my feet unsure of themselves, I kept my head down. I didn't want to engage anyone, although I imagined that my dishevelled, careless appearance was the subject of speculation by passers-by.

I was a wreck.

I had barely slept in three days; my bed was a twisted nest of discontent. I'd tried all the tricks – a couple of glasses of Scotch, keeping the bedroom cool, getting up to break the relentless churning inside my skull – but the mental bustle continued. It was unstoppable, obstinate, implacable. No distraction was enough to throw it from its orbit. Everything else was inconsequential, senseless.

I looked down at my feet – leaves carpeted the pavement. They had lain there long enough to decompose slightly and then be turned slick and sticky by the rain that had been falling on and off for the past couple of hours. Cars hissed by, their windscreen-wipers moving back and forth metronomically.

I noted the slapping sound the wipers made as they moved from side to side. Some people might have heard a thunk-thunk, but I heard something different. The noise echoed with my thoughts, conjuring a name that I kept repeating to myself:

Cait-lin

Thunk-thunk

Cait-lin

Thunk-thunk

Cait-lin.

It had been two days since she'd gone. Two days of checking my phone in case she'd called, two days of hoping that the footsteps in the front yard might be hers, two days of gnawing regret. I looked up to cross the road. The rain made the people on the other side indistinct as they hurried about their business beneath hats and umbrellas.

But wait: within the haze there was someone I recognised, someone who attracted my attention, her walk as familiar to me as my own. As I focused on her it was as if my sight had switched from black-and-white to Technicolor. Everything about her was intrinsic to my own identity. It was Caitlin. It was my daughter.

I called to her, but she didn't respond, picking her way through the raincoat-clad passers-by.

'Caitlin!' I called again, but she carried on walking as I hurried along my side of the street, calling over the noise of the cars and the downpour.

'Caitlin!'

We walked in parallel. I was waving to her now, trying to catch her attention.

And then she stepped towards the road, making to cross it.

'Caitlin!'

She looked through the rain at me, her face doubtful as she stepped from the kerb.

Even as I did it, I knew that I had distracted her.

There was a pulse-quickening squealing of breaks, a hollow thud and a sickening, hissing silence.

I ran across the road to see my daughter, her limbs twisted

in rag-doll shapes, the rain diluting the blood spreading across the road.

She lay there, perfectly still. My love, her face undaunted.

PART ONE

Chapter 1

My desire to enter the commercial realm began innocently enough. I was eating a poached egg on toast (surely the most inoffensive meal known to mankind) one Thursday morning when my wife Amanda crashed into the kitchen. At times like this she was not so much a person but rather an amalgam of hair, perfume, breasts, heels and haste. She tore a packet of Pop-Tarts open with her teeth.

'Shit,' she exclaimed.

'What?' I asked.

She ignored me. This was not unusual.

'Is that the mouthwatering new flavour of Pop-Tarts?' I asked, looking up from the sports pages.

'Smudged my bloody lipstick,' she snapped back.

Amanda devoured the Pop-Tart, taking small bites and washing them down with a cup of lukewarm tea that I had made an hour earlier.

'Ugh.' She winced, clearly disgusted.

'I take it you're not going to bother toasting that delicious, nutritious breakfast.'

'MmMMMMmmmMMMMMM,' Amanda said.

I looked up at her expectantly. 'I'm not entirely sure what you just said. Did you tell me that you saw a unicorn in the garden?' I looked out at the well-tended lawn and herbaceous borders (courtesy of, I hated to admit, my wife) behind our red-brick Victorian semi. The day was strangely bright, despite the blanket of grey cloud rolling rapidly overhead.

'I'm late,' Amanda said impatiently.

'Oh, really?' I returned to my paper. 'Holy shit.'

Amanda clucked her tongue in disapproval, clearly irritated that I'd failed to acknowledge her frenzy of urgency.

'You could at least have made me a fresh cup of tea.'

'I did,' I replied, chewing my toast slowly. I was distracted by the preview of that evening's Champions' League games. 'An hour ago.'

'It's cold, Alex,' she said reproachfully. She moved towards the breakfast bar, still fussing with her blouse. 'What's that?' she asked, picking up a brochure that was at the bottom of a pile of post.

'Nothing you're interested in. It's research,' I explained.

'But what is it, though?' persisted Amanda. The concise answer was coffee-making porn, but I chose not to engage with the subject as Amanda quickly flipped through the pages of espresso makers, roasters and bean grinders.

'Whatever, Trevor,' Amanda said – I had no idea where she picked up these seemingly up-to-the-minute sayings – before lighting a cigarette and puffing furiously at it. Amanda smoked curiously thin menthol cigarettes that she ordered online. I had always been told that menthol cigarettes made you sterile, but I wasn't sure if that was just a myth: menthol cigarettes were popular with rappers, and rappers had *tons* of kids.

'Sorry,' she said, clearly not that remorseful.

'Can you open a window or something?' I complained, wafting the smoke away from my eggs.

'I'm in a rush, sweetheart,' Amanda said in between drags. Her use of the word 'sweetheart' didn't fool me. As far as she was concerned, it could mean anything – least of all that I had a sweet heart. I didn't have one, and I doubted whether my wife thought that I did. I stood up and opened the back door. Cold morning air rushed in. It was too much. I pulled it closed. By the time I had turned around Amanda had put the cigarette out, crushing it on a saucer on the breakfast bar.

'Bye, sweetheart,' (again with the sweetheart!) she said without a backwards glance – she was busy walking for the front door while digging in her bag for breath-freshening gum. All that remained of her was a trace of vivid-coloured lipstick on a mashed, still-smoking butt.

I caught the 8.27 to Waterloo and, as per fucking usual, I had to stand. I watched a woman nodding off to sleep, her mouth open, her double chin wobbling beneath her rouged lips, and felt faintly nauseous. I was sure that, if the woman could have seen herself, she would have fled into the sulphurous embrace of veganism and some radical form of yoga involving overheated rooms and strangely youthful middle-aged 'gurus' sporting uni-tards. Within the carriage, as it rattled through the ratty edges of London, there was a feeling of malaise, of compulsion. It felt like no one was bouncing through suburban London volun-tarily, they had all been taken captive. In one corner a man in a poorly ironed shirt and shiny, ragtag jacket read through his post before shredding the portions containing his address and stuffing them in a Styrofoam coffee cup that rested on a narrow tray just below the window. He surreptitiously stuffed the rub-bish under his seat, believing that he hadn't been observed. I had half a mind to expose him – litter lout! – but was convinced that I'd look like a bigger tit than him. Still, if you allow people to get away with that kind of thing, there's no telling where it might end . . .

God, I was bored.

I used to read the newspaper. I used to read books. Anything to make it seem like I was doing something useful, like the time wasn't being stolen from me. Now I didn't bother. It was too hard trying to wrestle the paper with its sections and supplements;

and anyway, the journey blurred into the office, which blurred into lunch, which blurred into the afternoon ...

It was all tedium, all the time.

I muscled my way off the train at Waterloo and through the migrating herd of commuters to the Bakerloo Line. I just wanted to bellow, '*Moooooo!*' A short march north to a grimy street just off Leicester Square brought me to the strip-lit and carpet-tiled offices of Knowles & Strauss, the travel agency where I had scaled the upper canopy of the corporate jungle and been appointed chief accountant almost three years ago. It felt like ten.

I swiped my ID card and pushed open the door to the office before greeting the thin-haired Scottish receptionist in the cheap shoes. I sometimes fantasised about her when I was getting it on with Amanda. That was how low I had sunk – a sordid crush on a workmate. Even my fantasies were clichés.

After significant amounts of bill paying, YouTubing and other forms of time-wasting, I settled down to take a look at a pile of vendor statements that needed my approval. Jesus. What a load of shit. Thank God that some smart arse had come up with a back-office software system that made my job something of a doddle. As long as I managed to stay awake for a few hours during the day (not including lunchtime) this was the kind of job that only an idiot could screw up. Which wasn't to say that I didn't consider it a possibility: the general tedium of the position could induce a coma in all but the most studious and ambitious of employees.

But I wasn't studious. And I was no longer ambitious, although I hated myself for surrendering to this shortcoming. As I munched my way through the latest 'sandwich of the week' from Pret A Manger, filled in my entry for the office Grand National sweepstake or collected my things before dashing out the door to get to Waterloo for the 5.56 p.m., I could not deny the undeniable: I had become that which I had always wanted to avoid – a queue mutterer. A service whiner. An escalator stander. Who would ever have thought it?

My walk home from the station was usually the happiest moment of the day. The stirrings of summer meant that there was blossom on the trees, the laughter of kids in back gardens, the smoke of it's-not-raining-so-we-might-as-well-light-it barbecues. It was Friday, so Amanda would go out with a couple of her cronies from work, sink a few bottles of Chablis and then come home pissed as a newt, stumble into the bedroom, wake me up and demand sex.

Which was okay with me. As routine as the sex was, at least we were still having it, which seemed not to be the case for a number of my mates with kids. Anticipating this, I thought that I would be best advised to pay a visit to my local for a couple of nerve-steadiers. Having sex with a drunk person is no fun if you're sober, but plenty of fun if you're not.

'Evening, Geoff,' I said.

'Ah, greetings, Lamb Chop,' said Geoff, the landlord, who had a habit of bestowing monikers on his customers that bore absolutely no relation to their character or behaviour. These nicknames changed almost as regularly as the bar towels that were neatly lined up on the counter, ready for a Friday-night pounding (in much the same way that I was).

I ignored the Lamb Chop comment. I was pretty sure that the last time I came into the Royal Oak I was the Cappuccino Kid. There was clearly a culinary theme developing.

'What can I get you?' asked Geoff. He gestured at the rows of bottles behind the counter in a way that I had once seen a salesman in a Moroccan bazaar gesture towards his wares.

'I'll have a pint of Heineken please, Geoff,' I said.

11

'A pint of Heineken,' he repeated, as if announcing the arrival of a society couple at a ball.

'Bag of cheese and onion as well.'

'Pushing the boat out, are we?' said Geoff, pouring the pint. He placed it on the bar in front of me and leaned down to retrieve a blue packet of crisps.

'Well, it is Friday,' I said, ironically.

'That'll be fifty quid, please,' said Geoff, ignoring the comment. Geoff never gave regulars the exact price of drinks. It was his thing. He was as likely to ask for 23 pence.

I handed over the money and, while Geoff was still at the till getting the change, took my drink and the crisps over to a corner table. Coming to the Royal Oak was a bittersweet affair. I liked that the landlord was pleased to see me, but I didn't always want to get into a conversation with a man who seemed to model his manner and banter on a Radio 1 breakfast DJ from the mid seventies. It surprised me that Geoff had never called me a 'pilchard' or referred to the 'falling-down water' that he sold.

I returned to get my change from Geoff, who subsequently entered a spirited instructional discussion with his Italian and Polish chefs as to the ideal Yorkshire pudding recipe. It was soon evident that Geoff was the only one of the three who had a strong opinion about the subject. Friday-night bliss: a newly poured pint, the fresh evening paper laid out on the well-worn pub table and no reason to get out of bed the following day. The evening stretched before me with seemingly unending promise.

'Evening, mate.' It was Mike Thomas, perhaps the only person in town whose presence did not make me sag from the sheer effort of engagement.

'Hello, Mike,' I said, relieved to be rescued from having to read about some TV company who thought that it would be a marketing triumph if they broke the world record for simultaneously bouncing space hoppers. Some clown in marketing was getting a pat on the back for dreaming up schemes like that. It was what was wrong with the world.

'Fancy a pint, mate?'

'That'd be nice,' said Mike. 'Stella, please.'

I went back to the bar.

'Ah!' announced Geoff, 'the return of the prodigal customer. What can I do you for, sir?'

I returned with the pint and set it down before Mike. We knocked our glasses together.

'To Friday,' said Mike.

'Friday,' I said.

Mike nodded at the open paper. 'Did you see that story about the world space-hopper record?'

'Too right,' I said. 'What a load of bollocks.'

'Too right,' said Mike. 'Sums it all up really, this country. We've become a nation run by pricks in marketing.'

'And accounts payable,' I added.

'Sorry, mate,' said Mike, 'I'm not disrespecting the accounts department. Far from it.'

'You doing anything this weekend?' I asked.

'God forbid,' said Mike. 'Julie will probably have me mow the lawn. Might have to round the kids up and go to Homebase. Maybe lunch with her parents, if I'm lucky.'

'You've always got Sunday lunch with one of her lot,' I said.

'Big family,' explained Mike. 'Catholics, see. What about you, then?'

This took me a little by surprise. I had absolutely no plans.

'Oh, you know. Might take Amanda out for a meal tomorrow night.'

'Nice,' said Mike, not sounding particularly enthusiastic.

The two of us sipped our pints.

13

'Mike,' I asked, matter-of-factly, 'do you think I should get a divorce?'

This was the kind of question to which most people might express a degree of surprise or shock but, as I knew he would, Mike took it in his stride. He swigged his lager.

'Why would you want to do that?' he asked calmly.

'There are lots of reasons,' I said. 'A lot of reasons. But the main thing I'm thinking is, I'm thirty-six years old. This might be, you know, my last chance for a second act.'

Mike picked up a beer mat and spun it on its side.

'What's wrong with what you've got?' asked Mike. 'Nice house, your wife's fit ... How's the sex?'

'It's always been good,' I said. 'Amanda has always been, you know, a sexual person.'

'Well, then, stop fucking moaning,' Mike said dismissively. 'Do you know the extremes you have to go to to get a fucking blowjob when you've got three kids? I reckon each one costs me a grand.'

I took a deep breath. It's not like I didn't care about the sex, but I was bored. Terminally bored. I was bored with Amanda, who I suspected was bored with me. Bored by my job, my commute, my routine; bored by being the epitome of dreary middle England.

'I just feel that if I don't change things soon, I'll never get another chance.'

'You're having a mid-life crisis, mate,' Mike said, like a doctor announcing a diagnosis.

'That's great,' I said. 'It's another fucking cliché to add to the list.'

A young couple walked in all done up for a night on the town. They looked good; hopeful, excited. I took a deep breath. Just the very *idea* of breaking away from the everyday, from the routine, was enough to raise my heartbeat.

'Talking of Amanda,' said Mike, 'I thought I saw her earlier driving through town. I could swear that Nick Belagio was in the car with her.'

Nick Belagio. Hearing his name made me clench my fist. Nick Belagio, City success story, local hotshot and all round arse-wipe. Nick Belagio, who loved being the centre of attention so much that he showed up in fancy dress – as a Gestapo officer – to a fundraiser for the local children's dialysis unit.

'Doubt it,' I said. 'I don't think she even likes the twat.'

'Well, she's in good company then,' said Mike. 'She might have been showing him a house or something.'

'Maybe,' I said, standing up. 'Fancy another?'

'Twist my arm,' said Mike.

Chapter 2

I rolled out of the Royal Oak a couple of hours later feeling gassy and a little prickly. Mike had decided to hunker down for the session. He was officially working late, according to the phone call home he'd made from the pub car park barely five minutes before. I had donated my *Standard* to Mike to save him from having to talk to Geoff – although Mike was hoping to break the ice with a group of sales assistants from the Boots perfume department who had arrived en masse only minutes before.

So there I was at home. Again. Sitting at the table where I had eaten my poached eggs this morning, on this occasion eating cod and chips from the paper, my cup of tea from this morning cold beside me. The house was quiet except for the ticking of the kitchen clock, a novelty gift from friends: two plastic flies were stuck to the minute and hour hands and the words 'Time flies' were written in script on the dial.

Quality.

Amanda had liked it. There were now two cigarette butts in the saucer on the breakfast bar. She must have come back to freshen up before going out, or nipped back for a sandwich at lunchtime. Her office wasn't that far away.

A life of comfortable convention was something I'd never really cultivated. It had just sort of happened. Not so long ago, shortly before I'd met Amanda, in fact, I was still on nodding terms with clipboard bullies at several noted London night-clubs. In my glory days there was the nod of approval from the fearsome Winston at The Wag as well as painless entry to City of Angels, RAW, The Mud Club, The Café de Paris, Quiet Storm ... I'd found being young, being hip even, painfully easy. I could just turn up at the Hacienda in Manchester, say, and I'd find someone (more often than not a female) who'd take me under their wing to usher me through the night. It didn't seem to matter that I did a boring job back then – the eight hours of work grind was respite from whatever was going to happen next. I wondered what happened to all those people I'd watched the sun rise with in Ibiza after we'd spent most of the night submerged in foam that had been pumped into the club. I'd met a girl from Bolton that night, and we'd spent most of the night applauding one another as we took turns dancing feverishly. I've never really been one for drugs, but Jesus, I missed ecstasy. Actually, forget that: I missed happiness.

I checked on the fridge door. This was Amanda and my primary mode of communication. Although Amanda spent at least three-fifths of her working day on her mobile, she rarely called me. I might occasionally ring her to let her know if the train was delayed or something, but otherwise we rarely communicated electronically. It wasn't like I had a lot of friends or family who needed maintenance. It was ironic, though, that while most people complained that technology had taken over their lives Amanda and I relied on good old pen and paper and a fridge magnet that friends of ours had brought back from Florida. It read: *Welcome to America – now speak English.* Our friends Mark and Tiggy had thought that this was funny and, somehow, instead of slinging it in the rubbish after a polite interval, Amanda and I had stopped even noticing it – it now simply existed in order to fix our semi-cordial messages to the fridge.

There was a note from Amanda: 'Gurmeet Singh. Solicitor. Urgent' and a London telephone number. I had absolutely no idea what this was about and was both intrigued and concerned.

Had I done something bad that I had forgotten about?

Impulsively I picked up the phone and dialled Amanda's number.

'Hello?' she croaked. There were shrieks and laughter and music and the general hubbub of women who are determined to wake up feeling like they need a day wrapped in seaweed in an upmarket spa to recover.

'Hi, love,' I said.

'Hello?' I heard her muffled voice, like she was conversing with someone else.

'Amanda, it's me.' The sour smell of the vinegar evaporating off my chips was making my nerves a little raw.

'Who's that?' she shouted into the phone.

I flinched. I should never have called. I'd hoped this might be a nice, flirty husband-and-wife 'when are you going to be home, sweetheart, because I'm waiting for you' experience, and had ended up on the line to a banshee who couldn't remember my name.

'It's me – Alex,' I shouted. 'Your husband. What's that note on the fridge about?'

'Alex?!' she said. I heard her tell someone that it was me, as if she were at a table and everyone wanted to know who'd called. 'What's the matter?'

'Nothing's the matter,' I explained, trying to keep my cool. 'I just, you know, wanted to see how you were. And I was wondering about that note on the fridge.'

'I dunno – some bloke left a message. I wrote it down.'

'Oh.'

'Look, I'm fine, Alex,' she said, sounding slightly perplexed. 'It's Friday. I'm out with the girls. What did you think?'

'I don't know what I thought,' I said. 'I was just checking in.'

'Well, I'm planning on checking out,' said Amanda with a cackle. A couple of her friends laughed at this, but I wasn't fully convinced that they got the joke.

'Well, I'll see you later then,' I said.

'See you later,' she said.

'Take care,' I replied, hoping to introduce a note of civility, of normalcy to the conversation, but I got the feeling that she had already snapped her phone shut. Forget that, she was probably back at the bar already.

I threw the rest of my dinner in the bin and pulled a bottle of lager out of the fridge. I flicked through a few channels on the telly. It was the same old bollocks, so I opened the French windows and followed the patio round to the back of the garage. I pulled out my keys – security was at a premium in the Home Counties; some fucker had broken into our garage last year and nicked the bloody lawnmower, for Christ's sake – and pulled out my golf clubs. I chucked them on the lawn and pulled out a five iron. In the twilight, with midges and bugs nipping at my cubicle-corrupted body, I practised my swing. I was at it for so long that I ran out of beer. No problem: Rory and Sue next door would have a couple of bottles I could commandeer.

Rory answered the door with a smile on his face. He was clearly in the middle of another conversation.

'Alex!' he said, and it was as much as I could do to restrain myself from hugging him, I was so happy to receive an unqualified greeting like that. 'How are you, sir? Come in, come in.'

I stepped into the carpeted hallway, where several sets of shoes in various sizes were lined up.

'Who is it, dear?' Sue called from the dining room.

'It's *Alex*,' said Rory, as if he were announcing the three wise men. 'Good old Alex.'

Rory led me through to the dining room where Sue was sitting at a large table covered in plates that had been pushed to the side, the remains of a meal leaving them slick with grease. Rory and Sue's kids, Matthew and Louise, both of whom I thought (but couldn't quite remember) had reached double digits age-wise, were hunched over a board game, the spoils of which – fake money in dusty hues, odd-shaped plastic tokens, cards offering advantages and punishments – were neatly lined in front of them.

'Hello, Alex,' said Sue. Following my gaze to the table, she added, 'It's getting pretty exciting, actually. Looks like Louise is going to go ahead and build on the site that Rory's had his eyes on since we finished the chicken tikka.'

At this point, Louise let out a demonic movie villain's laugh – *Mmmmmmmmmwahahahahahahah* – causing much merriment amongst the family.

'So what's going on then, Alex?' asked Rory. It was a general 'how's it going' question but, in my mildly intoxicated state, I took it as specific, and worried that I had intruded on a nice family's Friday-evening board-game session by stumbling into their living room hunting for booze.

'Oh, you know, the usual,' I said. 'Thank God it's Friday, eh?'

'Don't I know it,' chuckled Rory. 'I've had a hell of a week at work.'

'And his car packed up,' added Sue, shaking the dice. 'You should have heard him. He turned the air blue.'

'Yeah,' laughed Matthew, clearly relishing his father's fall from grace. 'He said—'

'Thank you, Matthew,' interrupted Sue. 'I don't think we need to go there, do we?'

'Bloody carburettor,' added Rory for my edification.

'Rory – language please.' Sue didn't look up from the blue plastic hat that she was advancing across the board.

'He said worse than that, too,' said Matthew.

'My turn,' said Louise. She rolled the dice before looking up at her father with a sad look on her face.

'Did you miss it?' Rory asked, excitedly.

'No!' said Louise, punching the air. 'Sucker!'

Rory rolled his head back in a mixture of mirth and frustration. 'That means that there's no way I can win,' said Rory to me by way of explanation.

I stood there dumbfounded. I had been practising my golf swing in the dark in the back garden for nearly an hour, and to find myself in this bright room with these happy people was, at the very least, disorientating. I needed a drink. Sue and the kids had turned their attention back to the game. It seemed like an opportune moment to strike.

'Rory...' I said, turning away from the others, hoping that my voice wouldn't carry. 'I was wondering: you haven't got a couple of beers knocking about that I could, um, borrow, have you? I'll pay you back.'

'There's a ton of it in the garage,' said Sue, who apparently had the ears of a fox.

'I'll grab some for you,' said Rory gamely.

'Have fun,' I said, waving to the rest of the family as I left the room.

'Byeee,' they all answered merrily, as they plotted each other's virtual downfall.

Rory led me round the back of the house – it was laid out in exactly the same way as my own, except inverted – to the garage door. He opened it and turned the light on. There on the floor, I saw what Sue considered to be 'tons' of beer: namely, a four-pack of unchilled Sainsbury's lager. Rory wiped dust from the cardboard packaging and surveyed the bottles.

'There she is,' he said, as if referring to a car or a boat.

This changed my thinking about Rory considerably. This was a disgrace: beer that had sat for so long in a man's garage that there was dust all over it? Was he trying to age it, like he would a decent Bordeaux, or was he thinking of staging an exhibition named 'The Saddest Beer in the World'? I wanted to ask Rory what on earth it was he thought he was doing.

But I didn't.

'Thanks, mate,' I said, before walking around the back of Rory and Sue's house to my own slice of suburbia and picking up my driver again.

I threw the beers in the freezer, but not before I'd flipped the top off one and started working my way through it. *Mmmmmm* ... Delicious, flat, warm beer. It was getting too chilly to go back outside and play golf, so my next move was my go-to Friday night at home on my own move. After learning that the company retreat was going to happen in Cyprus – an interminable five-hour flight from London – I had treated myself to a pair of extremely expensive hi-tech cordless headphones that were guaranteed to blot out any ambient noise as well as the dismal conversational gambits of Barry from HR.

And as I sat on the plane to Cyprus, what Barry from HR probably would not have guessed was that I wasn't listening to a BBC Podcast, nor U2. Neither was I learning a language. No, I had a singular taste in music, not to the exclusion of all else, but it was certainly a passion that the fiercest music fans would recognise. My particular area of expertise was hip-hop of the late eighties: consequently, when Barry was flicking through a Duty Free magazine and straining to catch a glimpse of air hostess thigh, I was rhyming along with the inimitable Biz Markie.

'Whether I'm in Connecticut or D.C.,' I said to myself as I searched for the headphones. 'I make I make a party cook like Chef Boy-ar-dee.'

That the head accountant for a mid-level travel agency should be so devoted to rap music was not that strange. After all, I was an impressionable teenager when hip-hop really hit the UK in the mid eighties, and despite my slide into the foothills of middle age (not to mention the deep valleys of career mediocrity) I had never forgotten many of the beats and rhymes that I'd first learned when I was working my way through bottles of Clearasil and scheming to get Melanie Sarfraz to give my tonsils a full examination on the back row of the Odeon on a Saturday night.

If I closed my eyes and really focused, I found myself onstage, the heat and sweat of the crowd all around me. I took a little while to get going, to really feel like I'm on top of my game, but, after a few tunes – Eric B and Rakim, Stetsasonic, Marley Marl, LL Cool J, The Juice Crew, Big Daddy Kane – I'm right there, where it counts. My rhymes and flow are *fucking shit up*. Tonight Alex Taylor– middle class, middle income, middle management – is dropping bombs.

'Cos I don't like to dream about gettin' paid
So I dig into the books of the rhymes that I made
To now test to see if I got pull
Hit the studio, 'cos I'm paid in full ...'
WHHAAAAAAAAAAA!!!!!!!!

The tap on my back nearly made my heart burst from my ribcage. I span round to see who was behind me, expecting the worst ...

One second I'm tearing it up for the kids in Bed-Stuy, the next I'm a drunk white man in his late thirties standing in his suburban living room in a house owned by the bank, staring at my even more inebriated wife, who's weaving in front of me unsteadily. *There is slut in her eyes.*

I peeled off my headphones. A faint ringing lingered in my ears.

'What are you doing?' slurred Amanda. She reeked of booze

and cigarettes and yakking. Other than the notes on the fridge, this is when we did our best communicating.

'I was listening to music,' I replied.

'Well, what about all this then?' asked Amanda, mimicking my aping of the mid-eighties MC style – gesticulating hands punctuated by my wrapping my arms around myself in a B-boy stance.

Thank God I didn't break out my electric boogaloo moves, I thought.

We could both hear the music – a tiny, tinny version of the thumping bombast that I had been lost in only moments before. I leaned over, turned off my iPod and put the headphones on the coffee table next to the empty beer bottles. All the lights were on, yet I couldn't remember flipping the switch. The glare was too much.

'Them's my moves,' I laughed, amused and mildly embarrassed by the absurdity of the situation.

Amanda cocked her head to the side. A sliver of fat gathered where she rested a cheek on her shoulder.

'So do you have any other "moves"?' she said, straightening her head and looking me squarely in the eyes.

'None that I've practised for a while.'

'Well, maybe you need to practise more regularly, then …' She put her hand under my shirt and started rubbing my belly. She came closer. I put my hand on the back of her head before pulling her gently towards me. We kissed firmly and sloppily. There was some kind of sweet alcoholic residue in her mouth. And the thick, toxic stench of cigarettes. Still, you had to take it where you could get it, and Friday night was generally when I could be assured of a result.

Nothing wrong with that.

Her hand slid down to my crotch. She started kneading – easy, love! – a little too enthusiastically. I pulled her shirt out of her skirt and started to unbutton it, my fingers clumsy in haste. She reciprocated while kicking off her shoes. Then my trousers were round my ankles, her skirt and underwear were slung onto the sofa and we were rolling on the floor and I was inside her: a Friday-night tumble with the curtains open and the light filaments burning bright in the suburban darkness.

And then she started.

'No ...'

'No ... No ... No ...'

The first time that I had encountered Amanda's spooky sex-moan it had stopped me dead in my tracks. The fact that we were on top of a pile of coats at a party we'd gate-crashed was distracting enough, but to hear this mysterious howl really put me off my rhythm.

'It's okay,' she'd said. 'Keep going.'

I got back to it.

'No, no, no ...'

Jesus.

'Are you sure?' I asked. 'Do you want me to stop?'

'*No,*' she insisted. 'It's fine. It's just my thing.'

Seven years later, as I lay on top of my wife, my face flushed with lager and exertion, my wife telling me 'no', all I could think was: Are you *sure* you don't want me to stop?

Chapter 3

Monday. Fucking Monday. I went through the early-morning motions at the office, pretended to be interested in my co-workers' pedestrian weekends while they made the first of the many cups of tea that would punctuate their working week. Once the clock struck eleven I usually allowed myself a resuscitating trip to the company vending machine. I reached in my pocket for a fifty-pence piece and found the scrap of paper with the mysterious Mr Singh's number on it. Returning to my office with a Toffee Crisp, I closed the door. I had been in a minor car crash last year; there had been some dispute over the insurance. Most likely, this Mr Singh was some ambulance-chasing dickhead trying to scare me out of a few quid.

I dialled the number.

'Singh and Lewis!' The voice was animated.

Bloody hell, calm down, love. It's f-ing Monday.

'Is Gurmeet Singh available please?'

'I think he's in a meeting,' said the assistant, hedging her bets. 'Who shall I say is calling?'

'It's Alex Taylor.'

'Oh, Mr Taylor.' The sunshine had gone from her voice.

There was a momentary pause.

'Mr Taylor?' The voice was male, well-spoken.

'Yes.'

'Hi, this is Gurmeet Singh – thank you for calling.'

'Look, I thought this car-crash thing was sorted out,' I said. 'My insurance company talked to Mr Vincenzo's solicitor and

26

everything was taken care of. I'm not paying out any more money, just so we're clear.'

'I think that we might be operating at cross purposes,' said Mr Singh. 'I'm not calling about a motoring accident.'

'Oh.' Far from calming me, this news made me even more suspicious.

'It's rather a delicate matter,' said Singh. 'It's something that we need to talk about in person.'

'I'm not following you,' I said.

'It's not something that I'm at liberty to discuss over the phone,' said Singh with a sigh. 'I'm sorry to be so mysterious, but you'll understand when we talk further. Is there any chance you could come to my office?'

'Well, I'm actually pretty busy,' I replied, tossing my Toffee Crisp wrapper into the waste-paper basket with a theatrical darts-player flourish. Double top ... *Yeeees*!

'Look,' said Singh, lowering his voice conspiratorially, 'I'm the executor of a will. Someone you know, or someone you knew in the past, has regrettably passed away. I'm in charge of the estate.'

I stood up.

Money.

I was going to inherit money. But from whom? Both my parents had extensive families squirrelled away in parts of the country I'd barely heard of. Chances were it was some great aunt whom I hadn't seen for thirty years. Poor old dear. Still, every cloud ...

'I'll be there at one,' I said, before writing the address down and high-kicking – kung fu-style – around my office in celebration.

Chapter 4

Because I was just about to become rich I decided to get a taxi over to Mr Singh's office in Kensal Green.

'Keep it,' I told the cabbie as he tried to hand me my change. As the tip amounted to around five per cent, his derisive look was probably no more than I deserved. I'd have to work on my playa act.

The offices of Singh & Lewis were on the second floor of a new 'courtyard' development behind a row of shops. I was buzzed in and found myself walking through a series of doors, each with its own complicated security system. Grilles, which could be folded back when the office was occupied, covered most of the windows.

A pale girl with curly black hair buzzed me into the inner sanctum.

'Sorry about that,' she said, acknowledging the complications of getting into the office. 'It's in case of unwanted visitors.'

'Oh, I see,' I said.

'That's not you,' she said with a laugh, revealing unnaturally spotless teeth. 'We get some, you know ...' She paused. 'Angry types occasionally.' She readjusted her smile. 'Mr Singh is waiting for you in his office – can I get you a coffee or anything?'

'I'm fine,' I replied. There was anticipatory moisture on my palms. I had made a bargain with myself. If I was getting more than fifty grand I'd treat myself to state-of-the-art golf clubs; more than a hundred grand would see me driving a Mercedes

S-Class; and more than one hundred and fifty...? Well, I'd strip off and run back down the Harrow Road naked.

Mr Singh – shortish, barrel-chested, mid-thirties, with an impressive mane of hair that was slicked back, eighties-style – stood and greeted me before closing the door behind us.

'Thanks so much for coming over at such short notice,' he said.

'No problem,' I said.

'I'll come straight to the point,' said Singh. 'I'm the executor of a will. The deceased died suddenly two weeks ago. A car crash. Rather tragic: she was blind-sided by a drunk driver.'

'Nasty,' I said, shaking my head while trying to guess which obscure relative might have snuffed it. Having lost both my parents by my early twenties I had been a little remiss in staying in touch with the rest of the clan. There was an occasional exchange of Christmas cards with a few people on my mum's side, but little beyond that.

'Fortunately, if such a word can be used in these circumstances, the deceased – perhaps because she was a young mum who was on her own – left very clear directions as to what was to happen in the event of her death. I have notified her beneficiaries and we're beginning to move forward with these matters.'

I settled into my seat. Here it comes, I thought: the business part of the equation.

'There is also a matter of some delicacy,' said Singh, looking away and rubbing his palms together.

I couldn't help frowning.

'The deceased had a young daughter. She's thirteen. As you can imagine this is a very, very difficult time for her, which hasn't been helped by the fact that she's currently in the care of the local authority.'

'Well, what about the father?' I said, shrugging. Not my problem, pal.

There was a pause while Mr Singh continued to rub his hands together.

'That's you,' he said so quietly that I thought I might have misheard him. I stared at Mr Singh, who nodded his head.

'You,' he repeated.

Chapter 5

The last time I had seen Cathy Meades, well over a decade before, things had not gone well. We had gone to the Cotswolds for the weekend with Cathy's friend Liz and her posh boyfriend Barney.

'I don't understand why we're doing this,' said Cathy.

'*What?*' I said as we sat on the M4 in soul-crushingly slow traffic. 'I might be wrong, but wasn't this, um, your idea?'

'I know that,' she said.

'I thought you wanted us to start, you know, doing the kinds of things that couples do rather than just going out to the pub and getting drunk.'

'Yes,' said Cathy. 'I know I said that.' She stared sulkily out of the window. 'And, in case you're wondering, going to clubs and getting drunk doesn't count as a break from the norm.'

The wipers slapped the drizzle to the edges of the windscreen. We had been on the road for over two and a half hours and were yet to reach Reading.

'This is what happens when you leave London,' I said. I left the smoke reluctantly and rarely. And Reading – which we appeared destined never to pass – stood for everything I considered imperfect and uninspiring in the world.

'When we booked this weekend I didn't know that Liz would be winding me up so much,' said Cathy. 'She's doing my head in at the moment.'

'She's just stressed out,' I said. 'You know what girls are like when they're getting married.'

'How would I know that?' said Cathy, tartly. I chose not to take the bait. Despite the traffic and the weather and the fact that I would be cut off from all means of watching the weekend's football, I was actually quite looking forward to the two days away.

I suspected that my sanguine attitude to the weekend might be explained by the fact that it would allow me time around Liz, who was uncommonly beautiful and, consequently, out of my league. I had a lot of time for Barney, too. There was an upper-middle-class dashingness about him that appealed to me, a devil-may-care approach to life that I aspired to but rarely managed to pull off. Liz and Barney would make the stuff that you did when you were in the country pretending to be grown up – like long walks (tedious), country pub lunches (passable) and nights in front of a roaring log fire playing Scrabble (a fucking waste of a decent evening) – tolerable.

After everyone had arrived at the damp, decrepit dump that we had shelled out five hundred notes for to be asphyxiated by smoke from a fireplace that hadn't been swept since Cromwell, shower under a stream of water the strength, colour and temperature of a jet of piss, and use kitchen equipment that would have been condemned by most health authorities, I had been thrilled when it was Liz and I who took it upon ourselves to drive to the nearest supermarket. Most of all, I liked the fact that everyone in the Spar would assume that we were a couple. I encouraged this perception by leaning in close to her when we were choosing vegetables for the evening's meal, succumbing to her every dietary whim and insisting on carrying all of the heavy plastic bags no matter how much the handles deformed my hands.

We got back to the 'cottage' and I felt almost giddy from my proximity to Liz. Cathy and Barney were ostentatiously busying themselves in the kitchen. Despite this they appeared to have

32

achieved absolutely nothing since they'd arrived: the bags were still in the car, neither of the beds were made and the kitchen had yet to be cleaned. Cathy was religious about this kind of thing: when we'd rented a villa in Mallorca the summer before she had insisted on cleaning the kitchen and bathroom as soon as we arrived because she hadn't trusted anyone else to do it properly.

'Where's the booze?' asked Barney, going through the bags.

I looked over at Liz. 'Did you put that bag with the beers in the car?'

She looked up at me blankly. 'I thought you did it.'

'Shit,' I said, slapping my forehead. 'I thought you did it.'

'For fuck's sake,' said Barney, pissed off.

'I'm sorry, mate,' I said, hauling another shopping bag onto the sticky kitchen table. 'I'm sorry that you're a total mug; I really am.'

I pulled a case of beers from the shopping bag.

'You bastard,' said Barney.

'Pass one in this direction,' said Cathy. 'I'm spitting feathers over here.'

We opened four bottles, which were clinked together roughly.

'Here's to not getting lynched by the locals,' I said.

'*You ain't from round here, are ya?*' said Liz in a hillbilly voice.

'Let's get all this stuff in the fridge and find a bloody pub,' said Cathy.

This was pretty much the last civil conversation that Cathy and I were to have. We bickered in the boozer over something that had occurred weeks before: Cathy thought that I had been rude to her friend Pat because Pat had kept us waiting in a cab outside her flat for too long. Later on we had a blazing row when, drunk, I dropped a roast chicken on the filthy farmhouse floor as I attempted to transfer it from a roasting tin to a serving dish.

Drunk and hungry, we resentfully played a game of Scrabble before hitting the sack for a cold night broken briefly by a bout of somnolent sex, followed by a tussle over the meagre blankets that we both tried to drag onto our respective sides of the bed.

I awoke the next morning feeling hungover, dirty and chilled to the bone. Liz and Barney were sitting at the kitchen table, fully clothed, drinking tea. There were three plates, each with crumbs on it.

'Morning,' I said.

'Morning,' they replied.

I shuffled around the kitchen, not knowing where to start in the unfamiliar surroundings.

'Um, where's the bread?'

'Over there,' said Liz. 'There's butter in the fridge.'

'Want a cuppa?' asked Barney, getting up.

'Love one,' I said, placing a couple of slices in the battered toaster. 'So I'll jump in the shower once Cathy gets out and then we can go for a walk or something. That's what we're supposed to do in the country, right?'

There was an embarrassed silence. Eventually Liz looked over at me.

'Cathy isn't here, Alex.'

I looked at her, confused. 'I don't follow you.'

'Look, I'm sorry, mate,' said Barney, 'but she asked me to drive her to the station this morning. She's gone back to London.'

'She said she needed to get her head together,' said Liz.

'Oh,' I said, trying to sip my tea nonchalantly. 'That doesn't sound good.'

And it wasn't good. The stone cottage in the Cotswolds was the last time I saw Cathy for some time. She sent two boxes of my stuff from her flat to my office by courier. She changed her mobile number. She refused to acknowledge my emails. She even moved flat. A friend told me that she'd moved back with her mum. There was talk of money problems.

Then, nearly four years later, Liz and Barney got married. It was a fancy affair up in Liverpool: a church service in Birkenhead followed by a meal and dancing in Albert Docks. I took my new girlfriend up to Merseyside for a long weekend and hadn't really given any thought to the possibility of bumping into Cathy. I strolled into the club where the reception was being held and there she was, wearing a black cocktail dress and chatting at the bar with a couple of friends from the old days. As much as I wanted to divert my course – I needed time to prepare for this – she caught my eye and smiled. I walked over and she opened her arms. We embraced. She smelled the same – perfume, hair products – and the shape and feel of her body seemed pretty much unaltered. I realised how much I missed her. I couldn't help wondering what would have happened if things hadn't got into such an unholy mess.

'Hello, you,' she said. The 'you' sounded indifferent. A little impersonal, but it was meant to convey the exact opposite. It was a 'you' that, with the syntactical complexities of the English language, conveyed specialness and warmth.

'Hello, yourself,' I said. We examined each other.

'I think you've still got some of my underwear,' I said eventually.

She laughed. 'Sorry, love, I sold 'em,' she said, exhaling smoke. 'Times have been tough and eBay's a wonderful thing.'

'I thought as much,' I said. 'I'd have done the same if the shoe was on the other foot.'

'Well, I can tell you that you'd have got a lot more for my knickers than I got for your pants,' she said, pulling a face of disapproval. 'They were full of bloody holes.'

'It keeps my tackle well ventilated,' I said, deadpan.

Cathy smirked. 'So what have you been up to?' she asked.

'Oh, the usual,' I said. 'Working. Playing football, you know. Got a new girlfriend, actually.' I cast my eyes across the room. 'There she is, over there.' Clarissa was standing chatting to some of Barney's family members.

'She looks nice,' said Cathy.

'She is,' I said with authority. I didn't mean it. I'd had enough of her. 'What about you, then?'

'I've been busy,' said Cathy with an enigmatic smile.

'Oh yeah?'

'I had a baby.'

'Oh, no you didn't,' I laughed.

I looked her in the eye. She raised her bottom lip and nodded her head in affirmation.

'Oh, yes you did,' I said slowly. 'Jesus.'

'Well, she's hardly a baby any longer. She's three.'

Wow. I was blindsided. This was news indeed. Cathy had had a child. This meant that she had had a relationship since we were together. Actually, maybe not even a relationship. Cathy had had sex with someone other than me.

'Um, when, how, what's its name?' I blurted this out too quickly. Cathy laughed.

'Well, when a man and a woman love each other very much ...' said Cathy in her best primary school teacher's voice. 'She's called Caitlin.'

'Sorry – it's not an it, it's a girl,' I said. This was all too much. 'Is she here?' I asked, looking around.

'No, no,' said Cathy. 'I left her with my mum down in Guildford. I moved back there.'

'*Guildford?*'

'I know.'

'I thought you—'

'Hated it there? Yes, but needs must,' said Cathy, signalling for another drink. 'You want one?'

'Yeah, Heineken, please.'

Cathy ordered.

'Wow,' I said, smiling at her. I felt a sickness rising inside me, a hollowness that I'd not experienced since our break-up. 'That's great. I'm, um, gobsmacked.'

'So am I,' laughed Cathy. 'You never know in life, that's the thing.'

'So who's the lucky fella?'

Cathy took a sip of her drink, leaving a faint trace of lipstick on her straw.

'Dad's not around,' she said. 'You know, it was one of those things. He made it clear that he wasn't going to be around, so the decision really fell on me. I decided to have her.'

'Good for you,' I said. This wasn't a platitude. I meant it.

'Well, you know, it's not easy but, as the cliché goes, I wouldn't have it any other way. My mum looks after her during the day while I'm at work. She's been bored senseless since Dad died, so she's happy to do it, and, actually, everything is fine. It really is.'

I nodded.

'I know some people think I'm mad,' said Cathy.

'Why?'

'Come on, Alex. Single mum, civil servant; it's not exactly a fairytale, is it?'

'Well, you know,' I said. I had noticed the unwelcome sight of Clarissa working her way through the dance floor towards us. I wanted to talk more. I wanted to be with Cathy. 'As we're talking in clichés, life is what you make it. Either you can enjoy it or you can let it become a burden. It's up to you, really.'

'Wise words, life coach,' laughed Cathy.

'I mean it,' I said as Clarissa closed in on us. I introduced the two of them before disappearing with Clarissa into the crowd. We spent the night on the dance floor, from where I kept half an eye on Cathy. I wanted to show her that I was okay, that I had a hot girlfriend, that I was having a good time. I watched her move through the other guests, hang at the bar, disappear towards the toilets with Barney. I wanted to show Cathy that I was having a good time, that I was doing okay. I caught her eye when she was on the way out the door. She emailed two weeks later, wanting to know if I'd like to go for a drink.

I never replied.

Chapter 6

'Caitlin.'

The woman spoke quietly to the girl, reaching out her hand in the light rain. Some people had umbrellas up, but the majority didn't. It was a mist as much as rain. She seemed tall for her age, although I wasn't quite sure how tall a thirteen-year-old should be.

We were standing in a graveyard in Guildford. Poor Cathy, she can't have imagined that it would have ended like this. In the rain, in suburbia, with her daughter standing next to an employee of Guildford Social Services, a motley collection of stunned friends gathered under a sky thick with menace, her mother's grave freshly dug beside her own. She'd died only two months before – a stroke as she was getting out of the bath.

I looked over at the daughter I'd never met, who stared blankly at her mother's coffin. Her eyes, young and uncreased, betrayed only exhaustion. She was wearing her school uniform – a grey jumper and skirt, a pair of woolly tights. Sensible black shoes. For some reason the clothes didn't look like they were hers – there was none of the customisation that teenage girls bring to sober school attire to demonstrate their singularity. It was as though she'd forgotten quite who she was. It broke my heart that someone who should not have had to witness the darker ways of the world so young had got out of bed this morning and got dressed knowing that she would be burying her own mother. The poor kid had lost all her moorings.

I could tell that the gathered adults were all trying not to stare at her, but were nevertheless drawn to the deep tragedy of Caitlin's situation. What happens to a child at a time like this? Are there professionals who offer comfort and guidance, pull together some explanation for the world's dark contrivances? How do you offer hope of any kind when capricious, hard, irrefutable events like this occur? I looked at the tissue-clutching, pink-eyed mourners and knew that I wasn't the only one thinking this.

'Caitlin,' the woman said again, slightly louder this time.

The girl looked up, surprised at being addressed. The woman smiled and nodded towards the white roses that the teenager was holding. Caitlin looked down at the grave and seemed to concentrate very hard, as if trying to communicate something to her dead mother. She clutched the flowers and her cheeks flushed intensely before she threw the roses into the grave. The flowers scattered across the wooden coffin lid – Cathy's coffin lid. A mourner sobbed, choking back tears. Caitlin turned her head slowly towards him. Her face no longer appeared child-like. She stared at the man who was unable to mask his grief. There was something else about her now, something pragmatic, disengaged even, something that seemed to say that she couldn't afford to associate with anyone who carried on in this way.

'Earth to earth,' said the priest. 'Ashes to ashes …'

I turned away. I could no longer hold the girl's gaze.

Chapter 7

How do you prepare to meet your own child? Most parents do so for months. They try out names, they paint a nursery, they spend money on *stuff* – a Moses basket, newborn nappies, breast pumps – that only months before would have seemed as exotic as a tiger-skin rug. I had had none of the lazy afternoons spent browsing John Lewis for stimulating mobiles or soothing Baby Mozart videos. There were no lazy gastropub lunches to mull over the inevitable changes that would occur once the baby arrived. I had not touched a tumescent belly, the most unarguable of the transformations, to consider and contemplate for signs of gender.

No, instead of being handed a mewling, pink infant wrapped hurriedly after having been slapped to life and weighed by the NHS's finest, I find myself encountering someone whom I've learned about only days before, someone who is fully formed, has opinions, has a history.

Someone who is bigger than some of my friends.

This isn't like finding yourself inheriting your mum and dad's house – this is like being given a safari park to run. ('Oh, here are the keys. Good luck, and don't forget to feed the tigers at five o'clock.') And while there is no training for becoming a parent at any age, I daresay it's easier to find your feet with someone whose skull is yet to fully form than with someone who, in all likelihood, is more competent with electronic devices than you are.

As I locked the car and walked the final steps to the care

centre, these are the things that were going through my head. I wished that there were loftier matters than this, but there weren't. Fear, panic and, to be honest – and this was not something of which I was proud – a degree of ambivalence stalked me as I steadied myself to press the bell. For this reason I had chosen not to inform Amanda of my visit. I had barely had a chance to get my head around the notion of the meeting, and I wasn't sure how I wanted it to play out. I was still prepared for my relationship with Caitlin not to go any further than today. Involving Amanda would just raise the stakes and complicate matters. I wanted to make my own decision with the least possible fuss.

I pressed the bell. What on earth was I doing?

I still had time to run. I could return to a life of … Of what, exactly?

The door opens. I'm invited in by a tired-looking young woman with short hair and big hoop earrings. I am not listening to a word she is saying. All I can think about is that I have a daughter whom I have never met before. A daughter who would walk past me in the street without knowing who I am. And I, of course, would do the same. We have the same DNA. Her blood group will have been (partially) determined by me. She will carry some of my visual characteristics and, who knows, some of my mannerisms. She may be carrying fatal physiological flaws courtesy of my genetic endowment.

And I'm trying to appear totally respectable, and nice and sensitive, because this is what the Social Services woman expects of me. And she's talking about the trauma that Caitlin has experienced over the past few weeks. And I nod and agree and speak in the hushed tones that we reserve for such conversations and I want to ask her: *So do you think that this has been a fucking walk in the park for me?* I mean, I know that us (almost) middle-aged white men are supposed to just suck up the disappointments, dust ourselves off and get on with the game (you'll be all right, son – here have a bit of the magic sponge). But I've just discovered that I have a thirteen-year-old daughter by a dead woman I have not seen for a decade and I would appreciate it if the woman who has, I'm sure, been on various sensitivity training courses, could show *me* a little bloody sensitivity, an ashamed little voice inside me says. Would it bloody kill her? Apparently so, because all she seems concerned about is letting me know what to expect from Caitlin.

Eventually she finishes telling me about grief and how it affects different people and how we need to take the process slowly to see how it develops, and I'm allowed to go upstairs to the room where Caitlin is waiting for me.

And that's when I go cold. As many times as I've rehearsed my speech and thought about what my first words should be to my daughter, the weight of the moment is so colossal that, as I walk up the stairs towards her room, I wonder if – really and truly – I can do it. I look back down the staircase and the woman from Social Services offers me an encouraging nod. I notice that one of the other bedroom doors is open. The walls are scuffed and plastered with colourful posters of chimpanzees. What is it about chimps that people like so much? Personally I've always found them pretty threatening – except for the babies; they're all right.

I knock on her door. I wonder if she's standing there on the other side, inches from me, wondering what awaits her on the other side.

It smells of stale, boiled food up here.

'Come in.' The accent is flat, somewhere between estuary and received pronunciation. I turn the door handle and walk in.

*

And there I came face to face with my daughter.

She was folded into an armchair, with jeans-clad legs tucked underneath her. She didn't get up. There was a boniness to her that most teenage girls (except for kids of a portly persuasion) seem to have. She was pale, although her cheeks were flushed with youthful bloom. There were suggestions of skin issues, a couple of red marks on her forehead betraying where blemishes had been excised. Her hair – dark and straight – was parted in the middle, ended at her shoulders and had been brushed neatly, as if for a special occasion. She had a high, broad forehead that seemed distinguished. Her dark eyes were set relatively deeply in her head. She looked at me briefly before turning her attention towards the window, which looked out on the leafy street.

Christ. I had no idea how to communicate with this creature.

'Hi,' I said.

'Hi,' she replied.

'Is it all right if I sit down?' I asked.

She nodded. I pulled a chair from underneath a desk. I positioned it well away from her – I couldn't process the fact that she was so big. So big that I would have assumed that she was around sixteen. *Sixteen*: an age when you're not allowed to drink legally, nor are you allowed to die for your country. But there are other things – things that I wasn't even remotely prepared to acknowledge – that every sixteen-year-old spends their waking hours either thinking about or acting upon. The thought was terrifying.

This was not a child.

But, then, of course, she was.

'So are they taking care of you all right?' I asked. I knew that it was a shoddy start, but I wasn't sure that any opening gambit would, in those circumstances, be the right choice. At that point I was more interested in just trying to make some noise, filling the silence.

She nodded again. 'I suppose so,' she said eventually.

I perched on the edge of the chair, leaning forward so that my tie touched my knees. My position was too intense. I sat back and crossed my legs, trying to appear relaxed and open, but my clothes were working against me. I was dressed for work in a suit and tie. It just didn't feel right. Too stiff. Caitlin had probably had enough of men in bad suits; case-workers, lawyers, people with files and dossiers. I made an effort not to stare, but I took a good look at her. I wanted to see myself. It was hard to tell, but the colouring seemed right and Caitlin had the high forehead of my mum's side of the family.

'So what have they told you?' I asked.

Caitlin looked up at me, wise to my tactic of starting the conversation. Somewhere in the house a clock chimed four.

'Not much,' she said. I couldn't tell whether this was the truth. Surely the social workers must have spent some time priming her for this meeting. I tried to imagine what it must have been like from her perspective. Maybe she just didn't want me here. And, honestly, who could blame her?

'You know,' I said, trying to encourage her, 'about us.'

She shifted her position a little and spoke quickly.

'Just, you know, that my mum had a will and stuff and that she said if anything happened to her they should contact you.'

I considered this for a moment. She didn't use the word 'dad'. She had made no reference to our relationship, or lack of it. She was just processing cold facts as they had been presented to her.

'Oh,' I said. This 'oh' was flat and slightly hard. I communicated disappointment when really there was none – it was more an acknowledgement of quite how distant we were. I smiled, not wanting her to think that I was disappointed when really it

45

was her that should have felt disillusioned, given the piss-poor show I'd put on. It's not like I'd walked in the room and solved all her problems. And, Jesus Christ, imagine the comedown of being underwhelmed after meeting your Mystery Dad.

There was silence for a few moments. I cast my eyes around the room, searching for something – *anything*! – with which to spark conversation, some kind of visual cue or prompt. I racked my brain, searching for the carefully worded gambits that I had prepared.

Nothing.

'So they told me that you're my dad.'

The D word.

But she said it in such an offhand manner that she might as well have been commenting on the weather or what was on telly that night. I readjusted my position, clasping my hands between my knees. It hardly seemed possible that the two of us were having this conversation – it was as if the relationship had, until moments ago, been coiled up, waiting to occur. And then, suddenly, Caitlin had released it in the most casual way. I looked around the room with its battered IKEA furniture, and somehow the setting made her bearing appropriate.

'That's right,' I said. 'I'm your dad.'

And I'm not even sure why – nerves probably – but I sniggered a little after I said this to her.

'What's funny?' she asked. Her look was different from before. She held my gaze until I was forced to look elsewhere. It reminded me of the way she'd looked at me at the funeral.

'Nothing,' I said. 'I wasn't laughing.'

She lifted herself, using the arms of the chair and unfolded her legs before crossing them. She was wearing black slip-ons that looked like ballet shoes.

'It sounded like you were,' she said.

'I'm sorry,' I replied.

'Yeah, but am I bovvered?' she said.

'Sorry?' I asked, at that very moment kicking myself that I hadn't picked up the TV reference. 'Oh, sorry, no, I get it. It's off that show, isn't it?'

She gave me a look that I can only describe as pitiful. 'Yeah,' she said drily. 'It's off that show.'

She tapped her foot in mid-air and began to twist a necklace around her index finger, screwing it into tight coils before releasing it and twisting it again. I noticed the final Harry Potter novel tucked into her bookshelf.

'So you like Harry Potter?' I asked.

She shrugged again, but this time quickly, as if the question had annoyed her. I sighed, frustrated.

'I read the first two,' I said, persisting, 'but I haven't had a chance to get to the next one. I've heard that—'

'Why are you bothering?' she asked, turning her focus back to me.

'I suppose I'd like to finish the series, I dunno,' I said.

'I don't mean that,' she continued. 'I mean coming in here and chatting away to me like you're my school counsellor or something.'

'Because I'm, you know, your dad,' I said, although the words sounded hollow as they fell clumsily from my mouth. 'I care about you.'

'Oh, really?' she said sarcastically. 'And did you care last week, or last month, or last year?'

'Well, I—'

'The answer's "no", *Dad*, in case you're struggling,' she said, interrupting me.

It was going really well.

'How could I?' I said, trying to keep my voice as reasonable as I could manage. 'I didn't ...' Oh, Jesus, why did I start down this road?

'You didn't *what?*' she said, shifting her body so that she wasn't even facing me any longer.

I took a deep breath.

'I didn't even know you existed,' I said eventually, knowing full well that this was where she wanted me to go.

There was a creaking on the stairs outside. In all likelihood we were being monitored.

Jesus, what a balls-up.

'So what do you want to do?' I asked her.

'Meet John Terry, climb Mount Everest, fly to the moon … What do you mean?'

'About us,' I said, feeling myself slowly deflating. The strain of the conversation was making me feel like my system was shutting down. Maybe this was what it was like when you began to die.

Caitlin shrugged. It wasn't (thank you, Lord) a shrug of rejection – a physical embodiment of dislike or, worse, disdain – it was more a shrug of ambivalence, embarrassment at having to open up to a stranger who introduced himself as Dad. She continued to twist her necklace. It was clear to me that, as few choices as she had at that moment, the proposition of going to live with a man who had just declared himself to be her father was about as appealing as signing up for fostering by Rose West.

I was lost. How to make myself a more appealing prospect than the workhouse?

'Look,' I said, 'I can't imagine how you're feeling at the moment. What you've experienced since … over the past couple of weeks is beyond me. And I know that you're probably wondering why on earth you've never seen me before—'

'You think?' Caitlin interrupted. It was sarcastic and sullen at the same time. Quite an achievement.

'You know, your mum and I, we … Well, things didn't work out.'

48

She stopped twisting her necklace and began to drum her fingers on the arm of the chair, but I suspected that she was listening, despite continuing to stare intently into space. If nothing else, it was making me feel better. Maybe, just maybe, I could communicate with someone so remote . . .

'Jesus,' she said eventually.

Clearly my communication was bearing fruit.

'You didn't even know I existed.'

'I understand,' I said, as if there was an answer to this that she'd find acceptable. 'I'm really sorry.'

She turned to look at me. He mouth was pinched with anger, but I could see something else there, something that tempered it.

I sighed. How to reach through the hurt?

'Look, you're a smart kid,' I started. 'You know, life offers a lot of surprises, things that don't go as you'd expected them to go, or as you'd hoped they'd might . . .'

She stopped drumming her fingers and looked away.

'We did our best,' I said eventually.

It felt strange speaking for Cathy, but I thought that if I could talk on her behalf, if I could channel her, than maybe that was a way of reaching Caitlin. Reaching our daughter.

'Do you see what I'm saying?' I asked.

There was more silence. Caitlin was perfectly still.

'I can't even remember your name,' she said flatly.

'Alex.'

'Your surname.'

'Taylor.'

She didn't react. Her father's name – *my* name – provoked no ripples outwardly. There was a squeal of tyres in the street. Caitlin was out of her chair and at the window before I could turn to see what she was looking at.

'It's nothing,' she said. 'Just some idiot driving too fast.'

She furrowed her brow and ever so briefly I got a vision from the past: someone I recognised. It was a dim, remote memory dug up from so deep within my mind that I was unable to recognise its provenance. Cathy? No, not her. Was it me, or an earlier version of myself? Maybe ...

But it somehow didn't feel right. There was someone else; I just couldn't think who.

It would come back to me.

The moment had passed. Caitlin was back in the chair and no longer in the mood to talk to the stranger who called himself 'Dad'.

I needed to get out of there before I ballsed it up any further.

'Look,' I said, 'I'm going to go now but, if you want, I'll come tomorrow and we can talk some more.'

Caitlin didn't reply. I stood up. What to do? I wanted to hug her, to show her I cared ... It was clear that such physicality would be unwelcome.

I said goodbye and closed the door behind myself.

Jesus. What a mess.

I stood outside the door for a moment composing myself for the social worker. She met me downstairs and we talked about my returning, and while I knew that it was the right thing to be talking about, the proper thing to be doing, part of me wanted to leave that house and never return.

And I couldn't help wondering if Caitlin would be happier that way, too.

Chapter 8

Driving home on the A3 I tried to make sense of what had just occurred. The rational part of me reasoned that Caitlin's less than enthusiastic response to my visit was a totally understandable reaction from an adolescent girl who had suffered a tragic loss. Attempting to comprehend or to sympathise was, in some ways, futile. I had to remind myself that, as her father (of ten days and counting) my most basic requirement was just to show up. Being present is what modern fathers do. Gone are the days when dads drifted home late at night with Harp on their breath, making a show of birthdays and Christmas: today's dad is *around*, making his presence felt in more ways than just doling out pocket money on a Saturday morning.

But this ideal supposes that the child *wants* you there in the first place, which, in the case of Caitlin, was a major assumption. It was getting darker. I turned on my headlights to illuminate my way home, following the car in front of me in a hazy afterthought. There was no rule that Caitlin *had* to like me. There was no preordained conga line forming just because we shared DNA. In fact, very often it's quite the opposite. I needed to give the girl a break. It was early days. She would come round. Her response was totally understandable ... I needed to concentrate. The traffic was getting heavier ...

Then a horrible thought flared in my mind.

The counterpart to Caitlin not having to like me was almost too awful to contemplate: there was nothing compelling me to love her either.

I pulled off the main road and found my way into town. I spotted a parking space and veered towards the kerb so dramatically that passers-by regarded me suspiciously. I fed the meter and started to walk. I needed air, or distraction. I noticed a teashop, a proper old-fashioned one staffed by no-nonsense old birds in pinnies, and settled at a corner table.

'Cuppa tea, love?' asked one of the women.

'I could murder one,' I replied.

'Oh, I don't think we need that,' laughed the old lady.

'And can I have a toasted teacake as well?'

A toasted teacake? Where the hell had *that* come from? I can't have thought about toasted teacakes since I was ten. The teashop reminded me of going shopping with my mum on a Saturday. Sometimes we would stop and have tea and sticky buns – Jesus, how I loved a Swiss bun – a thick, doughy cake slathered with teeth-jarringly sweet white icing. Still, here I was, sitting on my own twenty-seven years later, having just discovered that I had an adolescent daughter. A daughter who was not best pleased to find the underwhelming identity of her biological father.

Munching on a teacake, which had been singed a little before being slathered in margarine, I considered the irony of my position: having a child was something that I had coveted for most of my adult life. But, like much else in my life thus far, I just hadn't *done* anything about it.

Amanda and I had discovered that both the biological and scientific routes to parenthood were beyond us. I never really understood why. Apparently my sperm and her uterus just weren't a good mix. And after a while we became too jaded to care. The diagnosis had come after a long, tiring back-and-forth with various doctors and specialists. By the time we knew where we stood, we were so resigned to our fate that we were relieved just to have the process stop. The notion of having a child of our own had become a wholly abstract idea. We seemed to forget that we might have been the ones testing buggies at Mothercare and boring everyone rigid with conversations about sleep deprivation. But, as our friends had started families and the lads' nights out were fewer and farther between, I had a creeping realisation that there was something abridged about my life. On the surface, of course, there was little to complain about: the career, the successful (hot) wife, the house in suburban utopia, the three holidays a year, the two late-model cars in the driveway ... But there was still a dull nag at the back of my mind, a 'what if' that I thought would never be answered.

And now there was Caitlin. Was she what I'd been waiting for all this time? I mean, I knew that the general messiness of life meant that parenthood is rarely perfect, but what would I be letting myself in for? Would it really be better than what I had already? Was this a lifestyle upgrade? And how on earth was I supposed to sell the idea of bringing a stroppy teenage girl into the house to Amanda?

My wife would never agree to adopt. Too troubled by what she perceived to be her own failure, the notion of taking on someone else's kid was unthinkable to her. The very idea that she might embrace my teenage lovechild was laughable. I sipped my scalding tea. It was the colour of rust. Perfect. I thought about Amanda. There was something that I admitted to myself only occasionally: maybe our dud tubes or non-swimmers, or whatever it had been, were a blessing. If I was brutally honest, I wasn't sure (whisper it) that Amanda was outstanding maternal material or whether I was up to being a dad. She had always preferred to be out of the house, was constantly in motion: at work, at bars, at functions, getting her nails done, shopping ... Quite where a bereaved thirteen-year-old would fit into her schedule I wasn't sure. And how would I even talk to her about it? Our communication was limited to messages stuck to the fridge door and the occasional drunken fuck. There was no longer a connection, the transmitters were down. I polished off my tea. It was clear to me: Amanda would not like this one bit.

Which led me to another question. If – and at that moment it was a portly, corpulent if – I had to make a choice between them, who would I choose? Say we were up in a balloon and heading for the ground. Say that I wasn't able to gallantly throw myself over the edge, that I had to make a decision? Whom would I choose?

I walked slowly back to my car, weighed down by thought, only to discover a parking ticket fluttering on the windscreen. Fuck that. I pulled the object from underneath the wiper and ripped it up.

It drizzled all the way home, the weather matching my mood. I switched on more lights than I needed. In the kitchen I found a note from Amanda stuck to the fridge. She had gone to see a film with a friend. It advised that I shouldn't wait up; she'd be home late. There was a can of soup in the cupboard if I was hungry.

I had no appetite. I thought about Caitlin sleeping in a strange bed – the smells and noises of the house alien to her, the adults charged with her welfare near strangers – and I wondered what kind of life she now pictured for herself. Had she considered how the whole Annie the Orphan game might be played to her advantage? I couldn't imagine that this was so. Despite her dismissive mood today, surely she was just about as lost as a thirteen-year-old can be when the very sun about which you orbited had been snuffed out without warning.

I needed to talk, to try to work it through. I called Mike but got the answer phone. I opened the drinks cabinet and poured a couple of fingers of Johnnie Walker. It went down a little too easily. I poured another finger and turned on the TV: the usual prime-time bollocks. Some reality shit with exhibitionist morons being given their fifteen minutes of fame by well-educated programme-makers who believed in populist programming, especially when it came to making their mortgage payments.

I tried to care about what I was looking at, but I couldn't shake the image of Caitlin asleep, clutching a soft toy, her only companion a piece of her past that still felt and smelled like home.

What the hell was I doing?

I got up, grabbed my jacket and started walking over to the rugby club. It was too far to go on foot, but I was hoping that the elements would do what the television hadn't and clear my head. It was a fairly desperate move: despite my inability to settle, there were plenty of reasons why I didn't want to go to the rugby club. Foremost amongst them was the fact that Nick Belagio would be there, smug as a dog with two dicks, and secure in the knowledge that, despite the credit crunch, there would be no one at the club who had earned more money than him that week. I knew that Nick had earned more money than me that week not just because Nick was a partner at one of the hedge funds that had emerged from the market meltdown unscathed but due to the fact that I worked in an office where the appearance of a Milky Way in the vending machine was viewed as a significant perk. Aside from his Georgian pile on the outskirts of Cobham, Nick also had a house in the south of France, a condo in Barbados and was taking lessons so that he could pilot a helicopter. Nick did not fly scheduled airlines any longer.

Amanda had urged me, given my talent for numbers, to ask Nick for a job.

'It doesn't work like that,' I'd explained to her. 'I can't just beg him for a job.'

'Why not?' demanded Amanda, who had never been afraid to ask anyone for anything.

'I dunno,' I said. 'There's personnel, and all that stuff, isn't there? You can't just ask "if they've got any jobs going".'

Amanda remained unconvinced, just as she did every time I floated my notion that I would quit accountancy to open a coffee shop. I suspected that she struggled to camouflage the fact that I had inherited a lump sum when my parents died and, while I still needed to work, had a significant cushion should I decide that the daily grind was becoming just that. My grandparents had had a café in Old Street market back in the sixties and seventies and I had fond memories of the steam, clatter, banter and bustle, the snatches of conversation, the vibrancy of humanity coming and going. It just seemed to be the most vital place I could imagine. Cafés like that didn't really exist any longer, but I had always wondered if I could create something similar.

'A coffee shop?' she'd say, as if I'd announced that I was going to open a bordello stocked with Brazilian studs to service the haughty, well-groomed, 4x4 wives of the burgh.

'Like Starbucks.'

'Like Starbucks.'

'Yes.'

Amanda would shake her head, as if my statement hadn't been worthy of her attention, before punching something into her BlackBerry.

'So what do you think?' I asked her once, my voice barely masking my irritation. I always wanted my marriage to be a civil one, and the best way I knew to achieve this was not to allow my annoyance to surface beyond the confines of my own mind. I knew that the only thing betraying my anger was my throat, which flushed scarlet when I was aggravated.

'Are you sure it's a good idea?' she said, her eyes trained on the electronic device in her palm. 'I'm not being funny, but you make a terrible cup of coffee. And there already *is* a Starbucks, so ...'

I took a deep breath. She was missing the point. She *always* seemed to miss the fucking point. I wondered how to best explain.

'It's a bloody business,' I said, exasperated. 'Do you think Bill Gates could fix your computer? Or that Richard Branson could fly a bloody jumbo jet? It doesn't *matter* if I'm better with a jar of Mellow Birds than I am with one of those bloody great espresso machines. I'd just be running the business. I'd be, you know, the visionary.'

'Right,' said Amanda, reading a message. 'The visionary.' There was no spin to her words. There didn't need to be. The vocabulary was enough: I wasn't a visionary. I didn't know my Arabica from my Ethiopian but, by God, after this conversation I was going to learn.

'Thanks,' I said.

'Alex,' said Amanda, putting down her BlackBerry and reaching for her milky tea, 'I'm happy to support you in anything you do. You know that.' She smiled a pained smile, as if she were talking to a terminally ill patient in a hospital. She reached across and stroked the back of my hand with her aubergine-coloured nails. 'You know that, honey, don't you?' she said. Faint red lines arced from my knuckles to the top of my wrist. Momentarily I wished that she'd pressed deeper into my flesh, that she'd hurt me.

'Yeah,' I half-smiled. 'I know you do.'

As much as I didn't really want to be there, I have to admit to experiencing a certain amount of relief while I leaned on the bar of the rugby club. Two pints of lager to the better I had made a strategic decision: even at this early point in the evening, the deliciousness of the beer quickly persuaded me that I would not be walking home. Ever the planner, I went out to the hallway and plucked one of the business cards that local taxi companies stuck awkwardly behind the plastic frame to which the phone was attached.

I examined it: '24 Hour Taxi's' it read. Now I was no grammatical extremist, but the incorrect use of the apostrophe bothered me. I was fairly sure that the error wouldn't compromise my safety but, nevertheless, I felt that it demonstrated a certain lack of attention to detail. Maybe this would extend to the taxi's brakes. I was searching to see if there was a card for another, less syntactically cavalier company, when I felt the heavy clap of a hand on my shoulder. It was calculated more to unsettle than to greet, and consequently I knew exactly who was standing behind me.

'Hi, Nick,' I said without turning around.

'Hello, *mate*,' said Nick Belagio. The 'mate' was overwrought and aggressive. He smelled of limited-edition aftershave, or expensive leather, or the interior of a brand-new sports car. Something that I couldn't afford. I suspected that he had gone home to have a shower before he came out. He was the kind of man who worked hard to enhance his soap-star good looks.'What you doing standing out here then?'

'I was just getting one of these,' I said, holding up a card. 'I'm in the mood for a bit of a session.'

As was Nick's way, he ignored my answer and gazed over my head.

'So where is everyone?' he asked vaguely, as if disappointed that I was the only person he knew at the club.

'They'll be along later I expect,' I said, the lager earlier making me more amiable than I would like. 'Fancy a beer?' I hated myself for offering to buy Nick – rich Nick, arrogant Nick, Nick whom I couldn't abide but was willing to endure – a drink. There was nothing I wanted less than to spend the next few minutes – and my drinking fund – with Nick Belagio, but there was little else I could do. Wasn't that the way my life was panning out? A series of shitty compromises.

Nick brought out the worst in me. His self-assurance, his intrepid capitalism, made me strangely impotent. I could never find the right words when he was around.

'Mine's a Stella,' Nick said, even though he'd arrived at the bar first. I was aware that he probably drank wines that cost the equivalent of a small family runaround in Michelin-starred restaurants as a matter of course when he entertained other big shots and they swapped stories about their Caribbean holidays and their latest nine irons. But when he was out 'on the razz' as he referred to it, I could see that Nick liked to be one of the people, and indulged in brewed beverages. He surveyed the room like it was his own party, as if everyone were gathered just for him.

As we sipped our lagers, a steady procession of people stopped by to greet Nick, to pay their respects. Being around him made me feel marginalised, like a movie extra: in the frame, but only just.

Why the hell was that? I wasn't bad looking, had a 2:2 in Economics from a red-brick university, played both football and rugby (not to mention tennis and squash) at a respectable level. I didn't look for trouble, but in the few physical encounters I'd had in my lifetime I had acquitted myself fairly well. Yet I would go to parties and struggle to get to the centre of a conversation. My jokes were indulged but never really laughed at in that thigh-slapping I'm-gasping-for-oxygen way that all men crave. Before I married Amanda, women would go out with me – which, thankfully, was more than I imagined was the case – but none of them jumped at me. It was a great sadness to me that I was never propositioned with breathless offers of no-strings-attached sex. To be honest, sometimes I wondered about

Amanda's motivation for marrying me: was it so that she had no competition for an audience when we were out together?

Of course, I now had the chance to position myself at the centre of Caitlin's world. After our encounter at the foster home I had to admit that this seemed like a dim prospect. Even so, with some determination and time, there was possibility there; maybe even some hope.

But kindling our relationship was also tempered by fear. I felt as though I was bound in a straitjacket of mediocrity and, much as I wanted to reach beyond my current fecklessness, I wondered whether I would be able to live with the consequences of taking Caitlin on. Was fatherhood just something else at which I would prove myself to be undistinguished?

The thought had preoccupied me ever since Mr Singh had broken the news to me about Caitlin. But there was something else that followed on from this, a thought so terrible that I attempted to dispatch it as soon as it popped into my head: I would bring Caitlin into my life, rescue her from certain institutional brutality ... But I could always – I couldn't believe that I was actually thinking this – I could always give her back if it didn't work out. It would be like a trial period. I could give it, say, three months.

And, as awful as it sounded, my having an escape plan, a metaphorical button I could press that said 'abort mission', was enough to push me precariously close to the point where taking on a child – *my child* – was something that would become actual rather than theoretical.

As the bar began to fill up, my twitchiness about the decision that I was close to making, the one that yoked my future to Caitlin and rejected Amanda, prompted me to neck a succession of beers. The evening wore on, and my mood passed from wishing that Mike would show up to that of dazed interloper. I felt that I was not so much at the club as watching proceedings from the outside. After a while I decided that it was time to go home; I felt a little unsteady on my feet. I looked around for Nick to say goodbye, but couldn't find the unctuous git. Fuck him, I thought. Don't even like the twat.

I walked out of the club and into the clear evening and heard the unmistakable self-satisfied bray of Nick Belagio. The twat was regaling a group of smokers with some story or other while they were gathered around the corner on the path that led to the car park. I paused for a moment, secretly thrilled by the moment of quiet power: Nick Belagio doesn't know that I can hear him.

'And you've all seen her, right?' he was asking. 'She's not bad looking at all. So there I was, in the market to buy a place and I find myself in the kitchen of this house with my trousers round my ankles. She's up on the kitchen counter and we're going at it, hammer and tongs. And I'm thinking: What if the owners come back?'

The other men laughed. I waited for a moment. I was going to have to pass by the group, but didn't want to disturb them. Not now – they would know that I had heard the story. It felt like I was eavesdropping. Cigarette smoke wafted around the corner.

'And then I'm thinking: Is this what they call a full-service estate agency?'

Another peel of laughter. The mention of an estate agent was intriguing. I wondered if it was someone that Amanda knew.

'So there we are,' continued Nick. 'And I'm beginning to get into my rhythm when I hear her say, "no". So I ask her if she wants me to stop and she just goes "no". So we carry on and she says "no" again. And I ask her again and she's a bit annoyed by this and tells me to carry on, and then before too long all I can hear is, "No, no, no, no, no …" You know a lot of women are all, "Yes, yes, yes …" Well, this one is all about "No, no, no …" It's mental, but I soldier on anyway. It's not easy, but somebody's got to do it.'

Laughter. So much laughter that it flattened me like a wave, crushing the breath from me.

I could hear the group breaking up now, the sound of feet on gravel, backs being slapped and the odd chuckle. I wanted to duck into the shadows, to disappear from sight, but it was too late. I had to move forward, pass through the group of men who, as I did so, either looked at their shoes or sheepishly acknowledged me. Not one of them could look me in the eye.

They knew the woman Nick Belagio had been talking about, and they knew to whom she was married.

Chapter 9

I ran.

I raced down the path and into the street, my momentum causing me to skid across the road. I carried on, pumping my arms, my knees rising high, my jacket billowing behind me. I was barely aware of what I was doing, my body hitting a sort of uneasy overdrive that I was able to maintain for far longer than I expected. I kept moving towards the town centre, crossing roads with random, reckless verve, unconcerned by either pedestrians or road traffic.

I was in control. There was a quiet intensity to my flight. It seemed to be the most natural thing I could imagine: why wouldn't a man who'd had a few pints and discovered that his wife was having illicit sex on someone's kitchen counter be streaking through the streets at eleven o'clock at night?

The end came abruptly. The beer in my belly sloshed around disagreeably. I had thought that I could 'run it off', as my old cross-country teacher always said when faced with a pupil with a stitch. But by the time I got to the centre of town, not only were my lungs fit to burst but it also became abundantly clear that five pints of lager were not standard preparation for a typical Olympic long-distance runner.

My run became more of a stagger before I opened my mouth and threw up in the gutter, unleashing more fluid than I could remember ever having consumed in my entire life. It just wouldn't ... stop ... coming ... flowing down the gutter and puddling around a drain. A group of passing pub refugees cheered and chanted 'Chunderer! Chunderer! Chunderer!' – an undertaking they clearly had some experience and expertise in.

I stood up and wiped my mouth on the sleeve of my jacket, an act that repulsed me at the very moment I was doing it. I could see my reflection in the darkened window of a shop – a bloody travel agent, no less. There I was, hair matted to my forehead, my jacket hanging off me, doubled over trying to catch my breath, the modern-day cuckold, a man whose wife gets taken in a *Reader's Wives* scenario by the kind of arsewipe who stands in the middle of a car park bragging to his mates about it. What the hell was she thinking? The philandering – in a kitchen! – was bad enough, but getting it on with *Nick Belagio* . . .

Nick Belagio!

I couldn't look at the reflection of my heaving, sweaty body any longer. I turned to see a bus shelter. A fucking bus shelter! Right there – staring back at me. What the fuck was it looking at? Enraged, I walked over to the shelter, lifted my leg and stamped on an advertising hoarding as hard as I could. The plastic cracked.

Jesus, that felt good.

I looked around, suddenly self-conscious. Had anyone noticed? There was no one about. Good. I gave it another wallop and it split further. Still, no one in the street, so I kicked it again. And again. And again. Shards of plastic sprayed onto the street. I needed to make myself scarce before my luck ran out, but I wasn't going to run this time.

I walked through the deserted streets, the odd car flashing by, the thumping of house music on car stereos building and waning. Jittery and muddled, I needed to keep moving. I walked quickly around the town, doubling back and creating complex patterns and routes that I'd never considered before.

But even as my mind raced, my body was tired and, as much as the thought of returning home made me feel cold, I ached just to lie down.

I opened the front door noisily, a gesture designed to provoke. Booze and anger meant that I was prepared to have it out with Amanda. But, characteristically, she wasn't home. Bent over the bathroom sink, I drank as much water as I could in an effort to sober up. I didn't want to have to face tomorrow, and the inevitable apocalyptic confrontation, with a hangover. After a shower I went into the spare room and climbed into bed. The sheets were thick and fresh, brushed cotton, which reminded me of being a kid. And, even as my mind whirled with dreadful thoughts, to my surprise I tumbled into a sleep so deep and restful that I could barely believe it even as it came upon me.

Before I lost consciousness I had a vision of my daughter, asleep in a strange place. Her mother dead and her father just an interloper. After what I had discovered tonight, there was little doubt in my mind that my resolution – to try to make things work with Caitlin – had been right.

Maybe it was shock, but that night I was lost to such a powerful force – a phenomenon that shut my body down as if it were protecting itself – that I missed Amanda coming into the spare room and leaving a cup of tea on the bedside table before she left for work. Naturally, she assumed that I had simply gone out drinking and was too bladdered to share the marital bed. What a classy couple we were.

I woke around eight thirty, opening my eyes gingerly. I was encouraged to learn that I had only a light hangover. Nevertheless, there was a nagging tension at the front of my skull. A constant buzz that *something* wasn't right.

How was I supposed to respond? I knew that Amanda and I weren't exactly in line to win any awards from the marriage guidance council for empathetic and intimate handling of our relationship, but this ... I really had not expected anything like it. Never in a million years would I have thought that Amanda was capable of cheating, let alone two-timing in such a dramatic manner.

This wasn't an affair; it was an extramarital rampage.

I had a shower that lasted close to an hour. The steam and hot water offered a refuge from the laughter of the night before. I tried to shut it out of my mind, but it kept bouncing back, reviving the humiliation. It was like watching an accident in slow motion over and over again.

I tried to shake it loose, vowing not to do anything rash.

I would save that for later.

'*Hellooo*,' said the receptionist at Dyer & Liphoff estate agents. She always said it like that to people she knew. It drove me mad.

'Hi,' I said snappily.

'She's just with a couple of clients,' the receptionist explained in a conspiratorial whisper. She nodded her head towards Amanda, who was sitting at her desk trying to seduce – as I now thought of any conversation she might have – a well-groomed couple.

'That's okay,' I said.

'You'll come back in a bit, will you?'

'Actually, no,' I replied with a smile that I was later informed the receptionist described as 'maniacal'.

It started very softly, almost like a lullaby.

'Ooooooh ... Oooooooh ... Ooooooh ...'

The receptionist looked at me nervously. 'What are you doing?' she giggled.

I ignored her. My groans grew louder.

'Ooooooh ... Oooooooooh ... Ooooooh ...'

This caught Amanda's attention. She shot me a what-the-hell-are-you-doing-I'm-working-a-deal look, while trying to keep her clients focused on the task in hand.

Then I switched the noise.

'Nooooooooo …' came the noise. The receptionist sat horrified and rigid, like a rabbit hoping no one would notice it.

'*No, no, no, no, no, no, no …*'

Amanda stood up, smiling and reassuring her distracted clients.

'*No, no, no, no, no, no …*' I moaned, building towards a falsetto.

Amanda marched sternly between the rows of cubicles, coming towards the reception area. By this point I was reaching climax.

'*Nooooooo … Nooooooo … Nooooooo …*'

'What the fuck do you think you're doing?' she hissed. She kept her voice low, attempting to limit the damage to the deal she had been constructing. The couple at her desk stood up and were folding away the pieces of paper that they'd been analysing with her.

'*Nooooooooooooooooooooooooo …*'

'Get out,' Amanda said in a controlled but livid fashion. 'Get the fuck out!'

I stared at her angrily, maybe maniacally. Something passed between us, but I couldn't be sure that we were both registering the same thing.

'Shall I call the police?' asked the receptionist nervously. Amanda stared at me: the ball was in my court.

'That won't be necessary,' I said.

I took a couple of steps backwards towards the door before, in a sarcastically measured voice, saying, 'We need to talk.'

I looked back at the couple at Amanda's desk.

'Hi,' I said, waving to them. They regarded me nervously. 'Watch out!' I exclaimed, gesturing towards Amanda. 'She's going to try to have sex with you – she just can't help herself!'

Amanda had opened the door and was tugging at my sleeve to get me outside. We both tumbled onto the street and stood there panting with annoyance.

'I know all about it,' I said to her as we faced each other on the pavement.

Amanda stood with her hands on her hips and a menacing look on her face. The attempt to be intimidating wasn't having a huge effect on me; at this point, keeping her sweet wasn't high on my priority list.

'How dare you come into my office and embarrass me in front of clients?' Amanda snapped. 'What the hell has got into you?'

'Don't make a fool of yourself, Amanda.'

'What are you talking about, Alex?'

Was she serious? Was this the level of regard she had for me? Was she going to try to tough this one out?

I laughed. 'Don't insult my intelligence,' I said to her. 'You've humiliated me enough already.'

The punters to whom Amanda had been talking scurried out of the door. She turned to try and catch them.

'Judy, Robert, I'll be right back. I—' The couple didn't even make eye contact with her as they fled up the street. They wanted absolutely nothing to do with whatever was going on. I knew how they felt.

'I'll give you a bell later,' Amanda called over to them in her best this-is-really-nothing-to-get-worked-up-about voice. The message was: *everything is fine – get the hell back in that office and let's do a deal.*

'Don't embarrass yourself any more, Amanda,' I said firmly. She could tell that my mood had moved beyond the dementia that had driven me to instigate the scene in her office. I was focused now, maybe even persuasive. She looked at me timidly and nodded her head.

'All right,' she said. 'I won't.'

'So what have you got to say for yourself?'

'I'm not really sure what all this is about ...'

'Well, why not take a wild guess?'

She waited for a while before answering. I recognised it as the kind of look she would have on her face before she threw down a huge Scrabble score: thoughtful, yet competitive. But then the look dissipated. There was only plainness and something I had only ever seen during our months trying to conceive – vulnerability.

'We'll talk about this later on,' she said, before glancing away, not wanting to look me in the eye.

'Maybe,' I said. I turned and walked along the high street, passing a bus shelter that was being fixed by a couple of workmen.

I would talk to her. And I would tell her exactly how things were going to be. I was going to make some changes in my life. I headed for the train station. I had a work appointment to keep.

Chapter 10

'Morning, Steve.'

'Morning, Alex.'

I had been looking forward to this day since my arrival at TicketBusters. I had thought about it so often, and had constructed so many different versions of the fantasy, that now I was here, in the room where I was going to tell my boss that I was quitting, it seemed like an anticlimax. I had wanted to tell Steve what a loathsome, small-minded, petty whiner he was, and how everyone on staff mocked him and even risked getting caught making wanker signs behind his back as he progressed down the corridor, but as I sat in Steve's crappy little office, with its beige walls and flat-pack desk looking at the two dismal industry citations that passed for decoration, I simply couldn't be arsed.

'Thanks for making the time to see me today, Steve,' I opened.

'Not at all, Alex,' said Steve condescendingly. 'My door is always open.'

A fucking lie, if ever I'd heard one. Steve usually kept his door closed so that he could listen to the cricket, or the football, or whatever sporting event was in progress somewhere across the globe.

'I've come to tell you that I'm leaving,' I announced. Steve looked down at his desk before crossing his legs and brushing some lint from his thigh: some manoeuvre he'd picked up on some bullshit management course.

'Really,' he said.

'Yeah,' I said after a pause.

'And where are you going, then?' He said this testily, like I had behaved in an unprofessional manner.

'Nowhere,' I replied.

'Come, come, now,' said Steve, pushing his glasses up the bridge of his nose. 'We're all grown-ups here.'

'I'm serious,' I said with a shrug. 'I'm not going anywhere. I'm doing my own thing.'

'You're doing your own thing, eh?' said Steve, with a barely concealed chuckle. 'And what might that "thing" be, then?'

'A coffee shop.'

Did I just say that? I mean, I know that I've been thinking about it, been planning it even, but saying it to Steve, someone I didn't like, somehow made it real.

'A coffee shop?' Steve replied. For the first time he looked directly at me.

'So you're not going to counter-offer then?' I asked.

'What?'

'You're not going to make me a better offer,' I explained. 'To make me stay.'

Steve considered his response. He uncrossed his legs and leaned on his desk.

'Well, I'm not sure I know what I'm counter-offering against,' he said.

'I suppose I'm just interested to know if you can make staying worth my while.' This was a lie, of course. I would rather have battered my own balls and deep-fried them than stay at TicketBusters, but I was intrigued to know my worth to the company, and wanted to make this meeting as uncomfortable for Steve as possible.

'Um ...' said Steve. 'You know, I don't think I am.'

'Really?'

'Well, if you're leaving to follow a passion, I don't think I can compete with that, can I? It's not like there's a lot of leeway for me. I can probably offer you a couple more grand but – let's be honest here – it's not worth my while. Or yours.'

'Oh,' I said. I shouldn't have been surprised by his inertia.

'So I'll need a couple of weeks to find someone else,' said Steve. 'But I don't want to hold you up. I think we can say that, once we figure your holiday time out … You can probably have two weeks on Friday as your leaving date.'

'Sorry, Steve,' I said. 'Not going to be possible. In a bit of a hurry. Need to be gone, well, today really.'

'Well, that leaves us in the lurch a bit, Alex,' said Steve. 'I really feel that it's not fair of you to—'

'Well, I suppose that's it then,' I said, standing up. I didn't offer the twat my hand. 'Thanks for … Actually, I'm not sure what I'm thanking you for.'

'So you know that this means I won't be able to sanction an official leaving do?' said Steve officiously.

'Let me see,' I said, struggling to keep a straight face. 'Can I live with myself if I miss out on a TicketBusters farewell party with fifty quid bunged behind the bar at the White Horse? That's a tough one …' I drummed my fingers on my chin in mock thought before turning round and walking out of the door.

I was now single, unemployed and an unskilled father. Talk about a good catch.

PART TWO

Chapter 11

'Hello,' I said to Caitlin. I attempted to inject a cheerful energy into my words, but to my horror I sounded like a middle-aged man pretending to be an MTV DJ.

'Hi,' she replied. The words were colourless, empty. She looked at me and I could see resignation, not enthusiasm, in her eyes.

'Do you want me to carry your things?' I asked.

She was standing in the bedroom of the foster home, clutching a small suitcase with a faded Virgin Atlantic sticker on the side. It was probably something that a social worker had found inside Cathy's house.

'No thanks,' she said.

'Are you sure?' I asked, immediately wishing that I hadn't. She bristled, irritated by my eagerness. I needed to be more composed, to demonstrate authority but be warm ... paternal ... Good God, this was tricky.

Caitlin was holding a small stuffed animal – a bassett-hound, maybe? – in her right hand. She noticed that I was examining it.

'He doesn't have a name,' she said, agitated. Clearly I was pathetically predictable.

'I was just about to ask that,' I said, chuckling, trying to bring her out of her funk.

She nodded. I *know*.

I reached into my pocket and pulled out my car keys. There was part of me – and I felt terrible even rubbing up against the thought – that wanted to say to her: 'Fine, you stay here. I'll go and lead the life of a carefree bachelor running amok with girls from the Boots fragrance counter while you're passed from foster home to care facility to foster home, because *everyone* wants to adopt damaged teenage girls.'

Instead, I took a deep breath. I had been through the Social Services wringer, had undergone various interviews and background checks in order to prove my worthiness. Frankly, part of me was amazed that they were handing her over to me. It was like putting a milkman in charge of a Formula One team. I needed to see it from Caitlin's point of view: she was simply dealing with another adult who, since the death of her mother, was attempting to bond with her.

'Right,' I said, trying to take charge, thinking that this was what she expected of me. 'Are you ready?'

Caitlin shrugged. The room contained a few knick-knacks and posters that were meant to make it look homely. None of it really hung together, though: it was like looking at a hybrid animal, a beast that had been made up of parts of several others.

'Come on, then,' I said. I watched Caitlin as she walked past me and out of the room. There was no final glance, no moment of farewell.

The woman who ran the home had made herself scarce. Perhaps this was procedure, not wanting to upset the departing kids. I pulled the door closed behind us and found myself on the street – no, it was more dramatic than that – out in the *world*, with my daughter. Just the two of us. Me and my girl.

The weather wasn't exactly auspicious. It was overcast and threatening rain. Dad Duty number one flashed into my mind: Caitlin was wearing a thin-looking T-shirt, her skinny arms pale.

'Are you warm enough?' I asked as we walked towards the car.

'Yeah,' said Caitlin, 'I'm fine.' I noticed for the first time that, despite her long hair, her profile was boyish; she had a slightly upturned nose, an impishness that suggested trouble.

'Here we are,' I said when we arrived at the car. I unlocked the door and held it open for her.

'I'm not allowed,' said Caitlin.

I looked at her. *What now?*

'I'm not allowed in the front of the car,' Caitlin said. 'Not if there's an airbag.'

She looked at me like this was further evidence of my idiocy. What kind of a dad would be oblivious to something like this?

'Ah, that's right,' I said, closing the door. I looked in the back of the car. Surely she was too old for a car seat or safety harness?

'Are you all right in the back with a seatbelt?' I asked.

Caitlin glared at me, flushed red and then looked back at the car. Was she embarrassed or angry?

'I don't ...' she started, searching for the right words. Did I notice a shiver? 'My mum ...'

Oh, for God's sake. How had this not occurred to me?

'Oh, yeah, wow ...' I said, cutting her off. I needed to try to save her this kind of discomfort.

Deep breath, Alex.

'Caitlin,' I said, rubbing her shoulder. It was cold. I pulled my hand away sharply. I had never touched her before. Was this inappropriate? I really had no idea what I was doing.

'I'm really sorry,' I said. 'That was really, um, silly ...' *Silly?* What was I – a kindergarten teacher? 'I don't know what I was thinking.'

I ran my hand through my hair. What to do next?

Food. Everyone loves food.

'How about this,' I said, trying to be conciliatory. 'Let's put your bag in the boot and we'll get some lunch. There's a shop nearby where we can pick up a car seat.'

'A car seat?' Caitlin said, smiling. It was the first time I had seen her break into a smile. 'What are you talking about? Only babies have car seats.'

'Well, I thought, you, um …'

Caitlin started laughing. I began to join in, thrilled that – at last! – we were enjoying a moment of shared humour. But after a few moments I came to realise that there was nothing shared about it. The joke was on me.

Caitlin had no time for my ignorance.

'What a *fool*,' she said, flicking her fingers together in some kind of street celebration that had no place in this suburb.

'Don't worry,' she continued, the laugh verging on a sneer. 'We can pick out a nice pink one.'

'Great,' I said, nodding enthusiastically, knowing that I was making a total mug of myself.

'And I can show you how to fix it in as well,' Caitlin continued.

'Sounds good,' I said, trying not to show her quite how much she'd got to me. Despite what had happened to her, the girl had power. She was strong. That was good.

She handed me her suitcase. She wasn't laughing any longer.

'It's about height, you know,' she said. 'If you're over a certain height you can just wear a seatbelt. You should look it up online.'

'I will,' I said brightly, trying not to let her know that she'd drawn blood.

'Good,' she said, as if she'd proved a point. She turned her back, waiting for me to put her bag in the trunk.

'Look,' I said, 'let's grab a coffee or something, shall we?'

'I don't drink coffee,' Caitlin said. I couldn't tell whether this was just her passing on information or whether she was presenting me with another challenge.

'Come on,' I said, closing the boot. 'There's a place just up here.'

These were the first few moments that I'd spent with my only child. It should have been the kind of encounter that's memorialised in a Hallmark card or a made-for-TV tearjerker. Instead – even taking into account what I'd been through with Amanda over the past few weeks – I felt utterly incompetent.

We walked to a local mini shopping mall and found ourselves amidst the homogenous, mediocre retail found in any British town.

'You hungry?' I asked. Caitlin had stopped to look in the window of a shoe shop. I followed her gaze towards something silver and heeled. Was that kind of thing allowed? Every pair should have been sold with birth control thrown in.

'Caitlin – shall we get something to eat?' I asked.

'Okay,' she replied, without looking away from the window.

I stood and waited for her to lose interest, but she remained rooted to the spot.

'What do you want?' I asked.

'Those ones, there,' she said, pointing.

'It's "those", not "those ones",' I corrected her, feeling like a prig. 'And I meant "What would you like to eat?", not "Which shoes do you want?"'

'I'm not really hungry,' said Caitlin, turning away from the shoe shop. A couple of teenage boys walked past trying to play it cool. Her eyes followed them before she realised that I was watching her.

'If you're hungry, though, I'll sit with you,' she added.

'Well, maybe we should wait then,' I said. 'You know, until we're both hungry.'

'Actually, I *am* hungry,' she said.

The total change in tune was hard to grasp. It was like driving a car that turns the opposite way from the way you're steering.

'Okay,' I said. 'How about this place?'

I gestured towards a faux French bakery named 'L'Eiffel' that served faux French baked goods and salads. Caitlin shrugged.

'We can get a burger or something, if you want ...' I suggested. If I couldn't find a way to her heart I'd find a way to her stomach.

Caitlin looked at me, horrified.

'I don't eat *meat*,' she said, as if I'd suggested that she might like to tuck into a pair of my old trainers. 'I'm a vegetarian.'

'Oh, sorry,' I said. 'They do vegetarian food at McDonald's now, you know ...' My voice trailed off. Caitlin was looking at me with barely concealed contempt. I had blundered again.

'You've got to be joking,' she protested. 'It's disgusting there – really unhealthy. Everything is deep-fried and they scrape meat off the floor. And they're destroying the planet. They're cutting down the rainforest for hamburgers.' She paused, realising that she'd just said something she didn't mean. 'They're not *making* burgers out of the rainforest. They're cutting down the trees so that they can put cows on the land.'

'Fair point,' I said. So much for crowd-pleasing fast food then. 'I never go there myself. I just thought, you know, it's the kind of place that kids, I mean young people, like.'

'Some of my friends go,' said Caitlin. 'They'll probably get Mad Cow disease or something.'

'Maybe,' I said, smothering a smile. 'So is this place okay?'

'Yes,' said Caitlin, nodding her head several times. 'It's much better.'

We walked into L'Eiffel and sat at a small table. A bored waitress took our order.

'I'll have the ham and cheese croissant, please,' I said, before catching myself. I turned to Caitlin. 'Do you mind if I eat meat?'

'It's up to you,' she replied, examining the wipe-clean menu.

'Do you have any vegetarian options?' I asked, trying to be helpful. The waitress tapped Caitlin's menu distractedly, looking in the other direction.

'It's okay,' said Caitlin, 'I'm used to it.'

She ordered a tuna mayonnaise 'croissantwich'. The food arrived almost immediately and we sat eating in silence. To my enormous relief Caitlin demolished everything on her plate. Thank God I don't have to deal with an eating disorder, I thought to myself. Looking at her I had no idea where she put it all.

'I'm a pescatarian,' she told me, mopping up the last of her food. 'That means I eat fish.'

'How was the food in the, um, home?' I asked. The word 'home' made it sound like a Victorian mental asylum.

'Pretty bad,' she said, taking a sip of her apple juice. 'They couldn't boil an egg without messing it up.'

I paid the bill and we returned to the cloying dullness of the mall.

'So ...' I said nervously. 'Just so I know ... You don't actually need anything for the car, do you?'

Without looking at her I could sense her eyes rolling into the back of her head.

'I thought not,' I said.

When we got back to the car I realised that I might need to reconsider my motoring options. I was so distracted when I first picked up Caitlin that I'd failed to notice that my silver two-door 3-Series might not be the appropriate car to ferry a kid around in. There was barely any room in the back – but cramming her in there was preferable to letting her sit alongside

me in front where it could look like she was, um, my *girlfriend*.
I needed to invest in something more family oriented.

We headed off. It was strange knowing someone else – a
child! – was in the back seat of my car. It made me feel different,
more *established* somehow. I was someone to be reckoned with.
I drove a little more slowly than I normally would, stopping
whenever I noticed a pedestrian within stumbling distance of
a crossing.

'So I've sorted your room out,' I said. 'I think it looks pretty
cool …' Jesus, if anything was guaranteed to fill her with dread
it was my thinking that something was 'cool'. 'But you tell me
what you think,' I added quickly.

'Okay,' said Caitlin. She was leaning against the window, her
face pressed against the glass, which was steamed up where she
was breathing.

'Because we can go out at the weekend and get you some
stuff, if you—'

'Do you have a job?' Caitlin asked, cutting me off.

'Yeah …' I said, before catching myself.

Jesus, I'd actually forgotten that I'd quit.

'Actually, you know what,' I laughed, embarrassed at my
forgetfulness, 'I did have a job. I had the same job for seven
years. I quit a few days ago.'

'Why?'

'Well,' I started. What to tell her? That I hated it? Which I did.
That I had enough money to last for a couple of years? Which,
if I was reasonably frugal, I could. 'I decided that I wanted to
do something else.'

'Did you leave because of me?' asked Caitlin.

Hmm … Should I answer in the affirmative to demonstrate
how much her presence in my life meant to me? Or should I say
that actually, no, it was a number of different factors all coming
together?

82

'I want to do something else with my life, Caitlin.'

'Oh,' she replied, as if this was the kind of thing that grown-ups often said, as if it didn't really mean anything. I felt a degree of pressure, like I had to demonstrate to her that her father wasn't actually feckless, that he was a man of drive, energy and vision.

'I want to open a café,' I said, looking in the rear-view mirror to check her reaction.

Silence.

'What do you think about that?' I asked.

'Wicked,' said Caitlin without a high degree of enthusiasm.

'Yeah,' I continued, attempting to warm to the subject. I racked my brains for something to add, but discovered that I had nothing to offer other than: 'It's going to be great.'

We passed through another couple of miles of M25-land. Flash houses, petrol stations, traffic jams, schools with fancy uniforms: white people who just want to get home and turn on their satellite TV.

'Are you married?'

There was no easy answer to this question. I was still married, of course, although I had moved out (despite Amanda's protests and promises) immediately after I had come to the decision that I needed a fresh start – a fresh start that coincided with my agreeing to become Caitlin's guardian.

Dauntingly, however, Social Services had added various conditions to this, most notably that Caitlin would find herself in a 'settled family environment'. I had managed to fudge the issue of Amanda and I for the time being, but Social Services had assured me that they would be making regular visits. This was a problem that I would have to deal with but, at that moment, I wasn't able to think that far ahead.

I would have to manage the marriage situation equally delicately. Amanda must not know about Caitlin. And vice versa. I had yanked my ring off immediately after we'd fought outside the estate agency and slipped it inside my jacket pocket, where it still sat. I tapped my ring finger against the steering wheel. There was no noise of metal on plastic.

'No,' I said. 'Not any more.'

The car suddenly felt too hot.

'It's just you and me.'

Chapter 12

I had left Amanda the week before. There was stupendous un-pleasantness – recriminations, accusations, explanations – as I packed my bags and loaded the car. She had pleaded and then demanded that I stay, promising that her roving was a one-off. She swore that she wouldn't stray again.

None of this had really moved me, which was curious, as, despite Amanda's betrayal, there was still a large part of me that loved her. But I had made my decision: I would sample life with Caitlin, take on the role of dad – although I suppose it wasn't a role; it was more solid than that. It was the opportunity that I'd not been able to craft for myself, a chance to climb from the furrow into which I had fallen. And Amanda didn't need to know this. (Besides, I wasn't in a mood to explain myself.) Cynically I also calculated that, should my experiment with Caitlin fail and I had to extricate myself from my role as dad, Amanda's guilt and desire to absolve herself would allow me room to manoeuvre if I wanted to renew the marriage.

After Amanda slammed the door behind me I drove the ten minutes to my new home, the one that I'd come to think of as a family home. I had rented a three-bedroom semi on the other side of town, not far from the train station. I hadn't told Amanda where I was going to live, which had driven her mad with irri-tation. It was a cosy little house and met with the approval of a forbidding woman from Social Services named Joan Kennedy, who had come to look at it and commented on its warmth and the tidiness of the garden. It had gone well, although Kennedy had asked where Amanda was. She had stressed again that she needed to see Caitlin in a family context next time she visited.

I had put these thoughts out of my mind and focused on getting the place ready for her. From my limited experience, I knew that Caitlin was a tough crowd. I had my work cut out. There was no emotion on her face as we passed along the garden path towards the gabled porch and the front door. I wanted to tell her that I had spent the previous afternoon painting it green, but thought that this would not interest her a great deal. Honeysuckle grew up the sides of the porch. In the evening, its perfume enveloped visitors. It smelled like a home should.

'So this is it,' I said to Caitlin.

I let her walk into the house before me. She wiped her feet on the mat inside the door. I'm sure that Cathy would have been pleased with that. The landlord had repainted the place before we'd moved in and refinished the wooden floors. Although I had brought very little with me (part disorganisation, part keeping a foot in both camps) I had made an effort to add some personal touches: I'd tortured myself with a trip to IKEA and bought prints, furniture and lamps that would offer the place some character. 'Modern accents for a contemporary family', like it said in the brochure.

Caitlin looked around without saying very much. She was wearing her iPod. I wondered at what stage I could start ordering her to take them out.

'Do you want to see your room?' I asked.

'I suppose so,' she said unenthusiastically.

We climbed the stairs, which creaked a little, and I pushed open the door. I had given her the largest room at the back of the house so that she would be able to look out over the garden. There was only one downside which, thankfully, Caitlin would be unaware of: if you craned your neck you could see Nick Belagio's stately, detached residence, which I one day hoped

86

would be used by the RAF for target practice. I had painted the room mauve and bought furniture that I thought a thirteen-year-old girl might like. There was a bed (flat-pack), a desk (flat-pack), a beanbag (not flat-pack) and a bookcase (flat-pack) that I had laden with recommendations from the assistant at the bookshop. In addition I had chosen bedcovers that I hoped were acceptable. Otherwise I had arranged the things that Social Services had brought from her old room, touches of Caitlin's former life. On her bedside table I'd put a framed photo of Cathy.

There was no sign of emotion on her face, but when she walked over to the bed, sat on it and then placed her soft toy on the pillow it suggested that I hadn't totally screwed this one up. I went downstairs and collected her suitcase and brought it up.

'What's the name of the colour on the walls?' she asked.

'It's called Mountain Mist,' I answered. 'Do you like it?'

She giggled to herself. I had absolutely no idea how to read this.

'It's okay I suppose,' she said eventually. 'I don't really know.'

Deep breath, son, deep breath.

'Are you hungry?' I asked.

'We just had lunch,' she pointed out.

'Oh, yes,' I said, utterly at a loss as to what should happen now. 'I'll leave you to it then,' I said after a while. 'I expect you want to get things sorted out. Do you want me to close the door?'

'Yes,' she said. 'Does it have a lock?'

'What?'

She repeated the question.

'The door, you mean?' I said, finally realising what she was asking. 'Um, no, it doesn't.'

She didn't say anything else. I wasn't sure whether this meant that I should go out and buy a lock for her door, or whether we should talk about it. I imagined that being a dad involved lots of talking about things. I had no idea if teenage girls generally had locks on their doors, although I could understand why they might want them. Where the hell was I supposed to find out about this stuff? I had no mother, I'd never had a sister, and I couldn't exactly ask Amanda.

'I'll be downstairs if you need anything,' I said after a while.

I had turned to leave when I heard her say, 'Thanks.'

I smiled to myself at the simple word of vindication. I hadn't screwed it up! Unless, that was, she was being sarcastic . . . I was going to need to start to learn to read the signs.

Although the academic year had only just ended, I knew that I needed to get moving and enrol Caitlin at school. This would have the added benefit of buying me Brownie points with Joan Kennedy at Social Services.

I arranged for us to go and meet the headmistress at the local comprehensive, which had received a positive Ofsted rating, which probably made me the only parent in the district not to have moved here for the school.

'You're going to have to take those off,' I said to Caitlin, nodding to her headphones as we sat in the reception area. 'We need to make a good impression.'

'I'll take them off when she comes to get us,' said Caitlin.

'No,' I said. This might have been the first time that I'd said the word to her. 'You need to remove them now.'

She sighed. I looked at her and noticed something that made me even more alarmed.

'Are you wearing make-up?' I asked.

'*No*,' she replied, looking away from me. I wasn't expert

88

enough to be sure, but it looked like she might have applied some mascara.

'This is a good school, Caitlin,' I explained. 'I'm sure that your mum would have wanted you to give them your best.'

'How would you know?' she said quietly, as if to herself. She was right, of course; I had no idea what Cathy would have wanted. I was just about to take her up on this when a greying lady in a tweed skirt and half-moon spectacles appeared. Her hair was pulled back tightly into a bun. She looked like a cliché of Agatha Christie middle England, other than the fact that she was mixed race.

'Hello, hello ...' she said, striding briskly towards us as I struggled to climb out of my chair to greet her. 'Loretta Young. Very nice to meet you – you must be Caitlin,' she said, holding out her hand. I liked the fact that she had extended the courtesy to Caitlin first, but dreaded the girl's response.

'Very nice to meet you too,' said Caitlin. And I swear she nearly curtsied like she was meeting the Queen. Her smile illuminated the room. I'd yet to see anything like it. I noticed too that her iPod earphones had miraculously disappeared. We were led to the headmistress's study and furnished with scalding hot cups of tea.

'Now then,' she said, directing her question to Caitlin. 'How did you like All Saints?'

'It was really good,' she replied. 'I liked my teachers, the classes were interesting and ... you know, I liked it.'

'Good, good,' said Mrs Young. 'I know the school very well. A couple of their teachers have ended up coming to work here and we've sent some their way as well. What do you like best about school?'

'I don't really know,' she replied. I tensed, praying that she wouldn't say 'going home' or 'lunchtime'. Instead, she considered what she'd been asked. 'I think it's too early to start thinking

89

about cutting back on subjects like some kids are doing. I'd like to keep my options open. But I really like English and French and science.'

'Good, good,' said Mrs Young, examining a file. I couldn't imagine this going much better. I kept my mouth shut.

'How about sports?' asked Mrs Young.

Caitlin glanced over towards me, as if a little unsure of herself.

'They're OK, I suppose.'

'You're not a big netball or hockey player then?'

'Not really. I like swimming, though.'

'Good, good,' said Mrs Young. 'We don't have a pool on-site, but we have weekly lessons over at the municipal pool.'

Mrs Young removed her glasses and looked at Caitlin kindly.

'Right then,' she started. 'It was really very nice to meet you. If you could wait outside for a couple of moments I'll have a quick word with your dad.'

'Okay,' said Caitlin. The smile that she had delivered Mrs Young earlier had gone. She now looked anxious. She stood up and started to walk to the door.

'Well,' she said to Mrs Young, 'he's not really my dad ...'

I tried not to let the horror I felt inside transfer to my face. She was selling me out in front of her new headteacher.

'Well, he is my dad technically,' continued Caitlin. 'But we've only just ... reconnected. Because of my mum, you know.'

'I understand,' said Mrs Young calmly. 'And I know that you've been through a tough time recently. It's something that we'll all be able to work on together.'

I couldn't look at Caitlin any longer. I just waited to hear the door close.

'Sorry about that,' I said with an embarrassed laugh.

'There's no need to be,' said Mrs Young, slightly dismissively.

'I know about your circumstances through Social Services. She's been through as hard a time as a girl in early adolescence can experience. And it will take a long while for her not to feel sad and angry and lonely and all the other emotions that she has rolling around inside her.'

'Yes, you're right,' I said, wishing I'd been able to put it in such an articulate fashion.

'I can't imagine that it's been that much fun for you and your wife ...' Here she inserted a pregnant pause.

'Amanda.'

'... Amanda, either. Look, this is a popular school, and our results mean that parents want to send their children here. We don't actually have a place for Caitlin ...'

'Oh,' I said, deflated.

'But given her exceptional circumstances, I'm willing to bend the rules a little to accommodate her. However, you and your wife and I are going to have to monitor the situation closely.'

'I know,' I said, trying to pick up on her earlier theme. 'The grieving process is a long, hard road.'

'I'm not referring to that,' said Mrs Young, reopening Caitlin's folder.

'Oh?'

'I'm talking about her behavioural issues.'

'Behavioural issues?'

Mrs Young looked at me like I was insane.

'Mr Taylor, from the look on your face I assume that you don't know that Caitlin has been expelled from one school and was on suspension from another at the time of her mother's death?'

It took me less than forty-eight hours to realise that I was seriously out of my depth. Most of the time Caitlin was un-interested in talking; she kept moving when I asked her a question, greeted it with a shrug or just plain ignored it. This I could put down to pre-adolescent disposition and grief. But on discovering that she was the one-person Kray Twins of Surrey comprehensive schools (she had been expelled for stealing money from another kid's bag and then suspended for calling a teacher a 'knob jockey'), I began to doubt my stomach for the inevitable parent–teacher combat. It wasn't like I'd been able to spend years caring for and nurturing a child, shaping it into what I hoped was a decent and considerate member of society. It was more like finding yourself in a pub fight when you'd just popped in for a lager top.

Was I really equipped to deal with this?

I had not mentioned Mrs Young's information to Caitlin. I had tried Googling 'difficult teenagers' and 'behavioural disorders' and had been overwhelmed by the volume of information. Clearly I wasn't alone. But despite my worry I just felt paralysed, incapable of taking any action.

That afternoon we were sitting watching a movie – I was quickly getting up to speed with the oeuvre of Lindsay Lohan, *Gossip Girl* and Harry Potter – when Caitlin, who had been silent for almost an hour while I had read the marginal parts of the newspaper – the op ed columns, economics pages, equestrian stuff – turned and asked, 'Why don't you have a job again?'

It was a challenge more than an enquiry. It was like I was *in her way*.

I put the newspaper down. She had asked me a similar question only a few days earlier in the car. It sounded to me like she was annoyed that I was hanging round the house.

'I used to have one,' I said in a measured voice – the voice I'd read about in one of the dozen or so parenting books that I had stashed under my bed with the attention to concealment that, in the past, I had applied only to pornography. The books just served to make me feel exposed and untutored: I had started each of them with a degree of resolve, but had rarely reached the second chapter.

Here I was, theoretically responsible for guiding this fledgling relationship, yet I was flying blind.

'What happened to it?' Caitlin pressed.

'I decided to quit.'

'Why?'

'Well, I knew that you were coming and I thought that it was best that I focused all my energies on, you know ... us.'

'But you didn't need to quit your job just because of that,' she said, her eyes still on the screen.

I folded my newspaper and looked at her.

'It was a little more complicated than that,' I explained. 'I didn't really like it very much anyway.'

'Grown-ups never like their jobs,' said Caitlin. 'My mum didn't like hers.'

'What did she do?'

'I'm not really sure,' she said. 'She worked at a hospital, but she wasn't a nurse, or a doctor or anything. She came home from work and she was always stressed out.'

'That's what work is like sometimes,' I said. I felt a little defensive towards Cathy. It's not easy being a single parent, after all.

'I used to run her a bath,' said Caitlin.

'I bet she liked that,' I said, but Caitlin didn't respond. It was as if she was trying to shut the conversation down. Maybe it was too painful for her. Maybe she just didn't want to talk to me about her mum. She continued to watch the film for a few minutes. I switched my attention to the screen as well in the hope of gleaning some valuable conversational nuggets.

'I think you should get another job,' said Caitlin after a while. She had tuned out of the movie again.

'Really?' I said. Was it so obvious that a man without a job was no man at all? Surely my new 'purpose-driven existence', as the self-help industry might define it, was enough to offer me a role in life?

'What about that café you keep talking about opening?'

'I'm thinking about it.'

'Well, it's not going to get done if you just think about it,' said Caitlin. She had clearly picked this up from her mother. It was said in a voice that was kinder than the sentiment. Nevertheless, the sentiment was fairly clear.

'I suppose you're right,' I said.

Which, of course, she was. I got up from the sofa and went to search for my espresso machine brochures.

Chapter 13

'What kind of lunacy is this?' demanded Mike severely. Over-weight and sweating profusely, he wiped his forehead with the back of his hand before crouching down on the squash court and attempting to catch his breath. We were at the local sports centre for a winner-takes-all Tuesday-night throw-down.

'Let's talk about it afterwards,' I said, trying not to let him see that I was happy to take a breather as well.

'What's the score?' he asked distractedly.

'Eight–six; my service,' I said. Mike liked to talk on the squash court. His banter distracted me. I didn't want to natter; I wanted to win. I was a competitive sod when it came to sport.

Other than the game of squash, the evening centred around my seeking Mike's counsel on the various issues weighing on my mind. Mike had offered some sage advice on Amanda – 'fuck her' – and, although initially sceptical of the arrangement (he had tried to persuade me to take a paternity test before accepting any legal obligation for Caitlin), he had given a thumbs-up to my decision to abandon the marital home and go it alone with Caitlin.

'I'm sorry, mate, but I still don't understand why the hell you've suddenly decided you want to open a coffee bar.' He was bent forward now, holding his racquet, ready for me to bring the noise.

'I mean ...' He inhaled deeply. 'Bloody hell, Alex: one thing at a time, mate. Haven't you got enough on your plate?'

'Have you any idea how much bloody Starbucks is worth?'

'No,' he said. 'Have you?'

'No,' I admitted after a pause. 'But it's a lot. A lot more than a lot, actually.'

'Is it your expertise in accountancy that gives you that kind of valuable insight?'

'Actually, yes. The way we express that kind of amount is: a fucking shitload.'

We played a point. Mike always seemed less mobile than he actually was, which could be problematic for me: he had good feet for a big man, and, on the next point, I ended up handing service over to him on a shot I really should have killed. Mike put his hands on his knees and sucked on the dank air.

'I'm not following your argument, Alex,' he said. 'Giorgio Armani is worth a fortune but I don't see you trying to start a fashion company.'

'It'll work,' I insisted, trying to keep my head in the game. 'Around here, all these rich bastards, they've got nothing better to do than sit around drinking lattes all day and worrying about their kids' after-school classes. Can you imagine? The money is going to be up to my fucking ankles.'

'Actually, Alex,' interrupted Mike, 'truth is you might find yourself up to your neck in shit. You're a bloody accountant. What do you know about making coffee other than putting the kettle on and getting the Gold Blend out?'

'That means nothing,' I said, gesturing with my squash racquet. 'Nothing. Starbucks coffee is piss. We can do the real thing. The real McCoy. Like in Italy. We'll do it properly. People will pay more if you give them something they see as better, or authentic or something.'

Mike made a small gesture with his mouth, a tightening that conveyed scepticism. He nodded up at the gallery where Caitlin was reading a book.

'You've got enough to worry about.'

I knew what he meant. But I felt that, somehow, I owed it to Caitlin. Maybe if she saw me applying myself she would do the same thing.

'She wants me to do it,' I said.

Mike came a little closer. 'Mate, it might not have occurred to you, but she might not be best placed to offer you advice at the moment.'

I nodded, taking his point. But Mike didn't know the whole story. The café would give me purpose while Caitlin and I attempted to re-engineer our relationship. Beyond that, it might offer me meaning if my experiment with Caitlin unravelled.

Caitlin balanced a tray with the salt and pepper, vinegar, ketchup, a couple of plates, a glass of Ribena and a bottle of Grolsch on her way to the table in the back garden. Long shadows stretched across the lawn and swallows circled in the air rising above us. She put the tray down on the table before carefully laying out the items. She hesitated with the plates.

'Maybe we shouldn't use the plates,' she said. 'It'll save on washing-up, which will help the environment.'

'You're right,' I said, unwrapping my cod and chips. 'Anyway, you know that fish and chips taste better out of the paper, don't you?'

She put the plates to the side and unwrapped her meal.

'If everyone can just do small things,' she said, sprinkling vinegar on her chips, 'they'll all add up and then, you know, it will make a difference.' She said it in a mildly provocative way, as if it was me who was entirely responsible for the knackered ozone layer above planet Earth, the razing of the Amazon rainforest and the poisoning of the oceans.

'From tiny acorns doth the mighty oak grow,' I said, pulling air into my mouth to cool my fish.

'Mum always used to say that you can't wait for other people to change things,' said Caitlin, as if she were continuing her thought, as if I hadn't even spoken. 'You've got to do it yourself.'

'That's right,' I agreed. *Holy fucking shit.* We were having a conversation. 'It's all well and good to have ideas, but you've got to implement them.'

'What does implement mean?'

'You know, do them.'

The smell of the food attracted next door's pet, a portly ginger cat, which wandered out of a clump of rhododendrons.

'Here, puss,' said Caitlin, pursing her lips and making a kissing noise. The cat came to her, rubbing its body against the leg of her chair. Caitlin laughed. It was the first time I'd seen her this unguarded.

'I think he likes you,' I said.

'I think he likes the smell of my dinner, more like,' Caitlin giggled.

'There is that, I suppose,' I agreed. I pulled a bit of skin from the newspaper and dangled it for the feline.

'You don't want to encourage him,' said Caitlin. 'Before you know it he'll be up on your table every mealtime looking for scraps.'

It was such an old-grannyish thing to say. I really didn't know how to reply. One part of me wanted to tell her to relax; the other part of me knew that she was absolutely right. I put the skin back on my plate. The cat was too busy rubbing itself against Caitlin's chair leg to have even noticed the delicacy on offer.

Caitlin worked away at her food, intermittently pausing to take sips of her Ribena and squirt more ketchup on her plate.

'I think you should do it, you know,' she said.

'What?' I asked, thinking that she had changed her mind about the cat and the fish skin.

'The coffee shop,' she said. 'You need to do it.'

'You think so, eh?' I said, taking a gulp of Grolsch. 'What do you know about coffee shops then?'

'Nothing much,' said Caitlin, matter-of-factly. 'Just that half of the mums I see are carrying around one of those cardboard cups with the plastic lids. Seems like grown-ups can't get enough coffee these days.'

'You like coffee then?'

'Not really,' said Caitlin.

We continued to eat. A dove cooed somewhere in the distance and a breeze gently blew our food wrappings. I went inside to fetch another beer and Caitlin some more Ribena. When I came out I was overpowered both by a sense of contentment – the stresses and travails of the past few weeks had ended up here, in this garden, with this meal and (miraculously!) easy conversation – and by a need to do something that would offer the pair of us a challenge, a common goal.

'You know, I think we should do it,' I said, putting the drinks down on the table.

Caitlin was silent. She picked at one of her chips before discarding it in the wrapping.

I had miscalculated. She didn't want this kind of bonhomie. She wanted to pass judgement, not be *involved*.

'What's the matter?' I asked, my momentary upbeat mood beaten back down to earth.

'Nothing,' she replied.

If there was one thing that I'd learned during my brief exposure to fatherhood, it was that 'nothing' *never* meant 'nothing'.

'What do you mean?' I repeated purposefully.

She looked up at me and I could see that she was wearing eyeliner.

'Do I *have* to go to school?' she asked.

'Come on, Caitlin,' I said, irritated. I pushed my food away. 'What kind of question is that?'

'I don't want to go,' she said firmly.

'You have to go,' I said, equally firmly. 'It's the law.'

'Just because it's the law doesn't mean that we have to do it.'

'Actually,' I said, suppressing a chuckle at her teen poutiness, 'that's exactly what it means.'

There was a pause.

'So why should I listen to you?' she asked.

'Why should you listen to me?' I was both amused and faintly annoyed. 'First off, because you have no choice,' I said briskly. 'Second, what the hell else do you think you're going to do? Spend the day texting your mates?'

Caitlin moved her jaw from side to side disconsolately.

'Maybe I could just sit around on my arse like you,' she said, before getting up from the table. As she rose she knocked over both her Ribena and my Grolsch. She couldn't have aimed better if she'd tried: the beer and cordial were all over the front of my trousers before I could jump up.

'Come back here, young lady!' I said as she stormed into the house.

'Whatever, Trevor,' came the reply over her shoulder.

Whatever, Trevor. Was I the only person who wasn't using this phrase?

As I patted down my sodden chinos in the midsummer twilight I wondered if I'd managed to scramble out of one damaged relationship only to find another that was equally troubled.

Chapter 14

It had taken some arm-twisting, but I finally managed to get Mike to come and see the site I'd found for the café. Déjà vu, I thought to myself, having spent the previous few months countering Amanda's scepticism.

Amanda had always thought that if she didn't acknowledge my plans then the talk of tamping, water temperature and colour schemes would just disappear. Maybe she still hadn't recovered from having her own – now largely forgotten – dream of being an actor (she had been a dancer on a cruise ship for a few forgettable seasons) melt away with her twenties.

I pulled into Sainsbury's car park with Caitlin in the back seat. Two weeks after Whatever-Trevor-gate she was still punishing me. If her iPod buds weren't plugged into her ears then she was texting, her thumb a blur of physical accomplishment. Most of the time, though, she managed to do both at the same time. I tried not to let it get to me, but I couldn't help but think there was a clock ticking down when it came to our relationship, that we only had so long to get it right.

Mike had followed me in his own car, which he would need to get to the train station to go to work. Some early arrivals – mums with young families who had been up for hours already, old people with trollies – were making their way to the supermarket, as the three of us walked along the pedestrianised path towards the high street. It was a bright, fresh morning, but there was a chill in the air.

'You see?' I said. 'Just think about it. There's Sainsbury's' – I turned and pointed at the nasty, brown-brick low-rise building squatting behind them – 'and here is the café.'

I turned to see Caitlin ten yards behind us, fiddling with her iPod.

'Come on,' I said encouragingly. She shuffled towards me slowly, dragging her trainers along the pavement.

'She all right?' asked Mike.

'Oh, you know, teenagers,' I said with a beleaguered dad eye-roll. 'No big deal.'

Given that it was Mike who had strongly counselled me to enter this relationship wearing a figurative Hazmat suit, I wasn't about to get into the intricacies of the way it was panning out. I imagined that there were prisoners in Afghan jails who were having a better time than me.

Mike nodded but continued to walk briskly; he had to get to work.

'I know this space,' he replied. 'Didn't there used to be a record shop here?'

'Yeah,' I said. I pulled out a set of keys that I'd been lent by the leasing agent and proceeded to fiddle with the lock, turning it one way and then the other. The door wouldn't budge.

'Oh, hurry up, mate,' said Mike. 'I'm freezing.'

'You can't be freezing,' I said.

'I must remember to pick up some cigarettes after we've got this over with,' Mike said absent-mindedly.

'You make it sound like you're having surgery,' I said before finally wrestling the door open. 'A vasectomy or something.'

'I wouldn't get one of those,' said Mike. 'Wouldn't fancy all that—'

'Um, Mike,' I interrupted him, nodding towards Caitlin.

'What's a vasectomy?' asked Caitlin. She said it with a slight smile, knowing that she had just got Mike in trouble. I noted that she'd managed to hear this through the headphones that were normally impervious to sound.

'I'll tell you when you're older,' I said.

'Is it rude?'

'No, it's not rude,' I said, getting the key out of the lock, 'it's more, um, complicated.'

'That's what you always say,' said Caitlin. Then she did an impression – a pretty good one – of a dull, suburban man saying: 'It's complicated.'

Mike looked elsewhere, determined not to laugh. I could see the humour but was tired of Caitlin's constant barbs. Mike read the situation. He stepped forward.

'Let's just get in there,' he said. We stepped over a pile of junk mail that had accumulated behind the door and into the repository of my commercial hopes and dreams.

'So here it is,' I said. I was aware that there was a hint of pride in my voice that was not immediately borne out by what Mike and Caitlin were witnessing, namely an abandoned shop that until a few weeks ago sold discounted CDs and DVDs. There were four rows of racks and a counter at the end. The muddy-coloured industrial carpet had grey tracks marked on it from the heaviest customer traffic.

'Well, it's going to need a bit of bloody work,' said Mike. 'Have you thought about that?'

'I've had three quotes,' I said, trying to summon a business-like tone into my voice. 'We're looking at just under twenty grand.'

'Twenty grand?' said Mike suspiciously. 'Are you sure? There's a lot of work to do here.'

Caitlin glanced over at me. She could see that I was being tested. Did I actually know what I was talking about?

The answer, of course, was no, but I was determined to put on a convincing show.

'Come and have a look,' I said, leading them both down an aisle. We walked through the shop to the counter, which I lifted to get behind, and stood there proprietorially. Despite the dingy, unappealing interior, I was excited. Finally I had put my money where my mouth was. I was going to be my own boss. I clapped my hands together and slapped them down on the dirty counter.

'See?' I said, grinning. 'Not bad, eh?' Although I knew that to both Mike and Caitlin the situation probably looked worse than bad.

'Cheer up – you've got a face like a slapped arse,' I said to Mike. Caitlin laughed, but turned away quickly to examine an old promotional poster for a boy band. She wasn't interested in sharing the joke with me.

'I'm not grumpy,' said Mike. 'I've just got to get to work, that's all. It's all right, mate.' He gestured behind me. 'How much more is there?'

'There's a back room,' I said, opening the door behind me and pointing to the space. 'It'll be useful for storage, and we'll have a small kitchen in there in case we decide to extend the range of food. Come and have a look.'

'You're all right, Alex,' said Mike, standing still. 'I get the picture.'

'I know it's hard to imagine,' I said, 'especially with the windows all fogged up.' I pointed to the double-exposure windows that had been covered in an opaque white substance that stopped people from peering inside. 'But I think it's going to be great.'

'Oh yeah.' Mike nodded, shuffling uneasily. 'It's going to be great, no doubt about that. How long is the lease for?'

'Ten years.'

'Ten years?' replied Mike. 'That's bloody amazing. How did you manage to swing that?'

'Oh, you know,' I said, mock-examining my nails, 'charm, skill, talent.'

'That's a good deal,' insisted Mike, who knew about that kind of thing. 'I'm sorry, mate, but I need to get going. Busy day and all that.'

'All right,' I said. I wished he could have stayed longer. I'd have liked to run through the numbers with him. Mike could see things in numbers that I couldn't. I saw numbers as function. He was able to see them as art. 'Thanks for coming, though.'

'I'll see you later, pal. See you later, Caitlin.'

'Bye, Mike.'

Caitlin gave him a shy wave, raising her hand a little and waggling her fingers. It was a slightly awkward, girlish gesture.

'What now?' I said, closing the door behind Mike.

Caitlin shrugged. 'It's a bit of a mess in here,' she said. 'Maybe we should tidy the place up a bit?'

'Did you remember the Hoover?' I asked.

Caitlin took me seriously for a moment. 'Hoover?'

I broke into a smile. 'Only kidding,' I explained. 'The builders are going to come in and make an even bigger mess of the place. We can leave it as it is.'

'All right, then,' said Caitlin. 'Shall we just go home?'

I wasn't sure, but I thought that that might have been the first time I had ever heard her use the word 'home'. It was jarring to hear it come from her mouth.

'Yes, let's,' I said, opening the door for her. We strolled back towards the car. Caitlin still had her ear buds in, but it was clear that she was now willing to talk. Her mood had altered in the space of five minutes. I was excited, but didn't want to push too hard and make her retreat back to her pouting and shrugging.

'What are we going to call it?' I asked. I hoped that the 'we' wouldn't send her running for the hills.

'Call what?'

'The café, of course.'

'I dunno,' she said.

Helpful!

I ignored her, stepping up my pace. I didn't even want to walk alongside her. Part of this was her doing; she was the one who told me to move forward with the business, didn't want me sitting at home cramping her style. Yet the second I actually did something about it, she subjected me to full teen disparagement.

Maybe she sensed my annoyance. She skipped after me, trying to keep up.

'How about something to do with beans?' she said. 'Like "Bean There" or "Bean Away". You know, because of the coffee bean.'

I carried on walking.

'Interesting,' I said, non-committally.

'You're going to do takeaways, right?'

'Yeah, people can drink it there or have it to go.'

'Right,' said Caitlin. 'How about "Bean & Gone"? That would be wicked.'

I looked at her. I tried not to look surprised.

'That is a really, really good suggestion,' I said.

Caitlin nodded. She was playing it cool, but I got a sense that she was pleased.

'I'll have to watch out for you,' I said. 'I reckon you're after my job.'

'Can I have one?'

'I think I'm going to need all the help I can get,' I said.

'Good,' she said. 'Then I won't have to go to school.'

I was just about to tell her that I thought we'd been over this when I heard the tinny clamour of her iPod re-starting. I needed to be bigger than this. I would rise above it. Or I'd try, at least.

I was researching coffee suppliers online that afternoon when the front doorbell rang.

'I'll get it,' said Caitlin.

This was a first, especially as she was in the middle of a feverish texting marathon. I had promised her that she could go online for half an hour after I'd finished.

She pretty much ran to the front door: she'd done a poor job of pretending she didn't know who was there. I didn't want to crowd her, so I stayed where I was and listened.

'All right?' she said.

'All right?' came a voice. The hoarse bray clearly belonged to an adolescent boy whose voice was not entirely under his control.

Who the hell was this?

'Yeah, wicked,' said Caitlin.

I heard the sound of footsteps going upstairs. I looked upwards at the ceiling and followed the progress of the feet along the corridor and into Caitlin's room.

Then the door was closed.

There was a stranger in my house and he was in my daughter's bedroom with the door closed. Nothing good could come of this.

I paced the living room. I could not let this go unchallenged, but how to do so without further damaging my flimsy relationship with Caitlin? My imagination ranged in coarse and predictable regions. A terrible sourness sank in my stomach. I was allowing something bad to happen on my watch and doing absolutely nothing about it.

What kind of father was I?

I went into the kitchen, got a couple of cans of Diet Coke out of the fridge and walked upstairs. I stood outside Caitlin's bedroom for a moment. Was I being Uptight Dad? Was I imagining dastardly deeds where none existed? My palms were sweating, making the cans difficult to hold. Loud music – a song that sounded similar to something I had once liked a quarter of a century ago but somehow different – was coming out of the room. There were no voices. They were not talking. Why would anyone come over to see Caitlin unless they wanted to talk to her? Was there something I was missing?

I knocked. There was no response. I waited a few moments before rapping on the door, this time more loudly. Still there was nothing. I really didn't want to walk in without warning. Heaven knows what I might encounter. More than likely something that I – let alone Caitlin – would rather avoid at pretty much all costs. I had read the reports about teen pregnancy and rainbow parties (secretly wishing, of course, that there had been such a thing when I was in my early teens).

Jesus. This kind of situation had never occurred to me. How could I have been so naive?

I knocked again. Nothing. My hand trembling, I turned the door handle and opened the door.

Entwined limbs, interconnected lips, stray hands . . .

There was nothing of the sort. Instead, what greeted me was Caitlin and a boy who looked to be a good few inches shorter than her sitting next to each other at her desk looking at . . . Jesus Christ . . . *algebra*.

'Um, hi . . .' I said, standing in the doorway holding the two cans of Diet Coke that were, by now, presumably around boiling point. 'I did knock.'

Caitlin didn't even bother to disguise her scowl.

'I brought you both a Coke.'

'I'm not allowed to drink Coke,' the boy said. 'Only on special occasions.'

I took a look at him. There was a definite bad-skin situation. His hair was thick and either cut in a highly fashionable way or just a mess. I was fairly sure that it was the latter. His jeans were full of holes and his trainers looked like they were likely to be rejected by homeless people. I was no expert, but I was fairly sure that I had a nerd on my hands.

'Oh,' I said. 'And you are … ?'

'This is Brian,' said Caitlin. 'He used to go to my old school—'

'I still do, actually,' interrupted Brian, correcting her.

Caitlin ignored him.

'He used to help me with maths,' continued Caitlin. I could tell that she was thrilled to have put me in a position where I had acted like a mistrustful, irrational despot. 'We're just going over some stuff from last year. I want to try to, you know, get up to speed for the new school year.'

'Right,' I said, as if this was *exactly* the scenario that I'd been expecting. 'So, Brian, can I get you anything else to drink?'

'I'm fine, thanks,' said Brian, his voice yo-yoing.

'Right, then,' I said, putting Caitlin's Coke down near her. 'I'd best let you two get on with it then, eh? Let me know if there's anything you need.'

As I turned I could feel Caitlin's withering look on my back. I had blown it again.

I made myself scarce for the rest of the afternoon, talking to the Polish builder (who was making good progress at the café), chatting with potential suppliers and organising for someone from the council to come and inspect the premises and give us the requisite paperwork. I felt like I'd accomplished something other than driving Caitlin from me even more than I had already. I picked up a voicemail from Amanda. She wanted to have a drink and, rather ominously, 'to talk'.

I definitely wasn't in the mood 'to talk' but I made a mental note to call her. As much as I needed to keep the Caitlin situation

109

from her, I sensed that keeping the lines of communication open was important. There was going to be a reckoning of some sort with either Caitlin or the council, and having Amanda in my corner wouldn't hurt.

I heard Brian and Caitlin come downstairs and her see him off. I was slightly nervous: it was fairly obvious what I had assumed when I barged into her room. My acknowledging this had created a whole new crisis zone, one that I was keen not to explore in any depth.

She walked in and sat down on the sofa. Without looking at me she asked: 'Can I watch some telly?'

Relieved at this simple request I told her yes and continued to tinker with my business plan.

After a while Caitlin looked up from the diabolical American tween comedy that she was watching.

'Why have we got three bedrooms?' she asked.

'That's just the way the house is designed,' I replied.

'I get that,' she said, pushing a strand of hair behind her ears. 'It just seems a bit odd. You know, unnecessary.'

Now the *house* wasn't right for her? What was with this kid?

'Well, when I saw the house,' I said, 'I wasn't so much thinking about the number of bedrooms but more the overall layout of the place, you know. I suppose we could live somewhere smaller but then we might not have a kitchen and a dining room.'

'I don't mean it like that,' Caitlin said. 'It's more to do with that bedroom.'

I turned from the computer. The word bedroom was one that I didn't want to hear at that moment.

'I'm not sure I understand what you mean.'

She turned back to the TV for a moment, readjusting her position on the sofa away from me. I waited. And waiting on Caitlin was one of the things I found hardest to do. I wanted to know how she was feeling, what she meant, what was going on in her head, and asking her seemed like the most obvious and logical way to go about this. But, of course, it was most definitely the *worst* way to go about this. Opening my mouth and attempting to drag the information from her would have nothing but the opposite effect.

Eventually she said, 'I think it would be nice if we could have a room for Mum.'

'A room for Mum.' I repeated the words back to her in a manner that suggested it was the most normal request in the world. She wanted a room for her dead mother.

'Yeah,' said Caitlin. Her eyes were still on the film.

'I think it would be nice if we put some photos of her in there, and some of her things.'

The week after Caitlin had moved in the solicitor had given us several boxes of Cathy's artefacts for safekeeping. I hadn't known what to do with them and Caitlin had shown little interest in taking a look. In the end, I put them in the loft because I didn't like them cluttering up the hallway – Caitlin had tripped over them more than once.

'Do you want me to get her things out of the loft?'

Caitlin nodded.

'Would you like me to do it now, or can it wait until tomorrow?'

'It can wait,' she said absent-mindedly.

So that was how Mum's Room came into being. It was the smallest bedroom in the house, and appeared to have recently been occupied by a young girl, as it was painted a shocking pink. We made up the bed in the best sheets that I owned, arranged Cathy's photos and knick-knacks and hung pictures on the wall. Caitlin insisted on hanging a crucifix above the bed, explaining, 'It's what Mum would have wanted.'

I couldn't help pausing to consider this: I had had a fair amount of experience of Cathy's preferences when it came to recreational drug use and was familiar with her fondness for sex acts that were unlikely to be sanctioned by Rome. Nevertheless, I was happy to indulge her daughter in any way that she wanted.

After we'd finished we stood in the doorway surveying our handiwork. Without thinking I put my arm around Caitlin's shoulder. By the time I realised what I had done I was too terrified to take it away. She didn't shake it off.

'Do you think she'd like it?' I asked her.

'She loves it,' said Caitlin. Just like that: present tense. 'She absolutely loves it,' she repeated.

'How do you know?' I asked. The second the words left my mouth I wished that I could learn to keep my mouth shut.

Caitlin looked at me serenely.

'I just do,' she said, before walking along the landing to her room. For the first time in days she didn't seem angry with me.

I watched her walk back along the hallway and close her door. The music started again. I turned to look at Cathy's room again before I had an impulse to look upwards.

'You know what?' I said to whatever or whoever I was addressing beyond the plasterboard, timber and slate. 'Maybe she's right.'

Chapter 15

'What's this?' asked Caitlin. She stood in the driveway, her arms folded.

'It's our new car,' I replied.

'What happened to the silver one?'

Oh, the silver BMW M3 that I once would have eaten broken glass just to smell its interior? At the dealer's with a resale sticker on its windscreen that was probably a good few grand higher than the money I got for it. Still, with that money I was able to move from being a man with a top-of-the-range sports car to a man who drives a generic estate car with exceedingly reassuring test ratings. It was the nearest thing I could imagine to castration, but a man in his late thirties driving around in a two-door BMW with a thirteen-year-old squeezed in the back is not a good look, especially when it's parked outside the school gates.

'I thought we should get a black one,' I said. 'You like it?'

'It's okay,' said Caitlin. 'The other one was cooler, though.'

No shit.

We got in the car and headed to the Royal Oak. I had a morning of job interviews for the café lined up. Taking Caitlin with me wasn't ideal, but I didn't want to leave her home alone, as much as she wanted to stay. So I'd dragged her out with the promise that we'd buy her a pair of excessively priced trainers that she had her eye on.

The shop fitting was proceeding well – the builders, uncharacteristically for their trade, looked like they would deliver on their promise of a fortnight's turnaround. Given that the opening was getting imminent I'd put an ad online to recruit an assistant. It took me an hour to put the thing together, although truthfully I'd spent five minutes writing the ad and the rest of the time browsing the 'casual encounters' section, in which I learned that, should I so desire, a girl who called herself 'GameGrrl' would for one hundred quid meet me in a bookshop in Kingston where she was willing to remove her knickers and give them to me. Seemed expensive for a pair of pants to me.

Once I'd got over GameGrrl, I'd written the following:

Wanted! Customer service professional needed for small, independent coffee shop that's destined for big things. Must be hard-working and personable. Experience preferred.

The last bit was important. As optimistic as I was about the new endeavour, I was conscious that someone who had actually brewed a cup of coffee might be a useful asset. Within a couple of hours I had ten responses. I'd shortlisted four of them and had arranged to meet at the Royal Oak.

We ordered some lunch and sat sipping our drinks.

'Wish I'd brought a book,' said Caitlin. She was, of course, bored. I should have thought about this. I was just about to give her some money to go to the newsagent to buy a magazine when the first applicant arrived. She was young, pretty and French. Her name was Beatrice. I found this encouraging – after all, the French know how to make a cup of coffee – but it soon became apparent that her enthusiasm and Côte d'Azur smile masked an insurmountable problem: she could barely speak English.

'Well, that's not going to work,' I said, confident that I could get away with it before the door had even *fermed* behind her.

'I think she was nice,' Caitlin said, mopping up some ketchup with a chip.

She was right, of course. Beatrice was nice, but I wasn't sure if Caitlin was saying this just to contradict me, or because she really believed it. What I had noticed, though, was that Caitlin had listened to every word of the conversation. Far from drumming her fingers or rolling her eyes, she'd tuned in to what was being said.

The second interviewee was a bloke in his late twenties. He bounded into the pub like a Labrador. I tried to get his attention, but he was too busy introducing himself around the bar and asking customers if they were Alex. When he eventually noticed me he came racing over to our table. Caitlin shuffled back in her seat to distance herself from him.

'Matt the prat, they call me,' he laughed.

I smiled and held out my hand. Caitlin looked unimpressed. I imagine that it was an expression she'd perfected on the boys at school.

'Sorry,' said Matt.

After some brief small talk I started my interrogation of Matt the self-declared prat.

'What would you consider your strong points, with regard to this job?'

'Well,' said Matt thoughtfully, 'I'm a people person. I like to be around other like-minded people and that. And I'm a laugh, you know, a bit of a joker ...'

Alarm bells went off inside my head. I would rather have had a nasty dose of the squits than spend my days with Matt the prat. I held his gaze with what I thought was an appropriate 'interviewer's face', although it was clear that whatever happened from this point on was a waste of time.

'And, I suppose working at Starbucks would be up there as well.'

Not so fast.

'You worked at Starbucks?'

'Yeah,' said Matt. 'For nearly a year.'

'Starbucks?' asked Caitlin. I could tell that she didn't want this to mean that Matt was now in the frame for the job.

Matt sniggered. 'Oh, it's just a little coffee shop chain that serves, like, millions of customers every day,' Matt continued, pleased with himself.

'I know what Starbucks is,' replied Caitlin after a beat. 'But what I don't get is how you had time to serve millions of customers.'

I suppressed a smile. Nice one, girl.

'Oh, no,' explained Matt earnestly. 'I didn't serve them. Not our branch. No, I'm talking about hundreds and hundreds of stores all over the world serving millions of customers.'

'Oh,' said Caitlin, clearly unimpressed. 'Like McDonald's?'

'Yeah,' said Matt, encouragingly.

'I hate McDonald's,' said Caitlin.

'You didn't mention Starbucks in your email,' I interrupted.

'Didn't I?'

I shook my head and leaned back. Touché.

'So tell me then, Matt,' I asked, thinking myself to be a regular Sherlock Holmes, 'what if I asked you to make me a latte? Could you take me through the process step by step?'

'Do you want foam on the top, or just milk?' asked Matt before quickly and flawlessly running through the various steps necessary for a bog-standard high street premium beverage. I looked at Caitlin; she didn't return my gaze. She didn't like this one bit. My instincts were to release Matt back into the wild, but his experience could be a huge asset ...

'When can you start?' I asked him.

'Well, I've got a couple of things I've got to take care of in the next few days, but I could probably start in a week or so.'

Matt's mobile burst to life – he had a 50 Cent ring tone. Something about 'fucking niggas shit up'. Matt checked the number, before apologising and telling me that he had to take the call. He walked over to the corner of the bar where he started whispering urgently into his phone.

'What do you reckon?' I asked Caitlin. I was excited to find someone who knew what they were doing.

Caitlin shrugged. Not happy.

At that moment Matt, who was over in the corner of the bar, began shouting into his phone and gesticulating. Some of the punters turned to look at him. Caitlin raised an eyebrow.

'Sorry about that,' he said, returning after a few minutes. 'My probation officer.'

Maybe I'd been a little hasty.

'Oh,' I said.

'Yeah.' He went quiet for a moment before glaring at me. 'It's my fucking anger counsellor ...'

Red alert. *Dive! Dive! Dive!*

Matt acknowledged Caitlin.

'Sorry, sorry ... I'm really sorry, sweetheart ... Look, it's just that he keeps telling my probation officer that I'm missing appointments.'

I needed to get this joker out of here.

'Well, it's been great meeting you—'

'*Fuck* that bitch!' Matt interrupted me. It was more of a growl than a statement.

A couple of people turned to identify the source of the noise. Thankfully, Matt was oblivious to the stares, glaring only at the Coke before him.

'Caitlin, there's a love,' I gave the girl a fiver, 'get yourself another orange juice, all right?'

'But I don't want another orange juice.'

'Go and get yourself another orange juice.'

By now, it must have been clear even to Matt that the chances of my employing him were fairly slim. He had buried his head in his hands and was scratching his scalp feverishly. Before I could start giving him the brush-off again, he threw his head back dramatically and then returned his gaze to me as if absolutely nothing had happened.

'So what were you saying?' he asked.

'Um, I'll let you know ...' I said sheepishly. At that moment I was extremely glad that there were witnesses around in case anything should go awry. I glanced over at the bar. To my relief Geoff gave me a wink: he had 'the equaliser', as he called his baseball bat, tucked safely under the counter.

'All right then,' said Matt cheerfully. He got up and extended his hand. 'No hard feelings, then?'

'Um, no,' I said, shaking his hand.

And with that he stormed out of the pub on his angry way.

I polished off a plate of sausage and chips while watching the door for the next interviewee. I knew only that the woman was called Eva and that she was a part-time aromatherapist looking for some steady work while she built up her client list. The door opened and a gargantuan silhouette filled the doorway. It seemed as if the pub might fall into darkness.

For fuck's sake.

Although I could see only a black blob, I just *knew* that this was Eva. Equally, I was aware that the bulk wasn't what I needed to keep the skinny mums of Cobham coming back for extra slices of double chocolate fudge brownies.

'You're here about the job, aren't you?' I said to her, resigned to never getting the next few minutes of my life back.

Eva offered a soft hand and managed to manoeuvre herself into the seat on the other side of me, which caused a degree of embarrassing table movement.

'What's your name, poppet?' she asked Caitlin, who had just returned to the table with a packet of crisps.

'Caitlin.' She smiled, clearly not fazed at the prospect of a person with multiple chins. It was clear to me: I was a bad person.

'My daughter,' I said. The words still felt strange coming from my mouth. Caitlin shot me a dirty look. I got the feeling that she had clocked my appraisal of Eva and didn't like it.

'Would you like a drink?' I asked Eva.

'Yes, please,' she gasped, fanning herself, as if the struggle of sitting down had undone her. 'Diet Coke please.'

'Diet Coke please, Geoff,' I called over to Geoff, who rolled his eyes as if to say, *what's the fucking point*? I hoped that Eva hadn't noticed. We had a cordial conversation, which I thought, for the sake of politeness and the fact that Eva had made the effort to come and meet me, should last for a minimum of ten minutes. I was aware that the sigh of relief I let out when she admitted to having no retail experience may well have been audible. While I would have loved to have given her the opportunity to make the leap to front of house, I knew that I was simply doing society's bidding – and society did not want Eva to be serving it cranapple muffins. I recommended that she train as an accountant.

Caitlin kept fairly quiet during the meeting, although she did ask Eva a few questions – 'What would you do if you were Prime Minister?', 'How would you stop global warming?', 'What was your favourite job?' – which Eva was game enough to answer. What pleased me was that I got the distinct impression that Caitlin had been asking the questions purely for show. She knew that I would not be hiring Eva, but she still wanted to connect with her on some level.

Once the woman had gone Caitlin disappeared to the bathroom, offering no comment. When she came back she put on her iPod and ignored me. The message was clear: I had brought this on myself.

Three down, one to go. Jesus. One who didn't speak English,

one psycho and one suited to a 'back office' role. I flipped open the manila folder in which I kept the candidates' details. (The folder was courtesy of TicketBusters – I'd nicked a load before leaving.) I pulled out the final candidate's CV. Her name was Melanie Fulton and her message had been fairly short and non-descript. I really had no idea why I'd shortlisted her. I closed the file and returned to the bar to get another drink.

'I'm not sure that we're going to have any luck today,' I said to Caitlin.

She took a sip of her orange juice and read the printout of the email that Melanie had sent me.

'I've got a good feeling about this one,' she said.

'Really?' I said. 'How come?'

'I don't know,' said Caitlin, with exaggerated impatience. 'It's a *feeling*.'

A woman walked into the pub and looked around, searching for someone. It was dark inside and her eyes took a while to adjust to the gloom.

I stood and watched her emerge from the shadows. She extended her hand; a late-twenty-something woman who looked me in the eye and seemed to have me all figured out.

'You must be Alex,' she said.

She was called Melanie, but she liked to be known as Mel and she was the first interviewee who'd asked for a pint when I enquired whether she wanted a drink. As it was just past mid-day, this did not appear to be a good sign. She smacked her lips when she took the first sip.

'I needed that,' she said, putting the pint glass down. I knew exactly how she felt.

'You know what?' I said. 'I'm going to have one of those too.'

As I stood at the bar waiting for Geoff to pour the pint, I

watched Mel chatting with Caitlin. They were laughing. I wondered at how easily she had made Caitlin shift from sullenness. Mel dressed and had the hairstyle of someone who perceived herself to be youthful. She reminded me of the office girls I used to see on my morning commute: freshly made-up and dressed to impress in the mornings, but a little bleary-eyed on alcopops on a Friday night. I supposed that Caitlin could just relate to her easily.

Even so, as I watched the two of them chatting I couldn't fathom why someone like Mel, someone with potential, with possibilities, would want to take the kind of job that *I'd* have to offer. I wanted to tell her that she could do better, not to sell herself short.

I raised my pint glass to hers.

'Cheers,' I said.

'Cheers,' she replied with a grin. 'This feels a little, you know, strange, doesn't it? Sitting in a pub in the middle of the day.'

What a relief. Although I then wondered what the other interviewees had thought about *me*; after all, it was my choice to meet in a pub, and with a kid too. Then I realised that I didn't give a shit. Anyway, I was the boss now. I could make my own rules.

'I owe you an explanation,' said Mel.

'Oh,' I replied. I had no idea for what.

'It's actually early evening for me,' she explained. 'I've been working at this call centre over in Hounslow doing the two until ten in the morning shift, so I've just come off work. It's dinner time really.'

'Or cocktail hour,' I said.

'Never really been one for cocktails,' said Mel. 'I like the sound of them, but they're either too sweet – you know, sickly – or they taste like medicine. A lot of my mates love them, though. *Love* them. Me, I'm more of a beer person.'

121

'Me too,' I said. Beer was delicious after all.

'And what do you like?' Mel said to Caitlin. 'Coke, I'll bet.'

'Beer,' said Caitlin with a poker face, before breaking out in a grin.

'My nan used to give us stout when I was a kid,' Mel said. 'Do you know what that is?'

Caitlin shook her head.

'You know, the black beer, like Guinness.'

Caitlin pulled a 'that sounds hideous' face.

'She said it would make us big and strong,' continued Mel. 'She used to mix it with milk, break an egg in there and stir in a little nutmeg.'

'What did she give you when you'd been bad?' Caitlin asked.

'It was actually quite tasty,' Mel said, fondly. 'So what's that then?' she asked suddenly, pointing at the two glasses in front of me. If I was a beer man why were there two empty tumblers slick with suspicious fruit juice residue in front of me?

'Sometimes even the keenest beer drinkers need a change,' I explained.

'Not me,' said Mel. 'I'm all right with beer as long as the day has got a "y" in it.'

This kind of plain-speaking can become a little tiresome – depending on who's plain-speaking it – but when it came from Mel it seemed to contain only brightness. I liked it because there was no pretence. The equation seemed pretty simple: because Mel was uncensored you could trust her; she wasn't hiding anything. She seemed reliable.

'Tell me about the call centre,' I asked.

'I wish there was something to tell,' said Mel. 'It's not exactly thrilling. We don't get many calls, given that it's the middle of the night. A few drunks, I suppose, although they do pick up towards the end of the shift. I sit in a cubicle under fluorescent lights in front of a computer wearing a headset. I answer people's questions. And if I can't answer them I follow a series of prompts on my computer. And if I still can't answer them I hand the customer over to my manager. I get two fifteen-minute breaks, and one in the middle of the shift for a half-hour to eat. They've got these vending machines with all this disgusting food that you buy and then heat up in the microwave. I usually take sandwiches or leftovers. It's mainly the blokes who eat that rubbish.'

'Doesn't sound like a lot of fun.'

'Oh, it's not that bad,' she said, taking a sip of beer. 'Believe me, I've done worse. It's steady work, but it's basically boring. You just feel very lonely, even though you're talking to people on the phone all day.'

I nodded. I knew the feeling.

'So tell me about this coffee bar then,' said Mel. 'When're you opening?'

'The builders have nearly finished, so it won't be long – a couple of weeks, maybe.'

'What are you looking for, you know, with your team?'

I was momentarily flummoxed. I knew the kind of people I *didn't* want – I'd met three prime examples in the past hour and a half – but I wasn't exactly sure if I could easily put my finger on the type of person I was looking for. I'd just hoped that they would show up and I'd know.

'Who do you think I should be looking for?' I asked with a brilliant bit of management jujitsu. *Take that.*

Mel considered the question for a moment.

'Let me see,' she mused. 'They've got to be good at communication,' she said eventually. 'You know, getting on with people, making sure that everyone is being taken care of. They've got to be able to do a lot of things at once, multitask. Mostly, though, people have got to want to come in there and see whoever it is behind the counter and think that they're, like, a friend. You know that thing in *Cheers*, a place where everybody knows your name? Something like that.'

'I suppose I'll be Sam then.'

'I could be Carla.'

'What's *Cheers*?' asked Caitlin.

'It was a TV show,' said Mel. 'It's not on any more.'

'How do you know about *Cheers*?' I asked. 'There's no way you're old enough. Whose memory implants are you using?'

'Satellite,' Mel replied. 'You watch a lot of it when you're a single mum.'

A single mum?

I considered this for a moment. Would it be a problem? Would she be knackered from being up all night? Would there be problems when the babysitter didn't show up? Would she be unkempt and splattered with vomit when she came in to work in the mornings?

'How old are your kids?' I asked.

'He's thirteen,' said Mel.

'*Thirteen*?' I said, unable to mask my surprise.

'I was young,' said Mel, as if it was something that she had had to explain on numerous occasions to employers, acquaintances, local government officials, school teachers. 'In my teens.'

'Wow,' I said.

'Yeah, well, you live and learn,' said Mel, taking another swig of her pint. 'But I wouldn't change a single thing.'

'Good for you,' I said, raising my glass to her. She clinked hers against it.

'I wouldn't either.' I had meant this generally, but Caitlin looked at me like I was directly referring to her.

'I'm thirteen too,' she said.

'No!' said Mel, mock-surprised. 'I thought you looked older than that.'

Caitlin blushed.

'So I'm looking for something local,' said Mel. 'All the travelling to Hounslow is doing me in, and I don't like being away from Oliver at night. He sleeps over at my mum's at the moment.'

'I see,' I said. The name Oliver always made me think of Laurel and Hardy.

'What about you?' asked Mel. 'You on your own?'

'Yes,' said Caitlin before I could answer. 'My mum is dead.'

Mel looked at her uncertainly. 'Oh, sweetheart,' she said quietly, 'I'm so sorry to hear that.' She touched Caitlin's arm. 'I'm sure that your mum's in a happy place, though, and that she's looking down on you, watching you, and that she's ever so proud. I know that I would be.'

Caitlin nodded. It was the kind of thing that people said to her.

'You just never know how it's going to work out, do you?' Mel said to me, changing the subject. 'Especially when you think you've got it all sorted.' She laughed at her own joke.

'I suppose you're right,' I said. 'Who'd ever have imagined that you'd end up working at a coffee bar in Cobham?'

Mel smiled at me.

'You serious?' she asked.

'I'm serious,' I replied.

'Good,' she said, holding my gaze for a little longer than was strictly necessary.

'So?' she asked Caitlin. 'You all right with that?'

Caitlin looked over at me and nodded. 'All right with me,' she replied.

Chapter 16

I couldn't sleep.

I lay there in the indistinct suburban night thinking about Caitlin and Amanda. Caitlin, my damaged daughter, who could hardly bear to be around me, and Amanda, a wife who turned out to be as flawed as her husband.

And I thought about Nick Belagio. I imagined multiple purple humiliations for him, none of them plausible without my being willing to do a stretch in prison. I would bide my time. He would know when I had decided to strike back. I wanted him to know that if you mess with the bull, you get the horns.

As all this bounced around my mind I tried to think about something I might actually be able to control: the café. More specifically, I thought of my recent purchase of a state-of-the-art coffee maker. As much as the rent and the shop fitting had taxed my financial capacity, the coffee machine had become the ultimate emblem of my endeavour. The lavish photographs in the brochures had fetishised the machine to such a degree that I couldn't remember wanting any object the way I wanted the Cyncra by Synesso. A few late nights browsing barista chat rooms had confirmed what I had wanted to believe: the Cyncra was a piece of engineering that was as carefully considered and artfully designed as any Formula One beast.

In a few hours I would have one.

I gave up on sleeping, showered and made Caitlin some breakfast (I had lost my appetite but was glad to see her, despite her languid exterior, sticking away a breakfast fit for a lumberjack).

We slipped out of the house and drove through the bleary morning. While I had yet to get any tangible information from Caitlin about her new school, if her attention to her homework was anything to go by it seemed that she was applying herself. And she appeared to have made friends; her thumb was usually working overtime to keep pace with the number of incoming texts she received.

'Just drop me here,' said Caitlin. We were a full ten minutes' walk from school.

'Why?' I asked.

'I want to walk the rest of the way.'

'Why don't I drop you just round the corner?' I said. It was a grim morning; surely she didn't want to have to slog through the mist when the car's heating system was fully cranked?

'No,' she said, insistently. 'I want to get out here.'

'But you'll have to walk in the drizzle and—'

'I said that I want to get out.'

I pulled the car over. Suit yourself, sweetheart. She got out without saying goodbye. She wasn't wearing a raincoat and she didn't have an umbrella. She was going to get ill, and there was absolutely nothing that I could do about it.

The way things were going I didn't just need a smart, adult female presence to tell me where I was going wrong; I needed a support group.

I tried to put Caitlin out of my mind and drove over to what I had decided would be called the Bean & Gone. I cracked open the door – it still smelled of paint and grout – and walked over to the counter where the Cyncra would be set like a religious artefact. I ran my hand over the countertop. I knew that, once the coffee machine had been placed there, if I ever saw that countertop again, then my business would have failed.

At half past eight a van pulled up outside. A shaven-headed

man in a Man United shirt, cargo shorts and Reebok classics rapped on the glass door.

'Delivery, mate?'

'Yeah,' I said, excited. 'Coffee machine.'

'That's the one,' the delivery man nodded. 'It's a heavy bastard.'

'I thought it might be.'

'Where d'you want it?'

'Over there,' I said, pointing to the counter.

'I'll just be a minute.'

The man opened the back of the truck and jumped in. He folded down a device that allowed him to lower the coffee machine, which was on a trolley, to the pavement then he hauled it into the shop and headed for the counter.

'Right,' he said. 'I reckon you're best off getting it up there and then unwrapping it rather than the other way round.'

'You're the expert,' I said.

'I'm an expert with a bad back, as well,' said the man, as if I was responsible for the problem. He wheeled the machine close to the counter and the pair of us paused, as if readying ourselves for something unpleasant, a moment of truth. Finally, we both squatted and pulled the machine off the trolley.

'Bloody hell!' I said. It weighed a ton.

'I told you,' shouted the man. We heaved it upwards, before flinging it onto the counter.

'Jesus,' I said, gasping for breath.

'Now you know why my back is crocked,' he said, wiping his brow. I looked at the guy, amazed not by the weight of the machine, but by his bloody performance. Given that this was his job – to transport heavy coffee machines around the country – every time he arrived at his destination, did he find it necessary to convey to the baffled recipients just *how heavy* the machines were and *how knackered* his poor back was? It was like a teacher moaning because he didn't like kids.

'You gonna make me one then?' he asked.

I gave him a look that made it clear our business was completed.

'Only joking, mate,' chuckled the man, wheeling his trolley towards the door. 'It's going to take you months to work out how to use it. It's like trying to fly the bloody space shuttle, that thing. *Worse*, in fact.'

'Thanks for the encouragement,' I said.

'It's what I do,' came the reply. Moments later I heard the screech of tyres as he headed off with his cargo of very heavy coffee machines that he would have to deliver with his very bad back.

I couldn't wait to get the wrapping off the machine. I grabbed a Stanley knife from the back room and sliced off large swathes of cardboard. The machine was entombed in layers of cardboard and bubble wrap. I pulled it off, creating a huge pile of waste in the middle of the empty shop, and stood admiring my acquisition. My God. It was beautiful in the way that only stainless-steel machines can be. I ran my fingers across its glossy surface, nervous in case I left finger marks on the pristine metal.

Beautiful. But beautiful.

There was a single fly in the ointment: there were disks of cardboard and plastic underneath the feet of the machine. Such imperfection polluted the whole effect.

I was considering how to lift the machine to get the cardboard out when I heard a knock at the front door. It was probably the postman delivering the menus, which I'd ordered from a fancy design company up in Liverpool I'd found online.

I opened the door to see Mel standing there.

'All right?' she said. She was dressed up, although I knew

she'd left her job the day before. She looked pretty, her face open and without make-up.

'Hello,' I replied, immediately wishing I had sounded a little more enthusiastic. 'Didn't expect to see you here.'

'Well, you know,' she said. 'I was passing. Thought I'd just stick my nose in and see how you're getting on.'

'Yeah, not bad—' I started.

'What is *that*?' asked Mel, interrupting me.

'It's a coffee machine,' I told her.

'I know that, Einstein,' Mel said. 'Just look at it, though. It looks ...' She paused for a moment. 'It looks like the Emerald City in *The Wizard of Oz*.'

'What?'

'You know, all gleaming and magical in the distance,' she said, walking towards it. 'Like some kind of glittering prize.' She had a nylon jacket on over a light summer dress and she was wearing what looked to be espadrilles with a fairly severe heel. I couldn't help noticing that she had great legs.

'I suppose it is,' I laughed. 'Not a prize exactly – I paid a bloody fortune for it – but a symbol of sorts.'

'A symbol of freedom,' said Mel. 'I know it's not exactly the Statue of Liberty, but it's something that shows you've escaped the daily grind.'

'Daily grind,' I said. 'Get it?'

'It was my joke in the first place,' she said, giving me a gentle elbow, 'so hands off.'

'Well, as long as you're here, give me a hand getting rid of all this crap underneath the legs, will you?' I asked.

I managed to lift the machine while Mel plucked the rogue bits of rubbish from beneath the legs.

'Job done,' she said as she threw the last one on the pile of rubbish. The two of us stood and looked at the machine again for a few moments. It was hard not to just stare at it.

'You know that this is rarer than a Ferrari Enzo, don't you?' I said to her.

'I do now,' said Mel. 'What's a Ferrari Enzo?'

'A very flash car,' I replied. 'It was named after … Oh, never mind about all that crap. There were only four hundred of them made, while there are less than two hundred of these in the world.'

'How come?' asked Mel.

'Because they're handmade,' I told her. 'In Seattle. In America. By craftsmen.'

'Really?' said Mel. I got the feeling that she wasn't too interested, but had decided to indulge my enthusiasm.

'Yeah,' I said, still entranced by the machine.

'So are you going to make a cup or what?' asked Mel.

'Um, no,' I said.

'Why not?'

'Because I've no idea how to operate it.'

'Well, that's no bloody good, is it?' she said, pulling the manual from my hands. 'I can see that I'm going to have to take you under my wing.'

She gave me a wink. I was going to enjoy working with this one.

Chapter 17

It had seemed like a good idea at the time.

'Of course,' I'd said, after Caitlin had asked if she might have a dog. I was happy just to hear her express some enthusiasm for something.

I regretted it immediately.

My desire to build bridges with Caitlin had bitten me in the backside several times already – going online and booking tickets for the Spice Girls reunion; the purchase of a top that, after consideration, I realised was too revealing for someone who might describe themselves as an 'adult entertainer', let alone a thirteen-year-old; approving a subscription to a magazine that had features on how to give the perfect blow job – so it was not the most difficult decision for me to opt to rescind an overly generous offer.

'You know we were talking about a puppy?' I said to her the next day when she got back from school.

She knew immediately.

'Yes,' she said cagily. She switched off her iPod. I was honoured.

'Well, I was just thinking that maybe we should start off more, um, slowly.'

'What, and get a tortoise?'

'No, not a tortoise.'

'Because a tortoise would be a slower start.'

I couldn't tell whether she was trying to be cute or sarcastic.

'I know,' I said, playing it safe.

'I don't think you can buy them now.'

'Tortoises?'

'Yes,' she said firmly. 'I think they made them illegal.'

'You can't make an animal illegal.'

She sighed, as if dealing with a really stupid and frustrating person.

'You can make *owning* them illegal,' she said. 'They stopped people being able to import them because it was cruel.'

'Really?'

'You don't believe me, do you?'

'Of course I do.'

'Well, I'm right. I know I am.'

'Okay, importing tortoises is illegal.'

'That's right.'

'I wanted to talk to you about something else, though.'

'You wanted to tell me that you don't think we should get a dog.'

'How do you know that?'

'Because of the way you started the conversation. Your voice.'

'Oh.' Was I that transparent? 'Well, that's right. I think we should ease into the whole puppy situation.'

'Ease in?'

'Well, Caitlin, a dog is a big responsibility. There's all the walking, and the feeding, and clearing up its mess. Maybe we should think about getting something else to begin with, some-thing that's a little easier to care for, so both of us can adapt to having a creature to look after.'

'Like what? A goldfish?'

Like an idiot, I walked right into it.

'Well, what would you think of getting a goldfish?'

'What do I think of getting a goldfish?' she said flatly. 'It's hardly a puppy, is it?'

'That's the point really.'

'Yes, but it's not even close to a puppy.'

'It needs to be fed, it needs to have its water cleaned, it needs attention . . .'

'What kind of attention does a goldfish need? It doesn't even know what day of the week it is.'

'Um, neither does a puppy.'

'But you take my point.'

You take my point? What was this? *Question Time*?

'It's like me asking for ice-cream and you giving me a stick of celery,' she continued. 'Or me asking you if I can watch *Borat* and you making me watch the news.' She puffed out her cheeks. 'You might as well just put a slice of carrot in a bowl and be done with it.'

'Look,' I said, trying to be conciliatory, 'I just think we need to try looking after an animal that's easier than a dog.'

She leaned on the kitchen counter, folding her frame over the surface and pressing her cheek against the granite.

'You're not supposed to go back on your word,' she said resentfully. For a horrible moment I thought that she might know about my doubts about our future. Had she worked out that I was close to calling Joan Kennedy at Social Services and discussing the arrangement? I realised that she couldn't, unless she was a mind reader. Although it must have been clear to her that things were not exactly a roaring success.

'How about a hamster?' she asked.

Like an idiot I replied, 'Okay,' without a moment's hesitation.

The purchase of the hamster was easy enough. We brought home a cage, some bedding and a large sack of food, most of which appeared to be sunflower seeds. Percy, as Caitlin had decided to call him, was a dozy creature with golden fur who

134

immediately curled up in the 'nest' that she had made for him and fell sound asleep. While able to empathise with this approach to life, I was concerned that it was not the behaviour of a pet that Caitlin would warm to.

However, she adored Percy, spending the rest of the day sitting by his cage attempting to rouse him with food and physical affection – without a doubt the best ways to a male heart. Percy was unmoved, his golden pelt nuzzled either in the crook of Caitlin's arm or in the tangled mess of his sleeping quarters. Relieved, yet unconvinced of the appeal of the creature, I went to bed pleased that I'd managed to sidestep the tricky dog situation and still manage such a direct hit on the pet front.

Moments after I started to drift off to sleep, I was rudely yanked back to consciousness by a squeaking noise. It wasn't immediately apparent where the noise was coming from but, after a few moments spent locating its source, I realised that the sound – constant, rumbling, insistent – was coming from Caitlin's room. More precisely, it was coming from Percy's cage, the result of his wheel-based nocturnal exercise regime. I wondered whether he'd woken Caitlin too and tiptoed into her room to investigate. Apparently the rodent's activity had absolutely no bearing on my daughter, who was breathing deeply, the sheets tangled around her limbs, which were thrown around with crash-test-dummy awkwardness.

Listening to her heavy, nasal breathing I wasn't entirely comfortable being in her room – she would not welcome my presence were she to wake up. Meanwhile, Percy, the little shit, continued to thunder round on his wheel. In the dead of night, it sounded like a drum solo. Feeling mildly guilty, I shook the cage to shut the bugger up. Percy scampered into his nest; in hamster terms, it must have felt like an earthquake. Job done, I went back to bed. I arranged the covers and pillow so they were just right and prepared to fall into a blissful sleep.

Some hope.

The rumbling started anew. Squeaky, constant, growling. I put a pillow over my head and tried to think about other places, people, scenarios … But Percy wasn't having it. He'd had a particularly restful day and was looking to burn off some of the sunflower-seed calories.

I must have eventually fallen asleep, but it was one of those nights where the tossing and turning and sighing seemed to go on until dawn. I woke the following morning bleary eyed, and quizzed Caitlin about the noise. Inevitably, she just shrugged, oblivious to what, to me, had sounded like a juggernaut steaming through her bedroom. I brewed a pot of coffee to revive myself and wondered whether my attempt to sidestep the puppy issue had, in fact, backfired.

I had acquired a rogue rodent.

Caitlin mumbled something about going into town to meet her friends (I think I heard the word 'shopping') before hogging the bathroom for half an hour. I lay in bed, forlornly hoping that I might get back to sleep. Then the hairdryer started and I gave up all hope. I was eating breakfast when she came into the kitchen.

'Can I talk to you about pocket money?' she said. She'd phrased it as a question, but she wasn't asking.

'Okay,' I said. 'What about it?'

When she'd first moved in I'd given her some cash to spend on things for her room. It wasn't a lot, but I was surprised to hear that she had got through it already.

'I think we need to settle on a weekly amount,' she said.

'All right,' I said. This actually seemed fairly reasonable to me.

'I was thinking about thirty quid a week,' said Caitlin matter-of-factly.

I nearly choked on my Alpen.

'*Thirty quid?*'

She looked at me as if I'd provoked her. 'It's what my mum used to give me.'

Oh, I see: if in doubt evoke your dead mother.

'It just seems like a lot,' I said, trying to diffuse the situation.

'It isn't,' said Caitlin.

'Look, I'm happy to give you extra when you need clothes, or shoes, or stuff for school or your room,' I explained.

Caitlin said nothing.

'How about twenty-five quid a week?' I asked. God I was weak.

'All right,' said Caitlin. 'But you'll help out with some stuff?'

'Of course,' I said.

'Then can you pick up some Tampax for me while you're out?'

And with that she left the kitchen and went back upstairs.

Jesus. Nobody had warned me about this. I paced the kitchen floor trying to think what to do. Twenty-five quid seemed like a more than reasonable amount to me, but what the hell did I know? I fetched my wallet, peeled off three tenners and left them on the table by the front door. I heard Caitlin come downstairs and, when I checked, the money had gone.

A fiver a week seemed like a small price to pay if it meant I didn't have to buy tampons.

Later that morning I opened the cupboard under the sink to fish out the washing-up liquid and noticed – of course! – a can of WD-40. Result: it would sort out the creaking, wheezing, grumbling wheel and restore my night-time hours to glorious deep slumber. I grabbed the can and went upstairs to Caitlin's room. Percy, the bugger, was fast asleep in his 'nest'. No wonder he was knackered: the little sod had spent the night running round the damn wheel.

I opened the cage, pulled out the wheel, yanked it apart and sprayed the two parts – the wheel and a spoke along which it hung – liberally with the lubricant. That would do it. I had saved myself from another night of prickly watchfulness.

Caitlin returned from town a couple of hours later and didn't mention the thirty quid. We had lunch together – ham and tomato on a baguette – while watching *Football Focus*. I had given up on my rule that we would always eat meals together at the kitchen table. Making Caitlin talk was nigh on impossible, so I thought I'd spare us the awkwardness. I was clearing up the lunch things when I heard her calling me.

She was shouting my name. I wanted to hear her say 'Dad!'

What I actually heard was, 'Hey! Alex!'

'If you want to speak to me you can come downstairs,' I called back. I wondered whether this wasn't the behaviour of a total tool.

'I need you to come upstairs now.'

I walked to the bottom of the stairs.

'This had better be important,' I said.

'Just come upstairs.'

I went up and walked into her room, where she was kneeling next to the cage.

'It's Percy,' she said.

'What's the matter?'

I leaned over her and saw that the rodent was curled up in his nest in the exact same position that I'd last seen him.

'He's not moving,' said Caitlin.

'They're nocturnal,' I said. He was probably just knackered after the previous night's activity.

Caitlin gave the animal a prod. It was not a gentle one.

'See,' she said.

'Um, yes,' I said. This did not look promising. I reached down

138

and touched Percy. The animal was distinctly cool to the touch, his furry back rigid and tense.

Shit.

'What do you think?' asked Caitlin.

How to approach this one?

'He's dead, isn't he?' asked Caitlin.

'Well, um, we should see what—'

'You can tell me if he's dead,' she said bluntly.

The truth was that I wasn't entirely sure. I felt exposed – dads are supposed to know this kind of thing. Our areas of expertise include changing flat tyres, taking out the rubbish and dealing with dead pets. I gave it another poke. The animal lost none of its shape. There was no arguing this one ...

I turned to Caitlin, who was now standing, her right hand inside her left. Her face was blank, her eyes expectant.

'Yes, he's dead,' I said. 'I'm sorry.'

'What do you think happened?' she asked. She needed an explanation. I had one: I sprayed a toxic substance inside Percy's cage and his little lungs are filled with it.

'I'm not sure,' I said. I didn't have an answer that she wanted to hear.

Actually, I killed poor Percy.

'Maybe he was stressed out,' said Caitlin. 'It's pet shops.'

Actually, I am the hamster killer.

I sat down on her bed. We needed to talk this one out.

Death stalked us.

'What do you mean?' I asked, although I knew. I'd never liked pet shops. They reminded me of Disneyland: supposedly happy, carefree places where dreams come true, yet with a sinister, phoney undercurrent. They were The Joker of retail.

'These animals are taken away from their mums much too early,' said Caitlin knowledgeably. I marvelled at her passion, at the expressiveness of her hands. 'They're just not ready,' she continued. 'And as much love as we think we're giving them, it doesn't matter. They're, like, totally freaked out' – I imagined she must have picked this sentiment up from a movie – 'by everything.'

'Well, I suppose they've only got small hearts.'

'That's because they're small all over,' said Caitlin. 'They're just little creatures. A little creature can't have a big heart.'

Strangely, she didn't seem to be emotional about Percy's untimely death. She was far more philosophical than I had expected.

'My mum told me that pet shops don't really care about the animals,' she said, slumping on a bean bag.

The invocation of Cathy made me nervous. It was easy to contradict a dead woman, but not when you were doing it to her doting daughter. It was not long since Cathy's passing, but somehow it seemed as if she'd never taken human form, as if she'd always been this character who meant very different things to both of us. It was odd that we both knew her so intimately, but had never been with her at the same time.

'Well,' I said, 'she's got a point. Pet shops are there to make money, not to look after animals. Looking after the animals is the job of the owners.'

'But it's hard to look after a pet if it's sick.'

'Yeah, it is,' I agreed. This was where I wanted to end the conversation. The pet shop owner was a Bad Person who should be blamed for the demise of poor Percy. Caitlin remained slumped on the bean bag, her hands folded between her knees. Her feet, with their chipped toenails, looked impossibly large for someone of her age.

I wondered whether I should 'fess up to the WD-40. It was probably the right thing to do, but I feared full disclosure would just cause a further rift. So I went into my bedroom and pulled a shoebox from my cupboard. Then I went into the bathroom and found a large packet of cotton wool, which I had bought assuming that Caitlin would need some – every female I had ever encountered seemed to have an insatiable need for cotton wool.

I walked back into Caitlin's room.

'I think we need to have a funeral for Percy,' I said.

Caitlin nodded. She stood and opened the cage and scooped up the rodent. His rigid body fitted perfectly in the bowl of her hand. She placed him inside the shoebox before leading me downstairs and out into the garden. It was a bright, sunny day: a rare moment of English optimism. I got a spade from the garden shed.

'Where do you think?' I asked.

'There,' she said, nodding to a spot about ten feet away.

'What, on the lawn?' I asked.

Caitlin moved forward and stood in the middle of the grass.

'Right here,' she announced.

'Caitlin,' I said, trying not to sound too whiney. 'This is the middle of the lawn.'

She shrugged at me.

'It's the middle of the lawn, sweetheart,' I repeated.

She showed no emotion. She just stood there. Held her ground. I sighed, walked over and pushed the shovel into the grass, through its fibrous roots, and into the soil beneath. I cut a neat rectangle about a foot deep and watched Caitlin place the box in the hole. She stood up and clasped her hands in front of her in prayer. I hesitated for a moment before following suit. This would give the neighbours something to talk about. After a few moments, I couldn't stop myself from interrupting the silence.

'Are you going to say something?' I asked Caitlin.

'Sssssssssshhhhh!' she hissed. 'I'm thinking.'

'Sorry,' I said. I closed my eyes and clasped my hands together. I could imagine the curtains twitching all around us.

'Dear God,' said Caitlin. 'I'm not entirely sure that you're listening, what with what's happened recently and all that. But, if you are, then I just want to say thank you for letting us get to know Percy a little bit. He wasn't with us very long. But we could tell that he was a nice pet. Please can you look after him and watch out that, if he's going to heaven, you keep him away from cats as there's a good chance that they'll eat him. Thanks very much, Caitlin.'

'That was lovely,' I said, squeezing open one of my eyes.

Caitlin remained in her prayer position, her eyes still closed. 'You need to say something now,' she said.

'Yes,' I said. 'Um, Heavenly Father, thank you for Percy. We had a great time playing with him, and we're sorry that he had to leave us so soon …'

I watched Caitlin listening, her eyes closed. I tried to make it meaningful, to make the words memorable and significant to help the kid through more loss, but there was just one thought going through my mind.

I had lied to my daughter. *I am a hamster murderer.*

'Hi, Mr Taylor?'

'Yes, that's me.'

'Joan Kennedy, Surrey Social Services child welfare support group. Are you all right?'

'Yes, I'm fine, thanks.'

I immediately felt a pang of guilt – the same guilt that I felt whenever I had to speak to a police officer – before I remembered that the lady from Social Services had told me a while back that they would call to arrange regular visits 'in order to monitor the transition process'.

'So we need to set up a time for us to come and visit Caitlin, you and Amanda.'

'Yes, yes,' I said, my palms sweating.

'Is next Tuesday, say 9 a.m., all right with you?'

'Yes, yes, yes ... Absolutely fine. Really looking forward to it.' I said all of this very briskly, as if I had *nothing* to hide.

'Ah, that's great,' said the social worker. 'So we'll see you at nine, then.'

I had been avoiding thinking about it, but as I was talking to her I knew that there was nowhere to hide: how on earth was I going to persuade the woman that Caitlin was part of a nuclear family? Amanda's absence would surely raise questions; it was, after all, part of the agreement that I had with the child welfare people – that Amanda and I were in a stable relationship. I put the phone down feeling nauseous.

Three days later, I was lurking round the corner from what I now had to think of as Amanda's house. She left home at her regular time, 8.45, with the usual cacophony of keys, bag, heels, clothes, hair and jewellery. Somehow everything about her made *noise*. She pulled out of the drive and headed up the road.

Once her car had turned the corner, I walked up to the house – *my* house – trying not to look too conspicuous (with a baseball cap pulled down virtually over my eyes and my hands stuffed into my bomber jacket) muttering my mantra: *please can she not have changed the locks, please can she not have changed the locks, please can she not have changed the locks ...*

My mission? To snag some of the family photos, make copies and leave them lying around my new house, so that when Joan Kennedy from Social Services showed up it would look like Amanda was living there. I was still working on how I'd explain her absence – 'She's upstairs with a nasty dose of diarrhoea', 'She got a message last night that there are some big waves coming into Cornwall, so she had to go', 'The dog was sick on her homework'?

143

I played around with the lock for a while and – hallelujah, praise the Lord! – I was in like Flynn. I walked through to the living room, where there was still a slight haze from Amanda's cigarette smoke and perfume, and was mildly surprised to see that she had left all of the photos of our seven years together (drunk in Mallorca, drunk in LA, drunk in Munich) in the same places they were when I walked out the door.

I couldn't figure out what this signified. Avoidance? Laziness? Hope that we might get back together? I pushed it from my mind: at that moment I felt like I was wearing a black-and-white hooped shirt, had a thin black mask covering my eyes and was carrying a black sack marked with the word 'swag'. I needed to get it over with, even if I wasn't sure whether I was technically committing a crime.

It didn't take long to gather what I needed and drive to the copy shop. On my way back, I relaxed. It was not even eleven: there was no way that Amanda would be returning home before lunchtime. Anyway, she preferred either to eat a sandwich at her desk or to go out for a proper lunch. With the copies of the photographs safely stashed on the passenger seat I cruised through the post-rush-hour suburban streets, running through my answers for the bleeding-heart busybody from Surrey Social Services when she showed up to judge me – a man who took in a child he had *never seen before* – as a parent.

I didn't deserve to be interviewed; I deserved a medal.

I let myself into the house and began placing the photos back in the right places. But then, while clutching a photo of Amanda and me at a wedding in Rome, I had a moment of panic – I had no idea where any of them went. Actually, that wasn't true: I knew that our wedding photo went on the Chinese chest where we stored the DVDs. But the rest of them . . .

Amanda would know. She would notice. She would sniff out

the fact that they'd been moved. I breathed deeply for a minute
– something I'd learned from a 'Self Nurturing' podcast that I'd
randomly downloaded while bored at work one day – and tried
to think of a solution. There had to be one . . .

I had it.

Amanda had bought a new camera for a Christmas party
we'd had last year and had taken a lot of photos of the occasion. If I could find that set of pictures then I could check the
backgrounds to see if I could identify where the portraits were
situated.

I started to dig around in the Chinese chest looking for the
relevant photos. There were all kinds of crap inside that I didn't
expect to find. After a few minutes I located the house party
photos and, sure enough, they proved an invaluable source. I
replaced each photo carefully, before putting the packet back
in the chest.

It was only just after eleven, but I was feeling a little peckish.
I opened the fridge and had a rummage around to see if there
was anything in there that wouldn't be missed. The primary
focus of my attention was a packet of M&S mini sausage rolls.
I picked one up and was just about to push the whole thing
inside my mouth when sense prevailed: Amanda would know
exactly how many of the things there were. She also knew that
M&S mini sausage rolls were one of my (many) weaknesses.
She would put two and two together. The last thing I needed to
do was alert her to the fact that I'd been sneaking around her
house when – very, possibly – I was going to have to engage her
help in dealing with Social Services at some point.

It was at the exact moment that I closed the fridge door that
I heard a familiar sound of a key turning in a lock and the front
door slamming.

Jesus.

It was Amanda. What the hell was she doing coming home

for lunch so early? I was outraged – how dare she sabotage my best-laid plans in this way? I knew that there was only one place she was heading: the kitchen. Seeing as this was exactly where I was standing I needed to make an important decision: come clean – explain what was going on and apologise for not letting her know that I needed access to the house – or hide in the dining room and pray that I wasn't discovered.

Being a bloke, clearly the only feasible option was the second one. At that moment, telling Amanda what was going on was about as enticing as a colonoscopy. As quietly as I could, I walked into the dining room and hid behind the floor-length curtains. My heart raced. This really was creepy, it was wrong, but I was going to have to tough it out. I prayed that she wasn't going to be around for long. I tried to keep as still as I could. I heard her go into the kitchen, pick up the kettle, walk to the sink and turn on the tap. The sound of running water had a powerful effect on me: I had to cross my legs – I was suddenly dying for a slash.

The fridge door was opened and I heard the rustle of plastic packaging; she was eating a sausage roll! Then I heard what sounded like a number of items being placed on the kitchen counter. A couple of eggs were cracked and whisked and the lever on the toaster was pressed: I was confident that she was making scrambled eggs on toast, a classic Amanda standby. Hearing her going about her daily routine made me wish that I could come out from behind the curtains and have lunch with her. A slash, some scrambled eggs and a cup of tea would be just what the doctor ordered.

It was getting hot behind the curtains. The midday sun was fierce and, given that I was sandwiched between thick curtains and the window pane, I was beginning to feel a little claustrophobic. The situation wasn't helped by the amount of nervy body heat I was giving off. I fanned myself to get the air to circulate. Amanda had turned the radio on and was singing along with Justin Timberlake. She was bringing sexy back.

I had always hated Justin Timberlake. In fact, I hated pretty much all of the crappy pop music that Amanda filled her head with when she was pottering about the house, in the car or at the gym. My God, the heat, desperation for the toilet and Timberlake were enough to make me miserable, let alone the prospect of being found out.

Fed up with breathing the musty curtain smell I shifted round and looked out of the window. What I saw made me panic: our neighbour, Sue, was hanging out her washing only a few feet from me and if she ...

Oh, no! She was turning ...

I tried not to move, like a terrified woodland creature caught in the headlights. Sue was pegging a pair of underpants to the line when her attention wandered over to the window where I was hiding. She did a double-take before realising that, yes, it was me. She had a slightly bewildered look on her face even as she waved. Compounding the absurdity of the situation I pretended to tap at the window pane, as if I was conducting some kind of pre-DIY analysis. I pretended not to have seen her before acting surprised when I looked up – 'Oh, hi!' – overly mouthing the words as if I were talking to someone incredibly old or simple.

Jesus.

After several more minutes of sweating it out behind the curtain it seemed like I might actually have got away with it. I could hear Amanda stacking her pots and dishes. Surely this was a prelude to her departure? The radio was switched off. The dishwasher hummed to life (*why does she insist on putting it on when it's not full?* I fumed to myself).

And then finally, blissfully, I heard her closing the door and double locking it. Oh, joy! I burst from my chintzy prison and fell to the floor, laughing hysterically. That was so close, it was almost unbearable. What on earth had I been thinking? If she'd stumbled across me it would have been beyond awkward. 'Oh, hi, yes, I'm just hanging around the house without mentioning it to you because, um, I've become a total psycho. Have you got a minute to talk about my estranged daughter?'

This near-death experience made me feel a little blasé. I had survived. This was reason enough to live a little, to celebrate triumph in the manner of a true victor. To this end I would eat one of Amanda's sausage rolls – consequences be damned.

I walked into the kitchen with the newfound swagger of the near-disaster survivor and swung open the fridge door to claim my baked delicacy.

My eyes told me what my stomach refused to believe: Amanda had eaten the bloody lot of them, the greedy cow.

'Sorry, love, I had the last one.'

I whirled round at the sound of the voice, even though I knew immediately to whom it belonged.

Amanda stood there, hands on hips that were sheathed in a figure-hugging dress. She looked good.

'Jesus,' I said, putting my hand out to lean on the kitchen counter. 'Steady on, Amanda. You nearly gave me a coronary.'

'Whereas I should be completely unsurprised to see you attempting to nick my sausage rolls from my fridge?'

'*My* fridge?' I said.

'Until you move back in it is,' she replied tartly.

I let it pass. One part of me wanted to tell her about Caitlin and Joan Kennedy and the bind I was in. But no, she'd forfeited that. I hadn't forgotten about Belagio.

'So what the fuck are you doing here?' she asked.

'I, er, came to collect some stuff,' I replied vaguely.

'Didn't you think to just call and let me know you were coming instead of creeping in here?'

'I didn't want to cause a scene.'

'Well, nice job on that front,' she said dismissively.

'How did you know I was here?' I asked.

'Sue told me as I was going out to the car. She wondered what the hell you were doing hiding behind the curtains in the dining room.'

Clearly my DIY ruse was a big success.

'Maybe I should go,' I said.

'No, please stay,' she said, light-heartedly. 'You won't respond to my emails or voicemails, so maybe I might get something out of you in the flesh.'

'I'm just going to get my stuff and go,' I said. 'This isn't the best time to talk.'

'Well, it's never a good time for you, is it?'

'Oh, come on, Amanda ... Don't start.'

'In case it slipped your mind, you and I are still married, Alex,' said Amanda.

'Well, I wish you'd remembered that when you were going at it with Nick Belagio.'

As soon as I said it I regretted it. I'd had the feeling that Amanda was moving towards some kind of reconciliation speech. Now I'd just succeeded in pissing her off.

'Just get whatever you need,' she said, raising her palms towards me in a gesture that meant 'enough'. 'But in the future I want you to call me before you come to the house. If you come in here again without informing me I'll change the locks.'

'You can't do that,' I said.

'Oh, really?' she replied. 'Well, how about you abandoning the marital home – is that allowed?'

I met her stare for a moment. The sides of her mouth curled upwards as if she'd delivered a knockout blow. I could have got into it with her, but I didn't want things to get thermonuclear. There were so many variables going through my head that I thought it best to go upstairs to the spare bedroom and pretend that I'd gone to all this trouble so that I could get hold of my football programme collection.

As I drove home, part of me wished that I'd played a little nicer. As much as the Belagio incident still burned sharply in my stomach I wondered whether I should try to keep the door open. As I found myself regularly wishing that I could turn to her for her brand of no-nonsense advice during the last few weeks, I remembered that there were so many things I missed about her.

Focus on the positive, I told myself. I had managed to get copies of the photos. The Social Services snoopers would be fooled and Amanda was still – how should I cast this? – passionate about me. Maybe this was overstating the case, but I was definitely feeling confident enough to ride out Social Services' questions about Amanda's whereabouts. I needed to stop worrying. Everything would be *fine*. I still had time to work things out with Caitlin. And if it didn't happen ... well, I'd cross that bridge when I came to it.

I spent the rest of the day tidying and cleaning the house in preparation for the arrival of the busybody Joan Kennedy the following morning. I scrubbed the bath twice, the kitchen floor was wiped to operating theatre standards, and the sofa cushions were plumped so that not even the most pampered aristocrat could complain. Of course, as Amanda would undoubtedly have told me, this was a displacement activity. None of my polishing, cleaning or dusting would have any bearing on the meeting that Caitlin and I were due to have with Kennedy, or our 'case worker', as she was known.

'Look, there's a lady coming to see us in the morning,' I said to Caitlin when she got home from school. She immediately gathered from my tone that this was not necessarily the kind of lady I wanted to have visit.

150

'What lady?'

'One of the ladies who took care of you after your mum passed. She visited you at the foster home sometimes as well.'

'You mean Joan?'

'Yes, Joan.'

'Why?'

'She's just checking you're okay,' I said, not wanting to build the visit into too big a deal. 'I wanted to let you know because she might want to talk to you on your own.'

She nodded. No problem.

'And I just wanted to tell you that there's a little bit of a tricky situation ...'

Caitlin closed her book and eyed me warily.

'It's just that ...'

How to frame it?

'The Social Services lady is expecting to see a woman here, a mum, but obviously there isn't one around at the moment.'

'But she knows what happened to my mum ...'

'I don't mean *your* mum,' I explained, packing away a bucket and a mop. 'We're talking about another mum. Like my wife.'

'The woman in all those new photos?' she said. 'You look young in some of them.'

'Well, I *was* young in some of them,' I said.

My explanation of the full significance of the photos that I'd placed around the house needed to be more direct.

'It looks like there's two people living here,' said Caitlin. 'And I'm not one of them.'

'Well, we need to remedy that then, don't we?' I said brightly. 'Let's get some photos of you up.'

'But if you're not living with your wife, won't it look a bit strange to them if there're photos of her everywhere?'

'Well, yes ...' I said. 'But, I, um, sort of told them that she did live here.'

'But that's a lie,' said Caitlin. Her tone was hard to decipher. She was vaguely amused, but I could sense that she was slightly anxious. She didn't need any further complications in her life.

'Well, it's what we call a white lie,' I said. 'I told them that because I thought that it was the best thing to do, because if they found out that there wasn't a mum living here then they might ...'

Caitlin nodded. I didn't need to explain any further. She turned her head and surveyed the room.

'Look at this place,' she said.

I did as I was told and looked around the kitchen and through into the living room.

'My mum used to have tons of *stuff*,' said Caitlin. 'Clothes, magazines, make-up, bags ... It was like living in a jumble sale.' And for a very brief moment, I was hit by a moment of recognition that overwhelmed me with longing: I recognised the woman that she was describing in all her chaotic shoes-stuffed-in-cupboards and 'Oops, I forgot that I invited people over for dinner and we've only got anchovies in the fridge' glory. I miss you, Cathy, I thought to myself. What we had was brief and intense but I haven't been the same since. I felt a ghastly sense of absence and longing before being wrenched back into the present by our daughter's voice.

'Look around you,' implored Caitlin. 'There's nothing like that here. It's like a kid and an old man live here.'

'Less of the old man,' I said.

'Seriously,' she continued, ignoring my attempt at humour. That was just like her mum. Cathy was back in the room.

I nodded. She was right. The only magazine on the coffee table was *Top Gear*. There were no scented candles and no trace of a decorative cushion on the sofa.

'If you want to get away with this, then we need to go and get some women's stuff,' she pressed. 'We need to leave it lying around so that it doesn't look like a museum. It needs to look like a place where a family might live.'

I checked myself for a moment. Unless I was mistaken it seemed that Caitlin had not only accepted the premise, but she was willing to take control of the situation.

'Right, get your jacket,' I said. 'We're going shopping.' And, for once, there was no shrug of the shoulders, no remonstration or obstacle put in my way. We went into town and plundered what we needed for the following day. It was the first time that I'd really seen Caitlin engaged. We didn't bicker or ignore each other, or regard each other with suspicion. We just got on with it — even if that involved buying second-hand bras from Oxfam.

The following day I was pacing the kitchen before six in the morning, while Caitlin arrived downstairs at her usual eight o'clock. I watched her eat a bowl of cereal while thinking that, actually, she could have tipped the Oat Clusters all over the floor: the surface was so clean that she could have eaten off it without fear of ill effects. Caitlin was often a little sluggish in the morning, so while she was coming round I took a little inventory of the female accoutrements that we (actually, mostly Caitlin) had purchased the afternoon before.

There was a jacket, which we had left hanging on the back of a chair, a big stack of women's magazines, a hairbrush, a vase of flowers, some scented candles, fancy cushions for the sofa, a bra that we had left hanging in the bathroom and bits of make-up. We'd also got some frames for the copies of the photographs that I'd finagled the day before.

I hustled Caitlin upstairs to get ready and hovered in the front room with my eyes on the street. Cars drove by, but no Kennedy. Eventually Caitlin slunk downstairs.

'You okay?' I asked, preoccupied with the road.

'Yeah,' she said lazily.

I turned to look at her and saw that her hair resembled a bird's nest.

'Your hair,' I said, barely hiding the panic. What if the woman from Social Services saw her bed-head? No woman would allow her daughter's hair to remain in that condition. Caitlin's unkempt mane was a clear indication that there was no female presence in the house. I didn't have long to fix it – Kennedy would be here any moment. I sat her down in the bathroom, despite her big, huffy sigh, and began the tricky work of detangling the mess that had miraculously formed on her head during the night. I paused momentarily, realising that I was a father who had never brushed his daughter's hair before. It was such an intimate act, yet so prosaic as well. Water, I needed water. I looked outside ... time was disappearing. I did the best I could, giving up on anything other than the bare minimum, then the front doorbell rang. I thundered down the stairs.

This was not an auspicious start.

As we greeted Joan in the hallway, my rictus grin was so intense that my face hurt. Joan too was smiling although, to my horror, I could see that she was examining Caitlin's hair, which, I had to admit, looked like a flower arrangement that had been done by a drunk. I was amazed that the girl had let me get away with it. What on earth had I been thinking? I was careful to offer Joan the chair that had the jacket on its back.

'So, how are you?' she said, all smiles, reaching into her bag to pull out some paperwork.

'We're fine, thanks,' I said, beaming back at her, desperately trying to get a glimpse of the kind of horror that was contained in the worksheets on Joan's lap.

'And how are you, Caitlin?' she asked, purposefully taking the cap from a pen.

Caitlin nodded.

Go on, I thought. Beads of sweat were forming on my upper lip. *Say something!*

'Can I get you a cup of tea? Coffee? Water? I'm afraid we don't have any Coke or anything – it's bad for Caitlin's teeth, you see,' I said. I sounded like a lunatic, a bona fide sitting-in-my-own-waste-blabbering-about-alien-spacecraft nut job.

'I'm fine,' Joan said, before making a note.

What the hell was she writing?

'Alex, would you mind letting Caitlin and me have a little chat for a while?'

'Oh, sure,' I said, the smile of a sad clown spreading over my face. 'No problem. I'll just be—'

'Upstairs is usually best,' said Joan with subtle but firm insistence.

I slunk upstairs and pointedly walked into my bedroom, which was above the living room, to make it clear to Joan that I was not eavesdropping. Once there I immediately dropped to the floor and pressed my ear to the carpet to see how Caitlin was doing. I couldn't hear a bloody thing. The lack of sound prompted me to begin wriggling, python-like, to get to the upstairs hallway where I stood a chance of overhearing what was being said below.

But my movements were not as smooth as I would have liked, my knees bumped the floor a couple of times as I tried to mimic the 'SAS leopard crawl' that I'd seen demonstrated on some TV show about survival. I settled into position, but for some reason was still unable to hear their voices at all. What the hell was going on? I needed to investigate. Sadly, I poked my head outside the bedroom door at the very moment Caitlin and Joan were passing on the way to see the girl's bedroom.

'Hi,' I said happily, pressing my fingers into the edge of the carpet. 'This thing has been worrying me for ages. When they fitted it, there was an edge that was just … not right.' I hopped back up on my feet. 'That's got it.'

Behind Joan's back, Caitlin rolled her eyes at me.

'So which one's yours?' Joan asked her.

'The next door on the left,' she replied.

'The biggest one,' I said with a chuckle. 'I, er, we, were insistent that a growing girl needed her space.'

'After you,' Joan said to Caitlin before following her into the room. She shut the door behind them.

I made a lot of noise going downstairs to prove that, whatever Joan's suspicions, I was *definitely* not eavesdropping. Eventually the pair of them came back down and – what was that? – did I hear a chuckle from Joan after one of Caitlin's answers? As they entered the kitchen it was clear that something had happened upstairs that I couldn't fathom, but it meant that somehow, Joan and Caitlin were now friends. What on earth had the girl said to her? I leaned against the cooker looking as casual as I could and tried to buy into the new atmosphere with a 'this is awesome' countenance.

'Caitlin seems very happy with her room,' said Joan.

'I am,' said Caitlin, beaming. She was like a different person. God bless her, she was turning it on. The threat of a return to foster care was clearly something of a motivator.

'Caitlin, would you mind giving us a couple of moments to talk?' said Joan.

As Caitlin left the room the smile disappeared from Joan's lips.

'Everything all right, then?' I said, clapping my hands together. At the very moment I did it I was conscious that I sounded like Basil Fawlty digging himself out of a hole.

'Caitlin seems to have adapted very well to her new circumstances,' she said. 'There are very encouraging signs here. But I have to talk to you about one major area of concern.'

'Right ...' I said, my stomach churning.

'Where is Amanda?' Joan asked, pointedly.

'Well,' I stammered. 'I, I ...'

And at that moment something quite incredible happened.

'I'm sorry to interrupt, Joan,' said Caitlin, returning to the room, 'but I couldn't help overhearing and I meant to tell you that Amanda said she was really sorry about this morning. She asked me to tell you.'

Joan examined the girl closely. I couldn't tell whether she was suspicious or impressed.

'She knew how important it was for her to be here, but there was a bit of an emergency at work,' continued Caitlin.

'I see,' said Joan.

'Couldn't really be helped,' replied Caitlin.

'Just one of those things,' I added.

'I see,' said Joan, although her tone suggested that she was referring to more than Caitlin's explanation. It felt like a broader reference to Caitlin and me.

Caitlin nodded sombrely. 'I'll leave you to it,' she said eventually.

After she'd left the room again Joan and I talked for a while, mostly about the practical details of our living arrangements, which I attempted to deliver with authority and clarity.

'Well, I think that's it,' said Joan, after a few minutes. 'Bye, Caitlin,' she said on her way to the door. The girl had come downstairs to see Joan off. 'I'll see you in a few weeks. And if you'd like to speak to me before then here's my telephone number.' She handed Caitlin a card, the sneak.

'Thanks, Joan,' said Caitlin. 'It was nice to see you.'

Jesus, this kid was good.

I walked Joan to the door.

'Thanks,' I said. 'We're very happy. She's a dream.'

I wondered if I sounded in the least sincere, given that it

was only sheer laziness that had prevented me from calling her after the pocket money incident to talk about what my 'options' might be if Caitlin didn't start settling better.

'I know,' said Joan, a cloudy look on her face. 'But I want to make it clear to you that I understand your wife's difficult professional circumstances. Be that as it may, I need to witness this family as a stable and nurturing environment. Although I feel that the latter is true, I am yet to be convinced of the former. I suggest that at our next visit in two months you ensure that your wife is here.'

'She will be,' I said.

I knew I was going to regret saying that.

Chapter 18

I decided that Bean & Gone should have a 'soft launch' – there would be no razzmatazz, no ribbon-cutting, no PA from Jordan and Peter Andre. Mel and I could work through the glitches that would occur – like piss-poor coffee – before too many customers had passed through the doors.

D-Day arrived, as I'd thought, two weeks to the day that I'd hired Mel. I didn't sleep much the night before and rose looking for portents. Caitlin had left early, explaining that she was 'working on a special project'. She'd shown some interest in the café, emerging from her self-imposed iPod isolation to ask the occasional question or make an observation, but our encounters remained largely uncomfortable and fractious. Before I could engage her or begin a dialogue she would slip back into the shadows.

I got in my Briefcase Bob estate and started driving to the café. The commute certainly beat the 8.27 to Waterloo with its row after row of mortgage hostages. I put Eric B and Rakim's 'Paid In Full' on the sound system for its musical excellence but also as a tribute to my new venture.

I was just coming off the roundabout near Sainsbury's when, out of the corner of my eye, I noticed a girl from Caitlin's school who had exactly the same bag as her. I slowed up a little bit, realising that, actually, it wasn't just a girl from Caitlin's school – it was Caitlin herself. I couldn't quite make sense of what I was seeing: the school was a good fifteen-minute walk from the town centre. She'd told me that she had to go in to school earlier than normal to get some work done . . .

And what really threw me wasn't the cigarette in her hand. It was the fact that some spotty Herbert – I couldn't see his face but I still *knew* he was a spotty Herbert – had his hand on her arse. A hand with what looked like a green ring on his little finger. More explicitly, the hand was on her arse in order to pull her closer to him for the purposes of a snog.

Yanking the steering wheel abruptly I pulled hard to the side of the road, causing the driver behind to beep me and deliver a volley of expletives.

Up yours too, mate.

As I pulled up I could see Caitlin had recognised the car. I jumped out ready to wring a scrawny teenage neck – I hadn't decided whether it should be Caitlin's or the spotty Herbert's – to find that they had vanished into the shopping precinct like a suburban Bonnie and Clyde.

If this was a portent, then it wasn't a good one.

Caitlin wasn't answering her phone. I started to leave a chastening voicemail, but deleted it. I needed to be calm. I needed to handle this right.

Mel was waiting for me outside the Bean & Gone when I arrived. Her smile and confidence were exactly what I needed. She could obviously see from my face that everything wasn't quite right. She reached into her bag and pulled out an envelope.

'This is for you,' she said.

I opened it. It was a good-luck card. I hadn't expected this. Thank you, Mel. Thank you.

'Let's get the show on the road, then, shall we?' I said and opened the door for her. I flipped the sign that hung on the back of the door to read 'open' and turned to survey my empire. It didn't really compare to that of Rome or the Ottomans, but it was – for the foreseeable future – mine. It was a simple set-up: at the back there was a counter with the coffee machine, a glass cabinet with pastries (which I was sourcing from a poncy patisserie in Richmond) and the till. Throughout the rest of the place were Parisian-style café tables and chairs. I'd set up a rack containing the daily papers. Mel had also made it her business to go around the local bargain bookstores and pick up paperbacks that patrons could browse while quaffing their lattes. There were plans to start doing sandwiches and a limited amount of hot food – this was where I'd make real money – but it could wait until the coffee machine had been mastered and there were enough customers to justify the expenditure.

'Right then,' I said to Mel, who was stacking coffee cups behind the counter. 'Are you sure that you know what you're doing?'

'We'll find out today, won't we?' she replied.

There were footsteps outside. My heart leapt – we'd only been open a couple of minutes and we had a customer already ...

A woman closed in on the shop, glanced quickly inside and passed by. I realised that I had been holding my breath. I exhaled.

'Don't worry,' said Mel, who had noticed. 'They'll come soon enough.'

'I know,' I said. 'It's just the first day.'

'And remember that you wanted to open quietly.'

'Well, it looks like I got what I wanted, didn't I?' I joked.

'Be thankful for small mercies,' said Mel. 'If we had a load of mums rushing through the door right now shouting for cappuccinos and croissants you wouldn't know what had hit you. Anyway, I think you under-ordered on the skimmed milk.'

'Really?' I said.

'Yeah,' she replied. 'I think we've got too much normal milk and not enough skim and soy. You know people round here; they're all into their health.'

'Well, you'd better hope we don't run out of skim,' I said.

'Why?'

'Because you'll be the one going to the supermarket to get more if we do.'

'Right,' said Mel. 'I'll be pushing the extra-fatty whipped-cream options then.'

Within half an hour we had had a dozen customers, mostly mums who had just done the school run and had popped into town to do some shopping. Mel and I smiled and made small talk, attempting to set up a gentle rapport with everyone. Some of them wished us well. One of them even said that she'd be back.

By mid-afternoon we had got into a rhythm: I was dealing with customers and the till and Mel was making the coffees. Thankfully, she'd got the hang of The Beast fairly quickly.

'You're going to have to teach me how to use that,' I said to her in a quiet moment.

'What?' she said. 'And put myself in a position when I'm dispensable? You've got to be joking.'

Then she winked at me and I felt something inside me melt. I caught myself staring at her a moment too long before grabbing a cloth and going to wipe pastry crumbs from the tables. When I looked up I saw her walking into the back of the shop. She might have sensed me watching her, because she turned round.

'Just going to the loo,' she said. 'Keep an eye on things, will you?'

The door opened and in walked a customer. He had long, straggly hair that was receding quite dramatically. He looked like he hadn't been out of bed too long. A studded belt, which was looped through his jeans, seemed oddly out of place on a man who must have been in his late forties.

'Hi,' I said brightly, 'what can I get you?'

He didn't smile, just looked me up and down suspiciously.

'I'm looking for Mel,' he said coolly.

'And you are?' I asked.

'I'm Kenny,' he said, 'her boyfriend.'

This was Mel's boyfriend? I couldn't quite fathom it. Kenny seemed not only to be a bad match for Mel – he could have been a much older brother or even, Jesus, her father and let's not even get into the sad state of his clothes or barnet – he just wasn't romantic material. I mean, these two actually …

I just couldn't comprehend it.

And Mel hadn't mentioned a boyfriend to me. Not that she had to, of course; it just seemed a little strange that I'd found out like this.

'She's in the back,' I said to him. 'I'm Alex.'

Kenny nodded. 'I know,' he said.

He didn't stop and chat, or offer his congratulations about the coffee shop. Rather, he just went and sat at a window table and waited for Mel.

She came out of the bathroom and gave me a smile. I nodded over to Kenny.

'You've got a visitor,' I said.

There was a flicker of something in her face – I couldn't quite tell what – before she went over to Kenny and had a quiet conversation with him. She came back and asked, 'Is it all right if I make him a coffee?'

'Of course,' I said. I wanted to appear magnanimous, like it didn't matter to me whether she had a boyfriend or not, but I had a strange feeling: resentment.

Moments later the door opened and in walked Caitlin. She waved to Mel, who made a fuss of her, rearranging her hair and fetching her a juice, before she acknowledged me. If Caitlin had been nervous about seeing me following my discovery of the nature of her 'special project' she didn't show it. Or maybe she did.

'It looks nice,' she said, which caught me by surprise.

'Thanks.' I stopped myself from saying: We've got to talk. That could come later. 'It's not too shabby, is it?'

Caitlin looked a little frayed around the edges after her day at school, or wherever she'd been. I tried not to think too hard about it.

'We thought that—' I continued, but Caitlin cut me off by raising her hand. She stuck her nose in the air, as if sniffing for something, and rotated her head 180 degrees.

'You need music,' she said finally.

It hadn't occurred to me, but she was right.

'It's too quiet,' Caitlin continued. 'People who come in and want to have a coffee on their own will feel, you know ...'

'Self-conscious?'

'Yes.'

There was a momentary pause.

'Well, I think we need some White Stripes.'

'How about Norah Jones?'

Caitlin pulled a face. '*Boring*,' she said.

She started to take off her school bag. I turned to look back at the street. Which is when I saw Amanda walk through the door. She looked a little nervous, casting her eyes around the café until she saw me.

'Hi,' I said.

I could feel Caitlin's gaze – she had seen the photos that I'd put around the house for Joan Kennedy's benefit. She knew exactly who Amanda was and could spot the tension between us.

'Thought I'd come through the front door rather than hiding behind the curtains,' she said. I think she meant it as a joke, but it came out wrong, like she was angry.

I smiled, but it was thin, humourless.

'So this is it, eh?' she said.

'Yeah,' I said, uneasily. Caitlin was still hovering. I willed her to walk away. 'First day today.'

'How was it?'

'Oh, good,' I said. 'We're finding our feet.'

Amanda glanced at Caitlin, who stared back at her. I had no choice: I had to introduce them. But how to introduce your estranged daughter and estranged wife when you don't want to let your estranged wife know that you have a daughter? Was there etiquette for that?

'Amanda, this is Caitlin, Caitlin this is Amanda.'

Caitlin gave Amanda a wave by holding her hand up and wiggling her fingers. Amanda smiled at the girl, but was clearly confused about her identity.

'And you're ...' Amanda looked to the back of the café where Mel was working the coffee machine. Mel looked over and caught my eye. She was trying to work out who I was talking to.

'She's Mel's daughter,' I said, gesturing to the back of the shop and praying that Caitlin would roll with my extraordinary fiction. I waited nervously as Amanda continued to examine Caitlin.

Maybe it was the opportunity to gain leverage over me that would counterbalance the incident that morning, but Caitlin didn't miss a beat. There was a reason her strange new father had introduced his wife to her in this way, and she wasn't going to question it.

'It's her first day,' said Caitlin, nodding over at Mel. 'Did she do okay?'

'She was great,' I said.

Thank you, thank you, Caitlin. But you're still not allowed to smoke or get groped.

'And Mel is ...' asked Amanda. It was clear at this point that her visit was a reconnaissance mission.

'She's my customer service manager,' I replied.

'Oh,' said Amanda. 'Is that a grand title for a shop assistant?'

I raised an eyebrow at her. 'If you're going to—'

'I'm sorry,' interrupted Amanda. 'I didn't mean to … I was just joking.' She sighed. 'Maybe it's just best if I go.'

She pulled her bag up onto her shoulder. Part of me was desperate for her to leave – this had been a close call. But there was another part of me that wanted her to stay. Seeing her had made me wonder if it might be possible for us to …

But no. Not yet.

As difficult as the Caitlin situation was, I had vowed to give the girl time. And then there was Mel … The whole situation just seemed too confused, too fragile. But I was going to have to be smart about it. The next meeting with Social Services was only five weeks away. I would have to tell Amanda the truth if I was going to get her there. I felt a burning in my heart – blow that and I'd end up on my own.

I gave Amanda a non-committal smile. 'Well, thanks for coming,' I said.

Amanda waited momentarily to see if I would move forward and kiss her. I didn't – out of the corner of my eye I could see Mel watching us.

'I'll be seeing you then,' I added.

Amanda nodded, but avoided looking directly at me. She slipped out of the door. I watched her go, trotting across the street, slipping in between the early-evening traffic. I turned to Caitlin to explain.

'Can I have a blueberry muffin?' she got in first.

'What's the magic—'

'Please.'

I needed to talk to her. The incident with the spotty Herbert, my telling Amanda that Caitlin was Mel's … It was all too much.

The door opened and a group of six people walked in needing caffeine and high-fat snack items. Caitlin and I would talk another time.

Chapter 19

We were sitting having a fishpie dinner when I decided to try to be Dad.

'So, about this morning,' I started. I was hoping that if I just started the conversation she might respond in a spirit of mutual trust. We would perch in the truth tree. Caitlin pushed some mashed potatoes onto some of her peas and scooped them up.

'What?' she said. Her hair was wrapped in a towel, drying from a shower.

'This morning,' I repeated.

She took a bite of her food. With her right hand, which wasn't holding anything, she flipped open her palm while lowering her head slightly to communicate bewilderment.

'You said that you had to go into school early because you were working on a special project,' I said. I was going to give her every chance to 'fess up. That's what modern dads did, right? We were gentle, nurturing, *present*.

'Yeah,' she said. 'I'm doing a project on apartheid. It's due next week and I wanted to get in the library.'

'Is that the truth, Caitlin?'

She put down her fork.

'Yes, it is.'

'Really?'

'Yes.'

I took another mouthful. The kitchen clock was the only noise in the house. How to deal with such a brazen lie?

'Look,' I started, 'I was driving through town this morning around nine, and I saw you.'

'Where?'

'Near the roundabout near Sainsbury's.'

She shook her head firmly. 'You can't have done,' she said. 'I was at school by then. No way.'

I paused. Was this just an honest mistake? Had I seen someone else who looked just like my daughter getting off with a little toerag hoodie? It was possible. It was the first day of the café; I was stressed and distracted and had been going at twenty or thirty miles an hour. She looked at me defiantly and I realised that, if I pushed it, I risked the small gain we'd made after she backed my story about Mel being her mother in front of Amanda. Plus there had been her handling of Joan Kennedy during the home visit. This troubled me – was I so weak that I'd capitulate in return for a quiet life?

'Anyway,' she said, 'I've got a question for you.'

'Really?' I said, encouraged that we might enter a dialogue.

'Why didn't you tell your wife that I'm your daughter?'

I took another mouthful of fishpie to consider my reply.

'Why?' said Caitlin, badgering me.

'Because it's none of her business,' I said, more sourly than I meant to.

'Well, it's my business,' she said.

'Some things are private,' I told her.

I was annoyed with myself now. Not only had I failed to punish Caitlin for what I had seen this morning, but now she had turned the tables on me and was making me look foolish.

'Well, if you're not going to tell her—' started Caitlin.

'Don't even think about it,' I snapped. She looked over at me with anger in her eyes. She thought I was a dickhead – and at that moment she was right.

'I'm sorry,' I said. 'I didn't mean to talk to you like that. I'm sorry that the situation is so strange at the moment. There's a right time for everything. I will tell Amanda eventually. I'm just asking you to be patient. With Social Services and everything things are really delicate.'

'When will you tell her?' Caitlin persisted.

'Soon,' I replied.

This was a lie, of course. I might never tell her at all. I would see how things developed over the next few weeks.

I looked around the kitchen and was reminded of another secret: in case things hadn't worked out with Caitlin I'd only rented the house on a short-term lease. Our home was as insubstantial as our brief and troubled relationship. What a wonderful father I was turning out to be.

The rest of the first week at the Bean & Gone was a blur: there was a steady stream of customers to keep Mel and me on our toes. Most of the punters were exploring, checking out the latest distraction from shoe shopping for the kids and trips to the health food store for flaxseed oil. But some reappeared, settling into purchasing patterns that, by Friday, were recognisable enough that Mel would start tamping the right blend of coffee or reaching into the pastry cabinet at the very sight of them.

Mel was a good worker and I liked having her around, although I was aware that she might prove a distraction to me. The only blot on the landscape was Kenny, who established himself as a regular presence at the café, one who appeared to find it hard to sit in a chair: he was either slumped or stretched out, as if his body was incapable of making anything other than gawky shapes. I'd not spoken to Mel about my rising level of irritation with her beau – I didn't want to piss her off – but at the end of the fourth day running that he'd spent leaning against the café wall, his legs extended in front of him, drinking lattes infused with peppermint syrup, I waited for her to disappear for a few moments before approaching him.

'Everything all right, Kenny?' I asked.

'Peppermint is very good for the digestive system,' he explained, taking a sip.

'Not working today then?' I asked by way of reply.

'No,' said Kenny. 'Taking some time off, actually. I'm tired. Need a rest. You know how it is.'

'Oh, right,' I said. The connoisseur of peppermint syrup had partially bleached his mousey hair, which was cut into a kind of shag. He was never clean-shaven, although his beard always seemed to be the same length. As I stood there in my Bean & Gone polo shirt and apron, he was making me feel like the squarest man on the planet. I made a mental note to ask Mel what it was, exactly, that Kenny did for money. I was beginning to suspect that it involved finding vulnerable women and shacking up with them.

'Kenny,' I said, scratching the back of my neck, 'I need your help with something.'

Kenny pulled his mouth into a sour shape. Clearly being helpful wasn't on his agenda.

'*Riiight* ...' he said warily.

'Oh, nothing like that,' I laughed uneasily. 'No, no ... Here's the thing: you like crosswords, don't you?'

'Yes,' said Kenny. 'I like all word games. But the one I like most of all is the cryptic crossword. The one in the *Telegraph* is my favourite.'

'Really?' I said, trying to feign interest. I was trying to lead Kenny in a particular direction before delivering the *coup de grâce*.

'Yeah,' said Kenny, tapping the café's copy of the *Telegraph*, which he had on the table. 'I can generally do it in about ten minutes. Sometimes longer, though, depending on how the old grey matter is working.'

'That's impressive,' I said. 'You know, it's interesting that you have that there, as I wanted to talk to you about exactly that ...'

Kenny straightened up and rested his chin on his fist.

'You know that I buy the papers for the use of all the customers,' I told him. 'People like to come in here and flick through them.'

Kenny looked at me, seemingly bored.

'Well, I was hoping, Kenny, that you might be able to resist filling in the crossword when you take a look at the paper. And I was also wondering if you might return the papers after you've had a look at them. I think, say, twenty minutes, is fair. What do you think?'

Kenny continued looking at me, his eyes half-moons of boredom.

'So you want me to look at the papers for only twenty minutes?'

'Per paper,' I clarified, feeling like a bloody traffic warden.

There was a pause.

'But what am I supposed to do the rest of the day?' asked Kenny. 'I mean, I have a very active mind. I need stimulation. And the crossword ...' His voice trailed off. 'That just seems a little, you know, draconian. I mean, we're not living in a police state, are we?'

'No, no,' I said, 'no police state, I just need to think about the other customers ... You know, the paying customers.'

'Hang on a minute,' said Kenny. 'Are you ... ? Did you ...? I think I need to make it clear, pal. The understanding Mel and I have is that anything I eat or drink here will come out of her wages at the end of the week.'

This was news to me.

'Didn't she tell you?' said Kenny, looking perplexed.

'No,' I replied. This bloke was a piece of work.

'Well, I'll have a word with her later, then,' said Kenny, snapping shut the paper, and stalking from the café.

'You do that,' I said to the closing door. I picked up his empty cup. I was disappointed that he hadn't asked me for another drink – it would have given me the excuse to turn and smash the mug on his head.

I hadn't wanted to make Kenny unwelcome (well, not totally, anyway) and I really didn't want to create a problem with the lovely Mel, but I was pleased that I'd established some pub landlord-style proprietorial boundaries. The only thing that peeved me about the incident was the way that Kenny had made me feel like a square, like the whitest man in the whitest town in England. I bet *he* couldn't name all the members of the Juice Crew (Marley Marl, Mr Magic, MC Shan, Big Daddy Kane, Biz Markie, Craig G, Intelligent Hoodlum, Kool G Rap and DJ Polo, Master Ace, Roxanne Shanté, T.J. Swan and Cool V), and didn't have a rare-as-hen's-teeth white-label copy of Mass Order's 'Take Me Away', or know every single word of the twelve-inch version of 'Rapper's Delight'.

'Is everything all right?' asked Mel, reappearing at the counter and looking at the seat that Kenny had just vacated.

'Yeah,' I replied.

'Just because I thought that maybe … Well, is it all right if Kenny is here so much? He's had a bit of a bad time recently and, well, I'm not sure that he knows what to do with himself.'

'What does he do?' I needed to work on my tone. Again, I sounded more aggressive than I'd meant to.

'He's a musician.'

'Really?'

I must have sounded a little incredulous.

'He's really good,' said Mel defensively. 'Back in the eighties, he did a lot of session work.'

'I daresay you're too young to know any of the songs, though.'

'No, he's played a lot of them to me,' she said. 'You know the guitar on "Sowing The Seeds Of Love"? That was Kenny. And you know the drum break on "In The Air Tonight"? Phil Collins asked him to do it.'

'Oh, *really*,' I said, wondering if Mel actually believed this fiction or was just toeing the party line.

'So does he still play?'

'Well,' replied Mel. She picked up some mugs and dishes from the sink and began to stack them in the dishwasher. 'He's mainly writing at the moment. He needs time to clear his head.'

Clear his head and get a decent bloody haircut, I thought to myself.

'Look,' I said. Mel stopped what she was doing. 'About Kenny,' I started, but I was interrupted by Caitlin.

'Is this how I do it?' she asked, taking off her coat with one hand and attempting to wrap a Bean & Gone apron around her waist with the other. Mel approached her and rearranged the apron, tying the cords around her waist twice.

'There,' said Mel, stepping backwards and surveying her handiwork.

'Is it all right?' asked Caitlin.

'It looks great,' said Mel.

Caitlin flushed a little, pleased with the compliment, and flattened the apron down.

'Right then,' said Mel, 'are you ready? Closing time is when your work begins.' There was warmth to her. It was clear that the way she engaged Caitlin absorbed the girl. Caitlin smiled and nodded.

'Come here, gorgeous,' said Mel, and gave her a hug. 'Right, first thing: I'm only going to let you help if you promise to save a few of those cuddles for me. Do we have a deal?'

Caitlin nodded. Mel stuck out her hand and they slapped palms.

'So we've got some dirty, nasty stuff over here,' said Mel, leading Caitlin over to the deep stainless-steel sink where we put washing-up while the dishwasher was in operation. 'Some of this stuff we'll need before the dishwasher finishes its cycle.'

Caitlin rolled up the sleeves of her school shirt.

'That's it,' said Mel. 'And why don't you use these as well?' She handed Caitlin a pair of yellow gloves, which Caitlin pulled on, waving her hands around for effect.

'Weird,' she said.

'If you've got those on you can make sure that the water is nice and hot,' said Mel.

Caitlin got to work on the various dishes and implements in the sink. I watched, leaning against the counter as she thoroughly scrubbed each item before rinsing it off. She was concentrating hard, inspecting every spoon to make sure that there was not a single blemish.

'If you keep going like this we'll be able to promote you to the pastry counter,' I said.

'Whoops,' said Caitlin, spraying herself with water from the cold tap by angling a dish wrongly.

'And if you break anything we'll have to spray you with more of that,' I said. 'That's the punishment.'

'We didn't discuss my wages,' she said.

'Oh, your wages,' I said. Was she serious? 'So what were you thinking?'

'Well, someone at school told me about the minimum wage and that I should ask you for that.'

'Well, your mate at school is clearly very on the ball, because there *is* such a thing as a national minimum wage ...' I replied. 'But, sadly, not around here.'

'Oh, why not?' asked Caitlin.

'Because around here we pay people in chocolate croissants that we haven't been able to shift during the day.'

'That sounds like a pretty bad deal to me,' said Caitlin.

I walked over to the pastry counter and pulled out a chocolate croissant, placing it on a plate next to her. 'So here's your first day's wages.'

I wasn't going to back down on this, I thought as I flicked down the latch on the front door and pulled down the blind. I was already giving her thirty bloody quid a week and she had the cheek to ask for more. Caitlin disconsolately finished the washing-up and sat down at one of the tables with her croissant. I watched as she pulled a book out of her bag and balanced it on her knees. She ate slowly, absorbed in what she was reading. It was a relief just to see her not texting someone or listening to her iPod. I wondered what was going through her mind, whether she saw this coffee shop adventure as normal, or a little kooky. Chances are she wasn't even thinking of it in those terms. It was what it was.

Mel approached me, wiping her hands on a tea towel.

'So, do you want to talk?' she asked.

I shrugged as if to say that everything was fine.

'About Kenny, you know,' she continued.

'What about him?' I asked.

'Come on, Alex,' said Mel.

Why was I acting like a dick towards her?

'I'm sorry,' I said, shaking my head. I was annoyed at myself for being rude to her.

'If you change your mind let me know,' said Mel, irritated. 'You know where to find me. Just so you know, I'm aware of Kenny's shortcomings, but underneath it all he's a good man.'

I nodded. She *thought* Kenny was a good man. I'd always considered myself better than someone as feckless and self-ish as Kenny. But, right then, I wondered if Kenny was a

176

paragon of masculine virtue when compared to my schemes and lies.

There was a sharp rapping on the door. I rested my mop against the wall and went to see who was there.

I pulled the blind up to see Amanda on the other side. My pulse shot up immediately. I followed her gaze: she was staring directly at Caitlin, who was looking up from her book to see who was there.

Jesus. Here was trouble.

I opened the door, slamming the frame of it into my toe and then back into Amanda's face.

'Oh, hi, yeah ...' I said. Smooth. Untroubled.

It was strange; even after several weeks of separation we instinctively moved to kiss each other before realising that there was way too much to be sorted out for us to engage in this kind of frivolity. We both drew back and became two awkward adults holding our hands in front of our chests to prevent any ill-conceived intimacy.

'So, how's your first week gone?' Amanda said enthusiastically.

'Yeah, not bad,' I said, underplaying my hand a little. I glanced back at Caitlin, wondering how I was going to handle Amanda's inevitable questioning.

'Good numbers today, then?' pressed Amanda. What a strange question. There was now no doubt in my mind that she was up to something.

'Yeah, yeah, pretty good today,' I said, unwilling to give her any more than the basics. 'You want a drink?'

Amanda looked over at the cold drinks. 'No, I'm all right at the moment,' she said. 'Got to get going.'

Got to get going? So she came round just to see if we'd had a good day? No, Amanda, I'm not buying ...

'All right,' I said. There was more, but I wasn't quite sure how to draw it from her. I put my hands on my hips – something that I would never normally do – but somehow it seemed like the right gesture for the moment.

'So do you want to sit down?'

'Oh, okay,' said Amanda, as if she had changed her mind and decided to stay. We sat at a table that was pressed against a divider. I leaned against the structure, while Amanda crossed her long legs, pushing them in my direction. Was she trying to tell me something? Certainly her legs were a distraction. I had always loved their paleness, and the galaxy of freckles running up and down her shins.

Amanda turned to take in Caitlin, who had turned back to her book. So that's why she's here.

'Hello, sweetheart,' Amanda said, craning her neck to see the girl whom it occurred to me only at that moment was her stepdaughter.

Was I totally insane trying to manage this?

'Do you remember me?'

'Yes,' said Caitlin, smiling sweetly. And then I realised that she was more than content to see Amanda and I sitting at the same table. I prayed that she didn't choose this moment to blow the lid on her real identity. Any thoughts I had of engineering a glorious marital reconciliation receded into the distance.

'He's got you working late, has he?' Amanda joked. 'Make sure you ask him for a pay rise, won't you?'

Caitlin laughed. 'I wouldn't mind being paid at all.'

'I do pay you,' I said. 'In chocolate croissants; the best kind of currency there is.'

'Yeah, but they're hardly good for my waistline, are they?' replied Caitlin.

'A young girl like you shouldn't be worried about things like that,' said Amanda. 'You look just right. Don't let them get inside your head and tell you that there's something wrong with you.'

In normal circumstances I would have loved Amanda for saying that. But I was too busy trying to send Caitlin signals to absent herself with immediate effect. No such luck: it was clear that the girl was being drawn into Amanda's dominion. It seemed that, for Caitlin, there was something hypnotic about her. It might have been her glamour, a powerful force for a girl without a maternal influence who is about to embark on a life of romantic adventure. But I thought it was more likely that Caitlin liked Amanda because it was clear that my wife knew how to handle boys, and all girls need this most particular expertise.

I had to do something – I needed to stage an intervention.

'Caitlin, can you do me a favour?' I asked rather too hurriedly. 'Can you go back and empty the dishwasher, please? Amanda and I won't be long.'

'But I've only just sat down,' protested Caitlin, aware that I was marginalising her on purpose. 'And then I've got to wipe down the tables.'

'That's all right,' I pressed with a tissue-thin smile, 'I'll take care of that.' Caitlin remained rooted to the spot. What to do? Then it occurred to me that my best course of action was to formalise the conversation – to make Caitlin think that there was something intimate happening between us.

'Amanda and I need to talk about something,' I said.

There was a pause.

'Oh, okay,' said Caitlin in her most docile voice. I thought that perhaps Amanda might also assume 'something' was a euphemism for 'reconciliation'. I'd have to handle that if it arose. For the moment, the most important matter was that I separated the two of them to prevent any awkward questions involving Caitlin's provenance.

'How's your mum?' asked Amanda provocatively as Caitlin passed by her.

I froze.

This, clearly, was the moment where my estranged wife discovered that I had a child that she knew nothing about.

Caitlin stopped and looked Amanda square in the eye.

'She's fine; thanks for asking,' she replied.

Now, *that's* my girl.

Caitlin walked slowly back into the kitchen. I watched her go, mystified but thankful for her ability to skip over the abyss so daintily.

Once Caitlin had gone Amanda seemed a little aimless, as if she couldn't quite remember something she'd forgotten to do. Eventually, after we'd made some small talk, she said that she had to get moving, she had a valuation to get to. I saw her off the premises fairly sure that she'd been evaluating something else for the past few minutes. I'd dodged a bullet, but it was clear that Amanda had sensed that something was up at the Bean & Gone.

When Caitlin went to bed that night, I took a look at the till receipts. We were doing all right, but only just. For the business to have a future we were going to have to get more people through the door. I needed to divulge this to Mel without letting her know that we were in trouble. In the meantime I would move some of my savings into the business account.

I just wished everything else in life was that simple.

Chapter 20

One night I dreamt that *every* table at the Bean & Gone was occupied by Kenny. There were fourteen of him, all drinking peppermint lattes and filling in the crossword. I woke with a start, switched on the light and shook the image of the shaggy shnorer from my mind. I was just about to get out of bed when I realised that I didn't need to: it was Sunday and I had agreed with Mel that I'd take the day off. I could stay beneath the duvet.

I lay there trying to get back to sleep, but my mind was already too active, so I heaved myself to my feet and went for a run. After a lazy few years I'd started pounding the pavement again. The stress of the past few weeks had occasioned a dull feeling of dread in my chest – long, unforgiving runs seemed to be the only way to dislodge the grizzlies that resided there.

That, and drinking, of course.

I got back around ten. There was no sign of life from Caitlin, so I made breakfast and tidied the house. I was just about to have a shower when the doorbell rang. I opened the door to find a young lad who seemed familiar waiting anxiously on my doorstep. Alarm bells went off: beneath his over-gelled hair and age-appropriate skin ailment he was a handsome devil. I wondered if he was sponsored by a sportswear company, or had just come from training: no piece of his clothing was free of a logo.

He didn't say hello.

'Is Caitlin in?' he asked as soon as the door was open.

'Yes, she is,' I said.

He nodded.

'And you are?' I asked.

'Ollie,' he said. He raised the heel of his right hand and wiped his nose with it.

'Ollie,' I replied flatly. I imagined that this was what the fathers of teenage girls had to do: make it known to all suitors that their quest begins with a paternal gatekeeper who, from that moment on, will subject them to constant, unforgiving – even menacing – surveillance.

'She's not mentioned you coming over.'

'Really?' He seemed a little hurt. He thought for a moment before pulling out his mobile.

'Look,' he said, holding his phone up so that I could see it. I stared at the screen and was unable to decipher the meaning of the language. Words had been replaced by single letters and acronyms, producing a language that was as new and unfamiliar to me as, say, Wookie.

'See,' said Ollie. 'CYT.'

'What does that mean?' I asked.

Ollie paused for a moment, as if he thought that maybe I was winding him up. Eventually it dawned on him that my question was genuine.

'See you tomorrow,' he explained.

'Oh,' I said. 'You'd better come in then.'

'Thanks, Mr Taylor,' he said cheerfully.

I watched as he walked into the hallway and wiped his trainers on the door mat. Clearly he wasn't as feral as he looked. He followed me through to the kitchen.

'Do you want anything to drink?' I asked.

'I'd love a cup of tea,' he said. This was the second time that he'd surprised me in a minute – wiping his feet? Asking for tea? It was like I had a visitor from the Women's Institute. I'd have broken out the Dundee cake if I'd had any. I set about putting the kettle on and gathering the mugs. Meanwhile Ollie made himself at home by stepping up onto one of the breakfast bar stools. He looked about the kitchen expectantly.

'Did you watch any of the football yesterday?' he asked.

'Not really,' I said. This was a lie. I had watched a couple of games, but I wanted to continue to play the role of remote parent.

'You didn't miss much,' he said. 'The United–Liverpool game today should be good, though.'

While I fetched the milk and put some laundry on he continued to chatter about football, apparently oblivious to his original intention of seeing Caitlin. I got the feeling that he just wanted to hang out.

'Do you have a tissue?' he asked while in the middle of telling me about a documentary he'd seen on mountain gorillas. 'Think I might have a cold coming.'

I passed him some Kleenex, and as he reached for the box it occurred to me: was this the lad who had had his hand on Caitlin's arse and his tongue in her throat? I glanced at his hand – there was no sign of the green ring that I'd seen when I'd spotted the pair of them.

I was relieved. My first impressions of this kid had been wrong: he was a nice lad. I relented on my Stern Dad act a little and, as he sipped his tea and worked his way through several HobNobs, we discussed Rafa Benitez's rotation policy. He had just moved onto the topic of the best Ultimate Fighter in the world when Caitlin walked into the room.

'All right?' she said to him. She leaned against the kitchen counter, her hip jutting out in his direction and played with the ends of her hair. She had taken some care with her outfit: she was wearing a short skirt but – thankfully – had leggings underneath. Caitlin was three or four inches taller than him; she could have been his older sister.

'All right,' said Ollie. He had apparently lost his ability for intelligent conversation, sitting there looking at her in the same way that a thirsty man regards an oasis.

This was a date.

Jesus Christ. Was Caitlin working her way through every lad in her year?

'Do you want to go upstairs?' she asked.

'Um, I thought you were going to go out to the shops,' I said.

'We are,' said Caitlin, yawning and stretching her arms outward, which pressed her cleavage in the direction of the bewitched Ollie. 'I just want to play Ollie a song I downloaded.'

Ollie hopped down from his stool expectantly and the two of them walked out of the kitchen. The change that had come over him when Caitlin walked into the room was spectacular: he'd gone from being chatty and extrovert to doing a passable impression of a slobbering village idiot.

'Caitlin,' I shouted up the stairs after them, 'be sure to leave your bedroom door open.'

There was no response.

'Okay, Mr Taylor,' came the eventual reply. But it wasn't from Ollie. My own daughter was referring to me as Mr Taylor.

They didn't stay in Caitlin's room long. A couple of minutes later they stormed downstairs, crashing out the front door.

'Bye, Mr Taylor,' shouted Ollie.

They were going 'into town', a time-honoured ritual of the teenager, which translated as driving OAPs from the benches in the shopping precinct, eating bags of chips and laughing loudly at the antics of histrionic peers.

I watched the pair of them disappear down the road, and

felt an odd stab of anxiety. Was it okay to let Caitlin out on the streets with a kid she barely knew? A kid who might have a packet of crack (I doubted that crack came in packets like crisps do, but had no idea what the correct terminology was), a Glock semi-automatic and a three-pack of flavoured condoms tucked inside his Adidas tracksuit. Was this a test by Social Services? Were they going to pick Caitlin up, bring her home and berate me for being the World's Worst Dad? Were there cameras rigged inside my house, filming me at this very moment?

Relax, I told myself. She's *thirteen* years old. She's mature enough to handle whatever the mean streets of Surrey throw at her. Kids much younger than her wander the streets of London, Liverpool and Birmingham every day without incident. What's the worst that can happen in Cobham? She has a run-in with a couple of girls from the pony club? There's an encounter with a group of prep-school kids who won't share their Yu-Gi-Oh! cards?

I was fairly confident there was very little in life that Caitlin would face that would prove more challenging than what she had experienced over the past few months.

Even the girls from the pony club.

Although I just wanted to crack open a couple of beers and sit in the garden, I had promised Caitlin that I'd make roast chicken for dinner, which meant getting in our family run-around and shifting my tired arse over to the supermarket. I couldn't be bothered to get dressed properly, or shave or comb my hair. I had a quick shower and threw on a pair of tracksuit bottoms. I looked like a vagrant who'd nicked some gear from the changing room at the local gym.

I'd pretty much got what I needed food-wise when I remembered that Caitlin had asked me to pick up some hair bands and other stuff – shampoos and creams and God knows what.

She'd even written me a list. She also wanted a copy of some magazine. I made a detour for these and was heading for the checkout when I turned the corner into another aisle and ran smack into Amanda.

'Blimey,' she said. She was holding a basket that she was struggling to carry.

'Amanda,' I said. 'Um, hi …'

When I'd decided to go with the hobo look for my trip to the supermarket I'd banked on not bumping into anyone, least of all Amanda, with her exacting standards of personal style.

'How are you?' she asked.

'I'm fine, yeah, just, you know, relaxing. Going to watch the football later.'

'Who's playing?' she asked.

'United and Liverpool. What are you up to?'

'Working – well, not literally. I made a little detour to pick up some things, but I'm in and out of the office today.'

'That sounds like fun.'

'Things have picked up now that the kids are back at school.'

'Right,' I said. I thought about removing the baseball cap, but didn't want her to see my full-on vagrant hair. I wanted her to talk to me, needed to hear her voice. 'Of course.'

'I'll probably take Monday off to make up for it. I haven't had a day off in a while,' she continued.

'Why not?'

'Oh, I don't know. Throwing myself into work, I suppose.'

'Me too,' I said.

'How's it going?'

'Oh, great, yeah.'

This wasn't entirely true. The café wasn't bringing in anything like as much money as it needed to. While I had enough money to keep it going for a year or so, I was beginning to sense my aversion to committing financial hari-kiri. The last person I was going to tell that we were struggling was Amanda. Her function as the town intranet meant that her role in the fortunes of the Bean & Gone should be as booster rather than forecaster of its demise.

'We're hoping to expand next spring.'

What a load of old bollocks. I wondered whether Amanda's bullshit detector was ringing yet.

'That's great,' she said. 'How so?'

'Well . . .' I said. Shit! My eyelids were flickering slightly – this was something that happened when I was about to tell a lie – 'we're partnering with a local chef to produce a line of organic snacks and sandwiches.'

'That's amazing,' said Amanda. 'I should tell Sarah – I'm sure that she'd be interested.'

Her friend Sarah worked at the local newspaper and was always looking for titbits for the rag.

'Um,' I said, cutting her off. It was now apparent that Amanda was testing me. 'Things are still being sorted. I'd much prefer it if we could wait for a couple of weeks, until we've finalised the plans. Don't want the competition finding out.'

'Oh, of course,' said Amanda. 'Just let me know when. I was thinking: have you got internet access there?'

'Not at the moment; you think I should get it?'

'D'uh,' said Amanda.

I liked this side of her, the knowledgeable, worldly side.

'I was worried that if I put it in then I'd just have a load of people buying one shitty coffee and then hogging the tables all day pretending to write a screenplay while they're just IMing their mates.'

'Jesus,' said Amanda. She sounded like her usual self again. Like the relationship had never gone off the rails. Like she could talk to me with the gloves-off familiarity of someone who had seen me naked and flabby. 'That's exactly what you want: you need the Bean & Gone to be one of those places where people just, you know, hang out. It's not a fast-food type place. You want people to think that they own the joint.'

'Really?'

'Alex, do I have a degree in marketing, or what?'

This was a bit of a bone of contention. Amanda was well aware that I didn't hold her higher education in much regard, on account of both its title and its alma mater. I was a major dick like that.

'Yes, indeed you do.'

'So keep your gob closed and give your arse a chance.'

This was one of Amanda's favourite sayings, no doubt a gem prised from her higher educational establishment.

'Look,' she said. 'I've got some post for you. Where should I send it?'

'Just leave it at the Bean & Gone,' I replied.

Amanda moved her basket to her other hand.

'Why don't you want me to know where you live?' she asked.

I bought some time by stepping aside to let a woman with a gut the size of a Benelux principality and what appeared to be a herd of kids pass by.

Because I live with my illegitimate daughter, I wanted to say. This would have been the truth, after all. But I wasn't ready. And part of me wanted to keep her guessing, to conceal the truth from her the way she had done to me. I wasn't ready to stop punishing her.

'Okay,' said Amanda. 'Why have you got hairbands and a copy of *Go Girl!* in your trolley?'

Goddamnit. She'd seen the stuff I'd got for Caitlin.

'Oh, my neighbour asked me to pick them up for her daughter,' I explained unconvincingly. 'Her car broke down and so

I'm picking up some bits for her while I'm here.'

'I see,' said Amanda sceptically. She looked me up and down. 'You seem different somehow,' she said. 'Something has changed.'

'New toothpaste,' I joked, lamely.

'Look,' she said, sidling forward and sliding a manicured index finger along my forearm, 'I know that things aren't easy at the moment, but maybe you could, you know, come over one night and we'll crack open a bottle of wine and, you know...'

I knew all right. The next words should have been something like 'sit and talk'. But, with Amanda, it was more likely to involve a horizontal rather than vertical form of communication.

'We'll see,' I said. I can't deny that I was tempted. There was so much that was unresolved between us, so much that I was only just realising that I wanted to say to her... What on earth was I thinking? Stay strong, Alex.

'I've got to go,' Amanda replied.

'Yeah,' I said. 'Me too.'

As tempting as it was to allow myself to be seduced, I knew that I had to hold off on getting too close to Amanda. The second visit from Social Services was coming up in a few weeks and I might need to enlist her assistance then. Before I could segue gently out of the conversation she was gone.

As she sashayed up the aisle I took a look at the contents of her shopping basket: two pieces of salmon, two large baking potatoes, enough vegetables for two, two individual tiramisus and a couple of bottles of wine.

That wasn't a shopping basket; that was a prequel to seduction. Amanda was having someone over for dinner and I doubted whether tiramisu would be the only dessert.

Chapter 21

Days of biblical rain in early October kept customers from the Bean & Gone. Casual passers-by virtually dried up, and I relied on a handful of regulars to get through the afternoon without calling the Samaritans. It was on the fifth day of subterranean gloom that I arrived at the coffee shop late – I had been called into school to discuss Caitlin's 'over socialising' in class, which meant another uphill conversation with her this evening – to discover that the lone patron was Kenny. Mel stood behind the counter and offered me a cheery 'morning' as I walked through the door, but nothing could mask the hollow thud of my footsteps as I crossed the wooden floor.

I tied my apron and waited for something to happen. The occasional spectre hurried by outside, identity masked by a low-slung umbrella.

'You all right?' Mel asked after a while. She had been examining her nails during the uneasy silence, having long since given up the pretence of keeping herself busy during the deadly lulls that had gone from being punctuation marks in her day to their entire content.

'Yeah, fine,' I said. I waited a little time before adding: 'A bit tired, I suppose. Not sleeping so well.'

The day dragged on and on. The difficulties with the shop, the complexity of the Amanda situation, and the looming threat of Social Services were all heavy on my mind. And I couldn't figure Mel out, either. I had started to wonder if she was happy with Kenny and had grown to like her more than was healthy for my head or my business. The last thing I needed was to complicate things further. But there was something about Mel, about her youth and optimism and apparent guilelessness that made it hard for me to cast her from my mind.

Kenny rustled a newspaper. He had camped at the same table all day. I looked over and saw that he had a pen in his hand. I sensed Mel looking over at me.

'Ken, sweetheart,' she intervened, 'please don't write in the papers, eh?'

Kenny looked over at Mel and then me before shaking his head slowly and raising both hands in mock surrender.

'Busted,' said Kenny. 'Guilty as charged.'

'Thanks, darling,' said Mel, before walking back into the kitchen. I wondered what she was doing in there: it wasn't like there was much that needed attending to. Maybe she just couldn't stand the silence any more. Maybe I should reorganise the muffins, I thought to myself. Maybe people didn't like the different types touching each other, or ...

Jesus Christ I was in trouble.

I had the money to keep going for another year or so, but did I really want to keep paying out for rent and Mel's salary – not to mention the coffee and food – while my life's savings dwindled? And there was the irritation of useless, sponging Kenny, sitting on his arse all day, drinking absurd beverages that I was comping ... I couldn't believe my eyes: Kenny was filling in the crossword again.

I walked over to him.

'Everything all right, Kenny?'

Engrossed in *The Times* crossword, Kenny didn't look up. His face was flushed. I wondered if he was a drinker and guessed at what that meant for Mel.

'Kenny,' I said, irritated, 'we've talked about the crossword, haven't we?'

'Yeah, we have,' said Kenny, looking up, a note of annoyance in his voice.

'So why are you still doing it?'

Kenny pushed the newspaper to the side.

'You said to me, right,' started Kenny, 'that you didn't want me to fill in the crossword because the papers were for all the customers, right?'

I nodded. What was so hard about this for Kenny to grasp?

'So what if I *am* all the customers?' Kenny asked triumphantly, as if delivering a championship-winning ace at Wimbledon. 'What if this is it?'

'Don't be childish, Kenny.'

'Well, you're not exactly run off your feet, are you?' said Kenny, a hint of mockery in his voice. 'It ain't exactly Piccadilly Circus in here, is it?'

'That has absolutely no bearing on this whatsoever,' I replied.

'Why not?' Kenny asked. 'Where are the other customers that I'm upsetting by writing in the paper?'

To my own disgust I couldn't prevent myself from looking around the empty room.

'You're missing the point, Kenny,' I said evenly. Although I couldn't see her, Mel would be listening in the back room. I didn't want to come off as a dickhead. 'The point is I'm asking you not to.'

Kenny seemed to consider this for a while then answered: 'I can't see the harm in it.'

'It's very simple,' I said. 'Here's the thing: are you going to write in the papers or not? Yes or no?'

'I'm not prepared to answer that question,' said Kenny pompously, as though he was at the Old Bailey giving evidence in a murder trial.

'Yes or no, Kenny?'

Silence.

'One last chance, Kenny: yes or no?'

'This is bollocks,' said Kenny, finally standing up. He was taller than me, but slighter. I fancied my chances if it got physical.

'Oh, it's bollocks, is it?' I said. 'Well, maybe it's bollocks that you spend most of your day in here drinking free coffees. Maybe it's bollocks that you can't do a very simple thing and stop yourself from writing in newspapers that, yes, I've paid for and leave out for all my customers.'

Kenny pulled his denim jacket from the back of the chair and laughed.

'But you don't have any fucking customers,' he snorted and walked towards the door. 'You're a joke. You think Java Jamboree up the road is empty because of a little bit of rain? It's packed, mate, *packed*.'

'On your bike,' I said.

'Mel, you better start looking for another job,' shouted Kenny. 'Cos this place is well and truly over.'

What a total wanker. (Although he did have a point.)

With that, Kenny opened the door and walked indignantly up the road, the rain soaking him. About twenty yards from the Bean & Gone he stopped and heaved his jeans up so that they sat snugly upon his hips. Rock and roll will never die, I thought to myself, but it's getting decidedly mangy.

I turned from the window to see Caitlin framed in the doorway staring back at me. She was dripping wet – there's something about teenagers that makes them physically incapable of carrying umbrellas or even wearing jackets in the rain. Beneath her sopping hair I saw something else in Caitlin's eyes: worry. I stopped momentarily and realised that she'd just watched Kenny and I arguing. She'd seen me lose it. We'd fought between ourselves before, but this was the first time that she'd seen me confront an adult. More than that, she can't have missed the doubt and fear in the way I handled Kenny. She knew that things were getting on top of me.

'Caitlin,' I said. 'Hello, love. You're soaked through—'

Suddenly I heard the chorus from Rihanna's 'Umbrella'. Caitlin pulled her phone out of her pocket, flipped it open and examined a message.

'Look,' she said, 'I've got to go – I'll be back in a bit, okay?'

I nodded, because there was nothing else to do. I wondered what drama was playing out inside her head.

'See you in a while,' I said. 'Oh, and why don't you take my umbrella, ella, ella, ella ...'

No dice. She'd already gone. I surveyed the empty café.

'Chin up, son,' I said to myself. At least I won't be handing out free drinks any longer. Life was looking up. Mel appeared from the kitchen.

'What happened there?' she asked. I knew that she was talking about Kenny rather than Caitlin.

'I'm sorry, Mel,' I said. 'I think I might have just really pissed Kenny off.'

'The crossword?' she said.

'Yeah,' I said.

'I warned him about that,' she said with a sigh.

'I know you did.'

Mel walked over to the window and peered into the downpour. Her breath steamed the window up.

'Oh well,' she said.

'Sorry, Mel.' What was I apologising for? She didn't say anything.

'I said I'm sorry,' I repeated.

'I heard,' she said.

I couldn't work it out. Was she annoyed with me, or just

preoccupied because she was going to have to deal with Kenny when she got home?

A middle-aged couple walked in, apologising for dripping all over the floor. They took a good five minutes to read through every item on the coffee menu before ordering two cups of English breakfast tea. I dropped the four pound coins into the till – thunk, thunk, thunk, thunk – and listened to the couple fret and fuss over the weather.

Be constructive, I thought to myself. Yet at the back of my mind I wondered if I should write to one of those TV shows where a famous businessman will come and take a look at your little concern and tell you exactly what you're getting wrong and how to fix it. I had a vision of a pair of TV entrepreneurs: a cockney wide boy and a toff standing in the Bean & Gone saying in tandem: 'There's no saving a business that's in a death spiral.'

I looked over and saw Mel's hands. Her nails were bitten close to the quick. I smiled at her but she looked away. I wondered where Caitlin had gone and where Kenny was headed.

'You mustn't worry, you know,' I said to her. 'We're doing fine.'

'Really?' Her tone was dry, distrustful even.

'Yeah, really.'

'I read something in a magazine a couple of weeks ago about how nearly all new businesses fail,' she said. She reached up and smoothed her hair back, retying her ponytail.

'That's true,' I said. 'I don't know the percentage, but it's really high ...'

Great work, Alex. Nice. Affirm her fears.

'But the reason that things are going to be okay at the Bean & Gone is that neither of us can afford for this business to fail. We both need it to work, for lots of reasons. Not least, our kids.' I sounded like a government minister. She wasn't going to buy that crap.

195

'Well, we'll see,' she said and went to tidy up the newspapers that Kenny had left scattered on his table. My heart sank. Was I lying to Mel as well? I had too many plates spinning with Caitlin and Amanda to bring her into play too.

The door opened and Caitlin came stamping back in from the rain. She was wet through.

'Caitlin, you're soaked,' I said. I threw her a tea towel. 'Dry your hair on this and I'll make you a hot chocolate.'

Then I realised that she wasn't alone. She was with a boy whose hair lay flattened on his face. He reached up and pushed it back and I saw that it was Ollie.

'Hello,' I said. 'Want some hot chocolate?'

'That would be lovely, Mr Taylor,' he said.

The two of them sat shivering at a table while I made them their drinks. I took them over and set them in front of them.

'Horrible day,' I said.

'Yeah, thanks,' said Ollie.

I was just ruminating on the boy's manners when I noticed something that made me feel very differently about him. As he reached for the mug of steaming milk there was a flash of green – a cheap silver ring set with a fake green stone.

So it was Ollie who had had his hand on my daughter's backside.

No sooner had I registered this than I saw Mel approaching us with her coat on.

'You two look soaked,' she said.

I was trying to focus, trying to stay in the moment, when all I wanted to do was pour the drink over Ollie's head.

'I need to get Caitlin home and into some warm clothes,' I said. 'And I've got to do the laundry. It never seems to stop.'

'Well, I should know,' said Mel, 'as a single mum.'

'I can't wait to meet your son.'

She laughed. 'You already have,' she said and clapped Ollie on the shoulder.

So this was Mel's son? *Ollie*? I wasn't that keen on Caitlin having a boyfriend, but at least Ollie could form a sentence and there was no sign of a Burberry baseball cap. While his presence in our lives had offered me glimpses of my daughter that I would otherwise have only guessed at, I still felt no closer to really understanding Caitlin. Despite her help with Joan Kennedy during her visit, her attitude towards me – if I expressed an interest in what she was up to – was to make it clear that she saw me as a tedious meddler, an irritant to be tolerated, a presence to be suffered silently.

The following Sunday, Caitlin absented herself from the house around midday. When I asked where she was going, she explained that she was going 'out'. I bit my tongue. We had barely spoken for almost three days, except for a brief skirmish after I had opened my credit card bill to discover that she had downloaded the most recent series of *Lost*. I didn't force it, I wanted to try to give her some space. This was, after all, what the touchy-feely parenting books (that had so far proved themselves about as useful as the proverbial one-legged man in an arse-kicking competition) advised. I'd tried to remain calm and objective, reminding myself that her behaviour towards me wasn't personal, but the consequence of hormones, a quest for independence and excessive hours spent watching teen movies set amongst the gloating, entitled inhabitants of Orange County, California.

Although it went unspoken, it was clear that my presence beyond the threshold of her bedroom door was strictly verboten. While I accepted my outcast status there was, however, the occasional necessary infraction needed: Caitlin liked to eat (thankfully) and over the period of a few days would amass quite a collection of crockery – mostly dappled with toast or cake crumbs, but I'd occasionally find evidence of something more substantial like a fried egg – that would be balanced precariously throughout her room.

I wandered in and opened a window to ease the teen funk that hung heavily in the air, piling up the dishes and cutlery on a tray. The room needed vacuuming, but I couldn't start that until I'd got her to tidy up a bit, which was a conversation I could do without. I went to collect a mug from her desk and looked at the mess of schoolbooks, papers, files and personalised detritus stacked seemingly randomly. It was impossible to see the surface of the desk. And amongst the piles of stuff, there was an item that caused me to pause before my heart started to beat a little faster: a diary.

I picked it up. I had struggled so hard for insights into the workings of my daughter's mind, to understand even in the slightest way her emotional composition, that to ignore its promise was impossible. It was simply too enticing to resist. Right there in my hand, I had an object more powerful than any awkward conversation that I might engineer: her words – uncensored, unambiguous and unguarded.

I opened it. The first page contained her name and address – the one she had shared with her mother. And then, inside a little heavily adorned box (all curlicues and laboriously rendered minutia), a note to anyone who might come across it: 'If found, please return to above address. Reward offered.' I bit my lip. The businesslike tone of the words, clearly gleaned from an adult source, caught me unexpectedly. It was like watching a child trying on grown-up clothes – even if they fit, there is always an awkwardness, something off-key.

I flipped through the pages. The year began ordinarily enough. Caitlin had gone to a friend's New Year's Party and

198

Cathy had allowed her to stay up past midnight, collecting her at 12.30. Caitlin noted that Cathy had showed up at the party wearing her slippers, which had clearly caused her significant embarrassment. I tried to recall if Cathy had ever worn slippers when we were together. It seemed unlikely, but then I suppose these cruel signifiers of maturity sneak up on us and we're barely aware of them. The reading glasses, the knee supports, the orthotics, all betray us before we're ready to call time on our youth.

The entries in January and February were significantly longer than those that followed. Around March Caitlin's thoughts about her friends, teachers and boys became less developed, although her commitment to well-rendered emoticons demonstrated that her artistic inclinations had not suffered the same fate as her literary pretensions. I also learned that the word 'sick' signified that something was really good.

Of course, I knew what was coming. It was as inevitable as the end of a corrida. I turned to the day before the accident and … I couldn't look. I reached for the page and pulled it back slowly, as if it were something I was scared to wake. Mentally apologising to Caitlin, I summoned my flintiest heart. The day before Cathy was killed Caitlin had gymnastics practice and pizza for dinner. Pizza. Does it get any more everyday, more prosaic, than a kid chomping down on a slice of pepperoni? The grim realisation that Caitlin was going about her early teenage life oblivious to the indifferent hand of fate that hovered above her pressed down on me. My breathing became shallower.

I flipped the page and … nothing. Just paper. Emptiness waiting to be filled. Birds chattered on a tree outside the window, the world still turning, ceaseless and neutral to all. I stared at the blank page and it occurred to me that I wasn't sure what I'd been expecting. A run-down of the day's events? A lucid description of Caitlin's unwitting final moments with her mother? Some kind of pivotal understanding that would change the tenor of our relationship? This, of course, was what I wanted: answers. And if I couldn't get those, then I wanted insight; even the most minor revelation would do.

I turned the page. And then another. And another. There were no words. For me, that meant more room for conjecture and speculation. I could only imagine. I flicked through the pages. Two weeks. Three. Four. And then, just over a month after Cathy died there was ink, noticeable not just because of its presence, but because it was a different colour from the reds and purples and aquamarines that marked the earlier pages: navy blue. Caitlin started to write again around the time that we moved to the house. I wanted to put down the diary now, to be rid of it. Far from not revealing anything, I feared that the returning tide of ink would tell me things that I shouldn't and – more significantly – *didn't* want to know. As Caitlin would say to her friends, 'TMI': Too Much Information.

I closed the book and returned it to her desk. I made to leave the room, keen to be done with the regretful episode, but hesitated. Was I being foolish to pass this up? My time with Caitlin had been the equivalent of someone stumbling over a barren wilderness; had I now come upon a signpost? Surely rejecting this chance was to reject an opportunity to alter the rocky course my relationship with Caitlin had taken? After all, wasn't parenthood about doing whatever you thought necessary for the welfare of your children? Surely it was more important that I should do anything in my power to heal our fractured relationship than to protect myself from whatever hurt I might encounter in Caitlin's diary or, indeed, to check myself for fear of breaking a confidence by snooping on a private document.

I picked up the diary again and began to examine the pages.

I was Mr Coffee.

Not Dad. Not even the Old Man or another, youthful synonym

for father. *Mr Coffee*. That was the first thing I discovered as my eyes scanned the pages. It was not immediately apparent to me what this meant, but calling someone Mr Coffee didn't seem to me like a way of declaring familial love (unless, I suppose, you're Mrs Coffee.) And there was more. Most of it fairly banal teen eye-rolling stuff of the 'He's really embarrassing' or 'I can't believe he said that in front of my friend' variety, but some of the words were more barbed. I found myself described as a 'total twat' at one point and a 'gimp' elsewhere. I reasoned that this was normal, that it was the healthy anger of adolescence spiked with bereavement. Who else was she to take revenge upon? But, Jesus, it wasn't easy to see those words written in Caitlin's elaborate cursive script. It hurt more than her telling me that I was a twat or a gimp because I imagined that teen-agers were prone to saying all kinds of things when they were upset and the words might just fall from their mouths. Writing them down was another matter. The written word felt more powerful, more considered, more noxious.

I stopped reading. I should never have started. I had never been a diary or email snooper before, and now I knew why. There were some things that it was best not to be aware of. The saying goes that knowledge is power, but knowledge – of Amanda's cheating, Caitlin's discontent, my inability to face up to parental responsibility – can also mean pain. Knowledge can be a real bitch.

As I stood up to return the book to Caitlin's desk it fell on the ground. Picking it up I noticed for the first time that there was a pouch on the inside back cover. The fall had dislodged something that Caitlin had stuffed in there, a letter. Although my appetite for the covert had vanished I couldn't help noticing that the envelope bore the stamp of Cathy's solicitors, Singh & Lewis. I pulled it free of the diary and examined it closer. It was addressed to Caitlin. Knowing full well that I was venturing further down a hole I'd only just emerged from, I pulled open the unsealed envelope. From the look of the worn creases on the piece of paper inside it had been read and re-read many times.

I recognised the handwriting immediately: Cathy.

My Darling Caitlin,

I hope that you never read this letter because, if you do, it will mean that we are no longer together. My love, I can't really get my head around the idea, to be honest, but the years have taught me that things don't always work out as you plan them. I'm writing this not long after Nana died because it suddenly occurred to me that, should anything happen to me, we have no other relatives. It was just you (the light of my life!), me and Nana and, somehow that's the way I always thought it would be. Nana and I are gone now (it feels strange sitting here watching you buttering toast, and pushing your hair back from your face) and I want to do what's best for you rather than leave the fate of my angel in the hands of other people and I think I should explain to you why I made the choices I did, my lovely girl.

First of all, the most important thing: I love you. I will always love you and I'm so sorry that you're reading these words. You're a wonderful daughter who has brought immeasurable joy into my life and I want you to always remember how clever, funny and strong you are. I remember the very first time they handed you to me at the hospital. You were bright pink and wrapped tight in a blanket and you opened your eyes and we just looked at each other. And in that moment I felt the strongest connection I've ever felt with a human being. I felt endless, bottomless, ever-lasting love and, while I'm not with you now, you've got to remember that that love still exists. It's still with you and will never go

202

away. Know that I will be looking down on you every day and watching over you at night. And while you can't see me, I'll be with you.

We went through so much together and I really wouldn't change a thing (especially not about you!), except maybe one. I always know how hard it was for you to grow up without a dad. It was the single biggest regret of my life that I couldn't offer you that. It just wasn't possible for your father and I to be together. Now I'm gone, however, I need to overcome what's passed and do what's best for you. I want you to feel loved and protected. I want you to be nurtured and cared for. I want you to be with someone who will make sure that you know quite how wonderful you are.

I've asked Mr Singh, who you will have met by now, to contact someone who I know will take great care of you. His name is Alex and he and I were together for some time before you were born. I'm sure that he will do everything in his power to look after you in the way that you deserve. My love, I know how unusual this situation is and, even as I write this at our kitchen table, watching you, I can't really believe that we will ever be apart. But, should it come to it, I think that it's for the best. Forgive me if I've ever let you down. Know always that if ever there were any problems in our relationship that the failure was always mine. I know that Alex will look after you. I've thought about this for a long time, and I think that it's the best option. I hope and pray that you will be able to find happiness and live a full, rewarding life, secure in the knowledge that there are people for whom you will always be the centre of the universe. Wherever I might be, know that I am with you. I love you always and forever,

Mum xxxxx

The hand holding the letter sagged into my lap. Poor Cathy. Poor Caitlin. How was the poor kid supposed to process this kind of emotion? It was too much to bear for an adult, let alone a child. As I processed this, Cathy's words 'I can see no other option' rang in my ears. As if I needed any further confirmation, I was not the knight in shining armour, the redeemer stepping in to save the day. Far from it. In fact, I was the last resort, the final throw of the dice, the last-chance saloon. I stared blankly out of the window, my eyes registering nothing. What did Cathy think she was doing? The whole situation was nutty enough as it was without Caitlin knowing that, well, if there had been any other possible course of action her mother would have taken it. I began to fold the letter to put it back in the diary.

'What are you doing?' The voice was hushed, unclouded by emotion.

I turned to see Caitlin in the doorway clutching a plastic bag from Top Shop.

'I was just …' I couldn't quite go on with whatever lie it was that I thought might absolve myself from the situation.

Busted.

She looked at me. There was anger in her face, a raw edge of betrayal. But what I noticed above all else was a gaze that mirrored my own hurt. I looked away, waiting for the scornful words to rain down upon me. But there were none. I looked up again. She had decided that I wasn't even worth shouting at.

Not only was I a last resort, I was a last resort she could have no faith in. I was the husband who half the town knew had been ploughed by the local douchebag. I was the man whose ex-girlfriend saw him as a bad solution to a terrible problem. I was the man whose estranged daughter had been forewarned of his mediocrity.

*

That evening I cooked dinner and served it at the usual time – 7.00 p.m. I had texted Caitlin twice during the afternoon. The first time had been a couple of hours after she'd stormed out of the house. The message had been conciliatory: DO YOU NEED ME TO PICK YOU UP FROM SOMEWHERE? As the minutes ticked by without a response, I kicked myself for my weakness – she would read this as a capitulation, an admission of my contrition. I should have toughed it out, waited to see what her next move was. My second message was more straightforward, although its intent was clear: DINNER IS ON THE TABLE.

I sat and watched the food grow cold. I looked at the clock – 7.30. I got in the car and drove. The movement was a relief – it felt like I was actually *doing* something. As I wove through the roundabouts and bounced over traffic-calming obstacles I scanned the pavements and streets searching for signs of life and wishing that Caitlin was sitting in the car with me acting dramatically bored.

Although I was still stung by what she had written I needed to see her again, if only for her to offer a final indictment to my inaction. I switched on my headlights in the twilight – it would be fully dark in a half-hour – and fished my mobile out of the change holder next to the gear stick.

No messages. I tried not to let my mind race towards dramatic scenarios – kidnappings, predatory boys – telling myself that she was probably skulking somewhere eating a bag of chips and wishing that she'd punished me enough to come home. I looked at my watch. It was nearly 8.30. I tried to pretend that I wouldn't be seriously anxious in half an hour.

In the middle of town, I pulled over to the side of the road and switched the engine off. Almost as soon as I'd done this my phone rang. I snatched at it, knocking the device to the floor on the passenger side. Scrabbling around for it, I checked the caller ID. It was Amanda. Just the person I didn't want to talk to – my state of concern was such that I could imagine spilling the beans within seconds. But I still felt her power over me. As much as I had planned to pull away from her, to freeze her out, there was another part of me – and the one that I was beginning to feel most attuned to – that was prone to melt when confronted with her.

'Amanda?'

'Hiya.'

There was silence, which was most unlike her.

'Everything all right, Alex?'

'Not really. Caitlin has gone missing.'

'What do you mean she's gone missing?'

'Well, I think that it's fairly fucking obvious what I mean by that,' I said, exasperated by what seemed like her game-playing.

'What I meant, Alex, was that she's not missing,' Amanda said after a long pause. 'She's here with me.'

The fact that Caitlin was with Amanda also meant that she was somewhere else: my house. (I'd tried to think of the rental as 'mine', but there was still a sense of the temporary about it in my mind.)

'Hi,' Amanda said, a smile teasing around the corner of her mouth as she opened the door. She seemed to be enjoying my discomfort. 'At least you decided to ring the doorbell this time – beats skulking around behind the curtains.'

'Well ...' I started, walking inside. My voice trailed off. I failed to find a witty riposte. Amanda was barefoot, wearing a yellow checked dress that was tied at the waist. My relief at finding Caitlin was tempered by the uneasy situation.

'Where is she?' I asked. It was a stupid question – there was only one doorway that led to both the living room and kitchen. Amanda tilted her head, gesturing with her chin towards the back of the house. I noticed then that she was holding a wineglass.

'Want one?' she asked.

'Of course,' I replied, trying to sound genial, although I felt anything but – was it possible that Caitlin had revealed her true identity to Amanda? They had been together for maybe a few hours. That would have given Amanda plenty of time for a full interrogation.

Caitlin was curled up on the sofa watching an American reality show involving a black midget and several young women whose breasts were of questionable provenance. Her hands were curled round a mug of tea. She didn't look up.

The sight of my daughter and my wife in the same place should have been one of the joy. Instead I felt like I was standing in the middle of a minefield: the smallest step in the wrong direction could see my best laid plans scuppered.

'All right?' I said to Caitlin.

The midget gave one of the girls a rose. Caitlin watched impassively. The three of us watched the television, not knowing what else to do.

'Come in the kitchen,' Amanda said.

We sat down at the table; a bottle of wine between us.

'I shouldn't be too long,' I said. 'Her mum wants her home.'

Amanda crossed her legs. She had a tan. Maybe she'd got one of those spray versions.

'Why are you taking such an interest in that woman's daughter?' she asked.

I hesitated for a moment. Danger lurked here.

'Are you going out with her or something?'

'She's *thirteen*,' I said, shocked at the absurdity of her question.

'The mother, for Christ's sake,' Amanda said. 'What's-her-name.' It wasn't a question. She was trying to get a rise out of me.

'She's called Mel,' I said. 'And no, seeing as you ask, I am not going out with her.'

'She's pretty,' Amanda said. I got the feeling that she was waiting for me to agree, testing to see if I had any feelings for my employee.

'Mel asked me to help,' I said. 'She was a bit freaked out.'

'That's nice of you,' Amanda said. 'The knight in shining armour.'

'Yeah,' I said, thinking back to Caitlin's letter.

'I saw her in the street,' continued Amanda. 'She looked upset. I could see that she needed a friend. She's a lovely kid.' Amanda poured another glass of wine. She waved the bottle at me by way of asking if I wanted one.

'I'm driving,' I said.

'Oh, come on, Alex,' she replied, 'relax for a few minutes, for God's sake. I feel like we haven't talked in ages.'

'That's because we haven't.'

'Well, whose fault is that?'

'Look, I didn't come here to fight with you, Amanda.' I sighed.

She raised her eyebrows and took a gulp of wine.

'We should, you know...' My voice trailed off. I was unsure if I wanted to take the next step.

'We should what?' Amanda asked.

'Get a drink,' I said.

'I'd like that.'

I nodded, trying to show that it was something that I had been thinking about. 'I'll text you in the week, then.'

'You do that,' Amanda said, smiling.

'I'd better go,' I said. 'Got to get Caitlin back.'

'She's a nice kid,' Amanda said.

'Yeah, yeah ... I know,' I replied, standing up and walking into the living room. Caitlin turned off the television, although she had yet to say a word.

'I'm looking forward to seeing more of you,' Amanda said to Caitlin.

I looked at Caitlin and then at Amanda, not sure what she meant by this.

'She's going to be helping me out,' Amanda announced. 'At work.'

I tried to smile, but I could tell that this was something serious, not idle banter.

'Caitlin's going to be doing work experience a couple of days a week,' Amanda said. 'After school. We've been looking for someone for a while and I reckon that she's going to be just perfect.'

I looked at Amanda. Was she for real?

'What?' I stammered. 'What about homework and the other things that you've got going on …?'

'We can work around that,' Caitlin said, with a smile. 'And the school likes us to do work experience with local businesses.'

Both of them looked at me expectantly. Surely I didn't have a come-back?

'Well, we'll see what your mum has to say, shall we?' I said, realising that my only hope was to evoke Mel. 'She probably needs to have the final say in this.'

'I checked with my mum,' said Caitlin with jaunty finality, 'and she said that it was all right.'

At that moment I wanted to both strangle and hug her at the same time. Jesus, she was a clever one.

Late that night I walked around the garden trying to clear my head. The father–daughter relationship was not progressing well. I needed to admit that, despite Caitlin's occasional lapses into affection, it wasn't working. I had to stop dreaming: As much as I had imagined myself as a proficient and loving dad, it was clear that Caitlin and I were failing to make the steps necessary for us to become a family. More than that, she seemed to be making it clear that she might never be able to accept me as a father. More than that, her new relationship with Amanda meant that, sooner or later, I would be exposed as a liar. I didn't want to give Amanda that kind of ammunition.

She had yet to call me Dad.

I pulled my mobile out of my jacket and punched in some numbers that I read from a scrap of paper.

There was a voicemail message. I waited for the beep, as instructed.

'Hi, Joan, it's Alex Taylor,' I started. 'I was wondering if you could give me a call back. I need to talk to you about Caitlin.'

Chapter 22

I had spent most of my adult life avoiding going to the doctor. There had been visits, of course – most of them prompted by Amanda after I'd had, say, a hacking cough for six months – but I had done all I could not to be a drain on our overworked and under-resourced NHS.

Caitlin was another matter. Even, in the event that things didn't work out between us, I thought that professional advice might help: the intense, dramatic life changes she'd experienced over the previous few months were more than anyone – let alone an adolescent – could be expected to bear. As much as I hated to admit it, I had demonstrated that I had no idea how to reach her, so I needed to help in some other way. I'd thought about going to the school, but they were already acutely aware of her needs (last week there had been a letter home about her clowning in class); telling them that I thought that she needed counselling might only further stigmatise her.

So I decided that a GP was as good a place to start as any. If nothing else just registering her would get me some Brownie points from Social Services.

We sat on grey moulded plastic chairs in what used to be the living room of a grand Victorian house. A digital board hung on one wall; it flashed up a patient's name when one of the doctors was ready to see them. When a new name appeared a loud buzzer sounded, reminding me of a joke-shop toy I'd had as a kid that I'd used to give unsuspecting relatives electric shocks. I would hide it in the palm of my hand and administer the treatment to relatives at parties.

Caitlin complained that she had forgotten her book and sat staring at the wall. She was dressed in her school uniform, which she had begun to customise – the tie was very short and her jumper wasn't regulation red.

'Why don't you read one of those?' I asked, nodding towards the well-thumbed magazines that were piled on a table next to a stack of informational pamphlets: 'You and Herpes' looked riveting.

Caitlin wandered over, sifted through the pile and sat reading until the buzzer sounded and Caitlin's name appeared on the board. I stood up, folded my newspaper and started to move towards the examination room. Caitlin just sat in her chair, oblivious. She was totally absorbed by whatever it was that she was reading.

'Come on then,' I said.

'Okay,' Caitlin said, her eyes still fixed to the page.

'Let's not keep Dr Locker waiting.' I was aware that a number of other patients were watching the situation unfolding: does this man have absolutely zero authority over this child? Eventually Caitlin stood up, but continued to hold the magazine up to her face, reading while she walked towards me. I smiled at a woman who was watching. She stared back at me disapprovingly. I wasn't going to get a look of mutual understanding from this killjoy.

'Caitlin, you're going to need to put the magazine down please,' I said.

'Okay.' There was no resentment in her voice.

I walked purposefully out of the waiting room, hoping that my movement would stir Caitlin into action. When I didn't hear her footsteps behind me I turned to see where she was, only to watch as she laid the magazine down on the appropriate table, leaving it open with great purpose, as if she would return to the same page later.

'Sorry about that,' she said. As we passed along a corridor there appeared to be a skip in her step.

'That's okay,' I replied. 'I just don't want to keep the doctor waiting. You know how busy they get.'

Caitlin said nothing. Of course she had absolutely no idea how busy or otherwise doctors got.

Dr Locker had been recommended by one of the mums at school as a GP who was good with kids. She turned out to be an older woman with a shock of white hair and a no-nonsense 'let's keep it moving, people' attitude that worked well with my own 'let's get this over with' philosophy on healthcare.

I was asked to remain behind a screen while Locker took various measurements, checked Caitlin's blood pressure, pressed her stethoscope to her chest and back and, to Caitlin's great embarrassment, asked her to go and fill a cup with pee.

After all this was done she said to Caitlin, 'Would you mind popping out for a moment, my dear? I need to have a very quick chat with your dad. Just so you know: you're doing very well. You're a healthy, strong young thing, so keep it up.'

Caitlin nodded, embarrassed, and closed the door behind her.

'So she's doing very well,' said Locker, jotting notes in her file. 'Heart, blood pressure, lung capacity, growth, everything is where it should be. We'll send her sample to the lab but I'm confident that everything is fine with her. We'll let you know. One other thing.' She crossed her legs and leaned towards me. 'When did she start menstruating?'

'Um ...' I couldn't believe that I did it, but I blushed. Went crimson, actually. This was Dad Kryptonite: even the slightest contact would surely kill me.

'I'm not actually sure,' I said.

'She's physically mature for her age,' said Locker, 'and we're seeing that girls are starting to menstruate much earlier than they used to. No one really knows why, but it's probably environmental.'

I told her about Caitlin and me, and our strange introduction to each other over the past few months.

'I can certainly recommend a clinical psychologist, if you want,' said Locker. 'It could be useful. For both of you.'

Both of us? *She thinks I'm mental?*

'I'm fine,' I said with a chuckle. 'Just a little stressed.'

'We're often the last people to know,' said Locker. She wrote a name and number on a piece of paper and passed it to me.

'I think it's important for single dads like yourself to be prepared for the changes that a girl like Caitlin is going through,' Locker said. 'She's going to be scared, confused, embarrassed, and you're going to have to be able to handle it. The worst thing you can do is pretend that it isn't happening. Ignorance isn't a strategy.'

'Okay,' I said. 'I just—'

'I know,' said Locker. 'But she's still a child. She's still a daughter. You just need to support her through whatever she's going through.'

I thanked her and walked back down the corridor to the waiting room to collect Caitlin. Dr Locker had totally blindsided me. Our disjointed relationship was as much about my own shortcomings as Caitlin's loss or adolescence. Perhaps this was why she was gravitating towards Amanda. There were no judgements, no Olympic opening cermony-elaborate attempts to establish a rapport.

Caitlin was sitting with her back to me reading the magazine that she'd been engrossed in earlier. I glanced over her shoulder and read the headline, feeling another heavy sensation in my stomach as I read the words: How To Make Him Love You.

It was peculiar watching my teenage daughter absorbing this kind of information. I knew that she was probably thinking about Ollie as she read the story, but I hoped that maybe, just maybe, she might have been able to apply the headline to me as well.

I dropped Caitlin at school. She seemed brighter than normal, had removed her earphones and chatted a little. Maybe she had forgiven me for reading her diary.

'I'll see you later,' I said as she jumped out of the door.

'Okay,' she replied. 'Have fun at work.'

Have fun at work? Usually I was lucky to get a grunt. This was progress. Unless, of course, there was something else going on that I wasn't aware of ...

I told myself to stop being such a cynic. She was making an effort and I should respond in kind.

I drove past Amanda's office and couldn't stop myself from trying to grab a brief glimpse of her. The day before, I'd been coming out of the dry cleaner's with some Bean & Gone uniforms and she'd been walking on the other side of the street engrossed in a conversation on her mobile. I had paused for a moment, just so that I could watch her for a while longer. I kept thinking about her supermarket basket for two.

The second unsettling landmark I passed was the local branch of Java Jamboree. Gazing enviously at the crowds of time-pressed office workers and mums with buggies, I wondered what it was – other than a global brand, of course – that they had that I didn't. The answer was a simple one: customers. This served to worry me further. Had I seriously miscalculated the Home Counties' desire for premium coffee and free WiFi (which had set me back a week's takings)? Perhaps they only wanted to do that in one place, and it wasn't the one I owned.

Mel barely said hello to me when I arrived at the café and,

although she worked hard all day, I could tell that she was pre-occupied. In fact, she'd been acting strangely for a while. There were a few more customers than the previous days, which meant that we were busy. I wanted to talk to her, but I didn't get a chance. At least that's what I told myself. With all the recent Caitlin and Amanda agita I really couldn't face any more conflict.

Caitlin appeared with Ollie (and his green ring) after school. I made a mental note to talk to Mel about them being an item (tomorrow, of course), imagining that parental surveillance from both sides was better than just one. Mel asked if I could mind the shop while she nipped out to the bank. While she was out Ollie, who had been doing his homework with Caitlin at one of the tables, walked up to the counter.

'Mr Taylor,' he asked, 'is it true that my mum is going to lose her job?'

'Who told you that?' I blurted.

'Kenny,' said Ollie defensively.

'Oh, really,' I said. My words sounded more pointed than I had intended, as if I were mocking Ollie himself rather than his mother's absurd boyfriend. 'And why does Kenny think that your mum is going to lose her job, I wonder?'

'Well, he reckons you might have to close the Bean & Gone because you don't have enough customers.'

So that's the thanks I get for pouring peppermint lattes down his gullet and keeping him in free newspapers, I thought, a fucking fifth columnist.

'Well,' I said, trying to do a 'I'm-not-fazed-by-this-conver-sation-at-all' face that was instead, from the way Caitlin was looking at me from across the café, clearly the kind of maniacal wide-mouth grin exemplified by Wallace in the Wallace and Gromit films. 'We've still got plenty of work to do here, but anything worthwhile has to be worked at. You can't expect something to be a big success from the word go.'

216

I now officially sounded like a day-time TV 'life coach' hunkered down on a sofa in a studio dispensing advice to disembodied people whose voices came across the airwaves with a slight delay. The kids exchanged a look that was a clear acknowledgement that neither of them had any idea what I was talking about.

'Is it true?' asked Caitlin. 'You won't have to close the café, will you?'

'No, no, no,' I scoffed. 'Look, you know Java Jamboree on the parade?'

Both kids nodded.

'It's always full, right?'

Affirmative nods from the teens.

'I just have a business problem to solve, that's all,' I said. 'I have to find a way to get some of their customers to come and spend money in our café, that's all.'

'But how are you going to do that?' asked Caitlin.

'I'm working on it,' I said, although what I was thinking was, I really don't have a clue. Worst of all, I was under no illusions that she hadn't already worked that out.

Chapter 23

It was Saturday. The first day of the weekend was formerly my favourite day of the week, but since opening the Bean & Gone, Saturdays had become loaded: they needed to be busy, otherwise I just couldn't see the café making it. Joan Kennedy had returned my call with one of her own asking me to ring her urgently. I made a mental note to call her as soon as I had a little quiet time.

I crept downstairs. I didn't want to wake Caitlin. She should enjoy a weekend lie-in, even if I couldn't. I walked into the kitchen to see her sitting eating toast and reading a magazine.

'Hiya,' she said breezily, taking a bite. She didn't look up, but I realised that she wasn't being dismissive – it was because she had grown used to me.

'Hi, Caitlin,' I replied. Our little interaction, so small yet so fulfilling, made me wonder at how empty the house would be without her. Maybe I'd been wrong all along. Maybe I didn't need to know everything about her. Maybe just sitting comfortably together over breakfast was enough. Sitting undisturbed with a bowl of cereal and a cup of coffee offered as much contentment as a prolonged chat.

This got me thinking: my change in attitude towards Amanda might be best served by not having a summit-style 'where are we going' conversation, but by small, everyday interaction. Caitlin had done a couple of days' work experience for Amanda and had enjoyed it. Perhaps I could find opportunities to slip in between their new-found friendship. I could see if I *really* wanted to get back with Amanda and, at the same time, figure out if the idea of the three of us being a unit was in any way plausible. Amanda's resistance to our adopting a child would surely crumble if she had, in a sense, already fallen in love with the kid. I would need to be cautious though – while Caitlin and Amanda became friends I would need to keep my role in her presence on the planet under wraps.

I was weighing this up while re-stocking the blueberry muffins at the café when I noticed Caitlin and Ollie come in. I checked my watch: Caitlin had told me at breakfast that they were planning on going to the movies, but the film that they had gone to see wasn't due to finish for a while. I wondered if they were okay.

'Hi, guys,' I said to them. 'So how was it?'

Ollie who, up until that point had been laughing about something, looked mortified. Caitlin hesitated slightly before speaking. There was guilt written all over their faces.

'It was good,' she said after a moment. I waited for further details. None were forthcoming. This just wasn't right. Usually when they came out of a film they recounted its events, re-enacted scenes and repeated dialogue. Their hazy response meant that they were hiding something and I wasn't sure that I even wanted to find out what it was. Direct questioning never worked; I would have to wait for the truth to emerge.

'Blueberry muffin?' I asked. They both nodded before taking one each and secreting themselves at a table in the corner where they had never chosen to sit before. I looked over at Mel, but she didn't meet my eye. It might just have been my imagination but it seemed that she had started to dress more sexily recently. The trainers and jeans had been replaced by heels and dresses. Was she trying to send me a message? I couldn't tell whether I was being punished ('look what Kenny's got') or encouraged ('look what you could have if you could only figure out how to reach me'). It was amazing how clueless you could be at even the ripe old age of thirty-six.

A few minutes after Caitlin and Ollie had walked in the bell on the back of the café door began ringing much more frequently than usual. The grind and complaint of the coffee machine became a constant and Mel and I found ourselves racing around just to keep up. The dishwasher was constantly running to ensure that there were enough clean mugs to satisfy demand. As I steamed another jug of non-fat milk I caught Mel's eye. She smiled at me for the first time in days, acknowledging the sudden upturn in pace.

'This is more like it,' she said, quietly enough that none of the customers could hear it. I seized this momentary thawing and winked at her. I'd never been a winker, but somehow the situation demanded a wink. It seemed to express the right level of intimacy, while its brevity acknowledged the unexpected but welcome time crunch. As I punched numbers into the till – were people really willing to pay three quid for an almond croissant? – it became apparent that we were enjoying the best day's takings since we'd opened the café. Incredibly, nearly all of the money had flowed into the tills within the past hour.

But something wasn't right and I felt strangely remote from proceedings, as if the customer surge wasn't really occurring. It seemed that, in my desperation, I might have somehow dreamed up the profit surge. I watched as customers waited patiently, steaming mugs in hand, for tables to become available so that they might sit for ten minutes and consume overpriced coffees and pastries. I wanted to ask each and every one of them what the hell they were throwing their money away on this crap for. But I didn't. I kept cranking the cappuccinos, steaming milk and plating the Danishes until the pastry cabinet was entirely plundered. This was a first, and quite why we were subject to this plague of Home Counties locusts I had no idea.

It was then that I saw Kenny slope inside. Since our falling-out, I'd seen him a couple of times sprawled at a window seat in Java Jamboree. On the second occasion the loafer had actually waved a newspaper in my direction as if to acknowledge that he was finally able to express his inner self and fill in the crossword without fear of reprimand. Good for him, I thought.

Kenny had a whispered conversation with Mel before hurrying out of the door. He glanced in my direction but neither of us acknowledged the other. His presence, following the customer avalanche, had me wondering what on earth was going on. Maybe the word on the street was that the Second Coming was scheduled for that afternoon at the Bean & Gone.

I sidled up to Mel to see if she would divulge some information. Clearly Kenny had had a reason to come by. Mel looked at me wide-eyed.

'Java Jamboree is closed.'

'What?'

'Kenny just told me,' she explained. 'Rats. Someone called the health inspector and they've closed the place down.'

I started to laugh. I couldn't help myself. Big riotous guffaws rolled from deep within me. I held onto the side of the counter, while customers waited for me to stop convulsing and deliver them their soy lattes.

'That is *hilarious*,' I said.

'Careful,' said Mel reproachfully. 'Don't laugh at the misfortune of others.'

'Oh, yes, that's right,' I said. 'Those poor shareholders. Excuse me for being so heartless.'

Mel half-smiled at me while changing a punter's fifty-quid note.

'Just get on with it, will you? Make hay while the sun shines,' she chided me.

'Do you have any other little pearls of wisdom to share with me, or are you finished for now?' I asked. I was trying to make a joke but I wondered, given the mood between us recently, whether she might take it the wrong way.

'I'm sorry to interrupt,' said a man carrying a sleeping baby in a sling. (Never having suffered the humiliation of wearing one of these emasculating contraptions was, to me, the upside of my not having met my daughter until she was a teenager.) 'Are my coffees going to be much longer?' The man had thinning hair and was making what Amanda would describe as a 'pooh face': a sour, passive-aggressive signifier of displeasure.

The Java Jamboree news had made me feel strangely cavalier. I thought about giving him a mouthful of impudence.

'I'm sorry for the wait, sir,' I said. 'I'm only going to charge you for one of these.'

Pooh Face warmed up a little. 'Thank you,' he said. 'That's very kind.'

Actually, no, just good business, I thought, calculating that I would still make two quid from the transaction. I got the feeling that Pooh Face and his uptight wife would be back but, more than that, I was smitten by the idea that, putting aside the inscrutability of my relationships with Caitlin, Amanda and Mel, this ridiculous fantasy of mine might actually be viable, might provide me with another life. And that was far more than I had hoped for when I'd got out of bed that morning.

Chapter 24

I told Mel to go home early. I was trying to be conciliatory about the Kenny situation, to get us back on the right footing. The afternoon had been overwhelming, but she had dug deep, never letting the onslaught of muffin requests and demands for less froth in chai lattes get to her. For the past few hours I'd envisioned the film *Zulu*, with me and Mel playing the plucky red-jacketed soldiers being overrun by the Home Counties hordes.

Caitlin was still helping out now and then at the Bean & Gone. While I was thrilled to see the effort (and glad of the help) I wondered if there was something going on that I wasn't aware of. Had she been kicked out of school? Was she playing some kind of mind game with me? Was Amanda dishing out advice during her work experience sessions, advising her to take a new approach? Had she and Ollie discovered something that neither of them had bargained for? It hardly mattered any longer, I supposed. I was still undecided about Caitlin. I had yet to speak with Joan Kennedy and was still debating whether I should just pull the plug on the whole happy families thing or use Caitlin and Amanda's burgeoning relationship as a means of getting closer to both of them. Certainly, I knew that I would be unable to prevent Caitlin's real identity from coming out for much longer.

As the customers began to drift away for the evening I looked up to see that Amanda had appeared and was chatting with Caitlin.

'Caitlin, can you go and empty the dishwasher?' I said, approaching them.

'See you later then,' Caitlin said to Amanda.

'See you, sweetheart,' Amanda replied, before turning to me, all business. 'We need to talk about Caitlin,' she said pointedly. She had lowered her voice and the words sounded almost like a hiss.

My heart sank. Caitlin and I weren't as clever as we thought we were. I opened my mouth to start telling her that, yes, I had lied to her, that Caitlin wasn't actually Mel's daughter. My rationale was this: we were square. Amanda had lied about Belagio. I had lied about Caitlin. I steered her over to a discrete table.

'It's about Java Jamboree and the health inspectors,' said Amanda. 'It's not what it seems.'

She glanced about, as if she was worried that someone might overhear. She leaned in closer to me conspiratorially.

'First of all I have a confession to make,' Amanda said. She looked down at the coffee table and traced patterns with a long red nail.

Oh, Christ, I thought; more Nick Belagio news. That's why she had a meal for two in her shopping basket.

'I stopped by Java Jamboree earlier today to pick up a coffee,' Amanda revealed eventually.

I breathed a sigh of relief. A Java Jamboree transgression I could forgive.

'Anyway, I was just getting my milk when I saw Caitlin and her brother – they look so different, don't they?'

'If you look closely I think you'll see the family resemblance,' I lied.

'Anyway, I thought it was a bit odd, two kids on their own in there. It wasn't like I was being nosy or anything. They sat at a table in the corner, and they were sort of staring at each other.

I was just about to leave when I saw her unzip a holdall and tip it on its side.'

Where on earth was this story was going?

'That's odd, I thought, so I paused a moment and you'll never guess what I saw next.'

I shook my head. I couldn't guess.

'Then a whole load of bloody rats crawled out.' Amanda shuddered at the memory. 'They were sort of sniffing around where Caitlin and her brother were, so the kids moved their feet to get the creatures to run off in different directions.'

'What?' I said. 'Rats? They emptied a bag of rats in Java Jamboree?'

Amanda nodded. 'Rats.' She shivered. 'I hate rats. No one noticed at first. Everyone was just sitting there sipping their drinks.'

'Let me get this straight,' I said. 'You saw Caitlin and Ollie walk into Java Jamboree and empty a bag of rats in the place.'

Amanda nodded. The look on her face was aghast, far more troubled than when we had fought over her sexual indiscretion.

I paused for a moment, trying to absorb the information.

'And no one else saw them?' I asked. 'You're sure of that.'

'Just me,' said Amanda. 'Once they'd got the rats out of the bag they just got up and left like they didn't have a care in the world.'

Somewhere nearby a clock chimed 7 p.m. It was time to go home. I rested my head on the table.

'You okay, Alex?' asked Amanda. She had noticed that I was trembling slightly. I raised my head: I could feel a mark on my brow where it had been on the table.

'That is absolutely fucking hilarious,' I said eventually. 'I mean, how do they even come up with a plan like that? Let alone get hold of the rats, then release them and get out of the place before the manager has seen them.'

Amanda's face remained stony. Clearly she didn't find it as amusing as I did.

'Come on, Amanda,' I said. 'Chill out.'

'It's a pretty serious thing to do,' Amanda insisted. 'What if some old lady had had a heart attack?'

'But no one had a heart attack.'

'They could be in a lot of trouble,' Amanda persisted.

'Well, they won't,' I said. 'Nobody saw them but you.'

I waited for her to tell me that that was just as well, as she had no intention of sharing the secret with anyone but me, but she remained tight-lipped. It felt a little menacing, like she was threatening to expose Caitlin.

'I can't believe it,' I said, trying to move the conversation forwards. 'I mean, where did they get a plan like that from?'

'I don't know,' said Amanda. She paused for a moment. 'You, maybe?'

'Are you joking?' I said, incredulous. 'You think I'd put two kids up to something like that? And you think that they'd even do it if I asked them?'

'Well, it does seem a little far-fetched that they'd come up with it on their own,' said Amanda. The volume of her voice had risen somewhat. 'And why would they bother? What's in it for them? The only person who gets anything out of this whole situation is you.'

'So what are you saying?' I demanded. I was baffled that she was thinking this way. 'That I put them up to it? That the Bean & Gone is in such trouble that I would ask two teenage kids to go and release rats at Java Jamboree?'

Amanda sighed. 'No,' she said eventually. 'I suppose it doesn't sound very plausible.'

We could hear the clanking of dishes in the kitchen where Caitlin was stacking the dishwasher. I was relieved that she wasn't eavesdropping.

'I just thought that I should tell you,' Amanda said.

It felt like there was more. I wondered if she'd already told the authorities.

'Look, I really appreciate you coming to me,' I said, trying to change the tone of our conversation. 'This is between us, right?'

'I best be off,' said Amanda, sliding out of her chair. 'Got to get back and cook dinner.'

'Right,' I said, walking her to the door. I needed to know that she wasn't going to reveal who had put the rats in Java Jamboree.

'I'll see you then,' I said, standing and putting my hands in my pockets. There was no kiss. 'And about the rats—'

'Oh, our secret,' Amanda interrupted me, tapping the side of her nose. She smiled at me, and for the briefest of moments, it made me forget that anything bad had happened between us. I floated elsewhere for an instant before landing with a thud, remembering that there was something else that I wanted to say to her. I could tell that she was waiting for something else, but I couldn't bring myself to form the words. It wasn't the right time. I wanted to talk to her about what had happened with Nick. I was still bruised by what she had done, but now I was ready to hear it from her. Maybe then we could move beyond it. I wanted to ask her to stay, to talk for a while ...

But I heard banging from the kitchen and realised that my thirteen-year-old daughter – the one whom I had told my wife was someone else's – needed to go home and get some rest.

That evening, as Caitlin and I drove home through the bleak November night, I turned down the radio and began my inquisition. My problem with talking to Caitlin was that I was unable to be the stern judge that the situation required. I was so affected by Caitlin and Ollie's spirited and novel approach to corporate competition that I just couldn't give her the talking-to that I was supposed to. Caitlin's intervention was a source of enormous pride and delight to me. The fact that she was keen to the challenges of the Bean & Gone and had formulated such a fiendish plan showed her to be both resourceful and – this was the best part – caring.

'So the movie was good, eh?' I said, peering into the rear-view mirror. I could see Caitlin resting her head against the window, taking in the foggy orange glow of the evening.

'Yeah,' she replied.

'What was it you saw again?'

'It was the new Pixar movie: *Two Gorillas Green*.'

'Oh really,' I said. 'I've heard that's really good.'

'It's okay, I suppose,' said Caitlin, not missing a beat. 'It's not one of their better ones.'

'Oh,' I said. She was doing well. 'So what happens?'

'It's complicated,' said Caitlin. 'I sound like you, don't I?'

Ah ha! I thought. Got her.

'Try me,' I said.

'Well ...' said Caitlin. She was struggling! I had her. 'It's about these two gorillas, one called Leonard and the other called Leonid, and they live in the rainforest in ... I think it's Uganda, or maybe Rwanda. Anyway, one day ...'

Over the next several minutes Caitlin went on to give such a thorough and detailed synopsis of the plot that I began to wonder whether Amanda had actually been mistaken. But this simply couldn't be the case. Either Caitlin had somehow seen the film or she had read about it online.

'Really,' I said, rather feebly when she came to the end of her speech. 'That sounds great.'

'It's pretty good,' said Caitlin, slightly dismissively. 'I wouldn't call it great. It's no *Wall: E*.'

'Right.' I was going to have to change tack. I needed to confront the issue head on. 'So I don't suppose that you heard anything about what happened at Java Jamboree today, did you?'

Silence.

'No,' she said, after a while.

'Well, apparently, they've been closed down by the health inspectors. They've got rats.'

'Oh,' said Caitlin carefully.

I was going to have to turn up the heat.

'There's a rumour going round town that someone put them there on purpose.'

'Why would they do that?' asked Caitlin.

'Well, for instance, someone who did something like that might have something to gain from putting rats in there.'

'I don't get it,' said Caitlin. 'Why would anyone want to put rats in there?'

It was a rhetorical question. I was hoping, however, that she might answer it.

'No one really knows,' I said. 'Although I daresay the people who did it – if the rumour is true – might eventually be caught.'

'Oh,' said Caitlin. She sounded troubled. I had done my parental duty by reminding her that bad acts receive punishment, yet I felt bad. I didn't want to scare her; I just wanted to try to wiggle the truth free like a baby tooth.

She remained silent for the rest of the journey. I cursed myself. She had done something that demonstrated her loyalty, her love even. I didn't want my response to cause her to withdraw, to drift back behind the adolescent iron curtain.

We arrived home. As Caitlin was unbuckling her belt, I said, 'I doubt they'll catch them, though.'

'Why?' Caitlin enquired as she turned towards me. I had piqued her interest.

'Because whoever did something like that is way too clever to be caught.'

I gave her a wink and – yes! – she returned it and followed it with a big grin. I would say nothing else about the matter. This would be our secret. Our shared bounty.

She grabbed her bag and jumped out of the car.

'That's what I think too,' she said breezily, before closing the door.

We learn things about those close to us all the time. I hoped that Caitlin knowing that I was on her side wasn't a revelation to her. For me, though, knowing that she was with me as I went about my everyday struggle was enough. I needed to try to embrace the positive: her rat attack on Java Jamboree was her way of expressing love. Surely even I wasn't too self-absorbed to recognise that. It was up to me, as the adult, to make this work.

My mobile rang.

'Alex, it's Joan Kennedy, Social Services. I'm sorry to bother you at the weekend, but I've been waiting for your call.'

Shit.

'Oh, hi, Joan.'

'You called about Caitlin. Is everything okay?'

'Yes, yes, everything's fine.'

'Well, what did you call about then?'

'Nothing really, it was—'

'Well, it must have been something,' she said, interrupting me.

'It's over now,' I said, turning away from the house so Caitlin wouldn't hear. 'Caitlin thought that some of the stuff from her mum's house was missing, but we found it.'

'Oh, I see,' Joan said.

'Thanks for calling anyway.'

There was an icy silence.

'Looking forward to our meeting in a couple of weeks,' I continued.

'Just make sure that your wife is there this time,' said Kennedy before hanging up.

Quite how I was going to achieve that I didn't know. But I looked up at the evening sky and felt hope – hope! – that Caitlin and I would finally be what I had wished us to be.

PART 3

Chapter 25

The doorbell rang at a bad moment: I was just towelling off after my morning shower. I looked at the clock. It hadn't even gone eight yet.

'Bollocks,' I said, pulling on my underwear. 'Caitlin!'

Silence. She probably had the radio on full blast in the kitchen.

I knew that the visitor was our landlord, Yossi, who had, as per usual, showed up on the dot. The poor bloke was only in his early thirties but had been cursed by the double whammy of male pattern baldness and simian hirsuteness of every other part of his body, including his ears. It was as if his hair had fled the barren part of his body that was his skull, only to find fertile ground almost everywhere else. Yossi had inherited the house from his aunt, decided that it was too big to live in himself, bought a flat and rented the property out. He had recently been offered a lucrative two-year contract in Dubai installing a computer network for a new Ukrainian-owned hotel. This meant that he was going to hand the maintenance of the house to a local managing agent – he didn't need the hassle of finding a reliable plumber back in Surrey while he was enjoying his tax-free salary in the Middle East.

'Caitlin!' I shouted.

'Yes?' The voice came from the bottom of the stairs.

'Could you do me a favour please?' I said. 'Can you get the door? It's just Yossi – he's bringing someone round to take a look at the house.'

The doorbell rang again. Then I heard another car pull up outside. This would be the managing agent. I pulled up the blind to take a look.

Jesus Christ.

The managing agent Yossi had hired was *Amanda*.

'Caitlin!' I shouted. 'Don't open the door!'

'What?' she called up the stairs.

'Do. Not. Open. The Door,' I repeated, jumping into my clothes as quickly as I could manage.

'What are you freaking out about?' she said.

Why hadn't I considered this possibility? I had gone to great lengths to conceal my location from Amanda: I could fudge Caitlin's presence at the café, but at home was a different matter. There was no way I could explain this away to her. I called down to Caitlin to get upstairs into her room, but she must have gone back to the kitchen.

I could hear Yossi on his mobile talking about interfaces and 'userbility'. I needed to get him in the house quickly and then smuggle Caitlin out of the kitchen, past the front door and upstairs before Amanda could see her. I hurtled downstairs, a picture of dishevelment.

'Hi, Yossi!' I said, all smiles, as I opened the front door. 'Come in.' He hesitated – he'd seen Amanda arrive. I grabbed his elbow and steered him indoors. 'Come in, come in,' I repeated, ushering him through the hallway. 'How are you?' I asked.

'I think that the person from the estate agency—' he started. I herded him towards the living room.

The doorbell rang. Yossi made a move.

'Don't worry. I've got it,' I said, cutting in front of him.

'Blimey,' chuckled Yossi. 'You been overdoing the coffee, haven't you?'

'Something like that.' I led him through to the living room. 'There's something I need you to take a look at.'

The doorbell rang again.

'Don't worry; I'm on it,' I said to Yossi.

On my way I stuck my head into the kitchen to see Caitlin.

'Pssssssssssst!' I hissed. 'Get upstairs quick!'

Caitlin made a 'wha—???' face at me.

'Quick!' I whispered. 'And don't let the man in the living room see you. I'll distract him.'

Caitlin's brow knitted.

'Don't worry,' I whispered to her as calmly as I could. 'Everything is fine. It's the landlord – remember I told you? Just give me a second to distract him.'

The doorbell rang again. Jesus, Amanda, give us a fucking chance . . . I saw Yossi making for the door and headed him off.

'So, Yossi . . .' I started. I racked my brains for the right button to push to sidetrack him. 'I think that we might have some damp coming through down there.' I pointed to a corner of the room. Yossi went over and knelt down to examine it. While his back was turned, Caitlin tiptoed through the room and crept upstairs.

'I'll get the door then,' I said. Now to deal with Amanda. I couldn't believe that she had inadvertently flushed me out. She'd get a shock when I opened the front door.

It had only been a couple of months since I'd moved out, but somehow I'd managed to forget how dressed up Amanda looked first thing in the morning: her hair ironed, her make-up applied and her BlackBerry clamped to her ear. I pulled the door open.

'Alex?' she said, as if this were the most natural situation for us to find ourselves in. Seemingly she was unfazed by the turn of events. Why was she able to take things in her stride so easily? 'What are you doing here?'

I stepped back to allow her inside.

'Actually, I live here,' I said.

'Really?' Amanda said. She glanced around. 'This place is big. And it's expensive. Why do you need so much space?'

Bugger. Good question.

'Well, it was really the first thing I saw,' I said. 'It just seemed right. Gut feeling, I suppose.'

'Bloody hell, Alex,' said Amanda breezily. She wiped her shoes on the doormat. 'Didn't I teach you anything? There's an old estate agents' saying: always walk away from the first thing you see.'

She put her hands on her hips.

'Now, where's Yossi? I want to talk to the organ grinder, not the monkey.'

Amanda seemed so blasé about encountering me that I couldn't help wondering if seeing me really was a surprise. We walked into the living room and it became apparent that, within moments of meeting Amanda, Yossi had relaxed, confident that this capable woman would look after his asset while he was making coin in the scorched metropolis of Dubai. There would be no leaking roofs, backed-up drains or broken windows that she couldn't handle. Yossi led her around the property, commenting on its various aspects while Amanda nodded sagely, took the occasional note and made pertinent comments. Watching her at work, I felt like I was seeing my wife in her natural habitat – this was where she was at her best. While I could not have predicted Amanda's presence, I felt vindicated that I had toned down "Mum's room" to make it look like a bog standard guest bedroom.

'It's okay, Alex,' Yossi said. 'You don't need to be here if you've got things to do.'

'Sounds good,' I said blithely and sauntered off to clear up the kitchen.

Then it struck me. I might have managed to conceal Caitlin upstairs successfully, but there was something I'd forgotten:

how was I going to explain to them that one of the rooms in the house was decorated with posters of boy bands? Let alone explain the fact that Caitlin would be lying on her bed listening to her iPod. I was in so deep with the charade that Caitlin was Mel's daughter that, if Amanda found out now – and in this fashion – I feared it would irrevocably damage our relationship at a point where it appeared to be defrosting.

Then something bad happened.

Caitlin moved a chair in her room, scraping the floor upstairs. Both Yossi and Amanda looked up at the ceiling before turning to me.

'Who's that?' asked Amanda.

'That?' I said, trying to brush it off. 'Oh, no one. Next door, probably.'

Neither Yossi nor Amanda seemed convinced by my explanation, but returned to reviewing the house. I strolled casually out of their line of vision then bounded upstairs to Caitlin's room.

'Sorry I didn't knock,' I said, walking in on her. It was a serious *faux pas*. Any dad worth his salt knows that one of the commandments of raising daughters is: *You do not enter an adolescent girl's room without knocking.*

'Isn't that Amanda downstairs?' Caitlin asked.

'Yes, yes, it is,' I said.

'Why is she here?'

'She's working.'

'Oh,' she said. 'That's a bit of a bummer, isn't it?'

'Yes, yes, it is ...' I said, running my hand through my hair anxiously. 'I really need a favour from you. It's very, very important that you don't come out of your room, okay?'

Caitlin rolled her eyes, exasperated by the games.

Yossi and Amanda were creaking up the stairs. There was no way that I could let them into the back room to see a grumpy Caitlin sitting on a floral bedspread with a Rihanna poster on the wall and her chemistry homework scattered across the floor.

I kneeled so that I was close to her and on her level. 'Please do this for me,' I asked quietly. 'It's important.'

Caitlin gazed into the distance. Oh Lord, please can she not have a teenage tantrum ...

Then she nodded.

'Good girl, thanks,' I said, standing up. 'I owe you one.'

As I backed out of Caitlin's room, I heard Amanda and Yossi stepping out of the bathroom.

'Hi,' I said, awkwardly. I had positioned myself in the hallway so that my body blocked Caitlin's door. 'How's it going?'

'Good, good ...' Yossi said. 'I just need to show Amanda that last room and we're finished.'

'This room?' I asked, gesturing over my shoulder with my thumb.

'Yup, that one,' Yossi replied.

Amanda, much like Caitlin, had crossed her arms and stuck her hips out. It was body language that was meant to convey the dubiousness of my position.

'Oh,' I said. I didn't know what to do with my hands so I pushed them deep into my pockets. Both Amanda and Yossi waited for me to speak.

'Well, you see,' I said, 'I'm going to have to ask if it might be possible to give this room a miss.'

Yossi raised an eyebrow. He was probably envisioning collapsed ceilings and blown plasterwork.

'Everything is fine with the room,' I said. 'It's just that I have a, um, friend staying.'

'A friend?' Amanda asked. Her tone suggested that this would be a first.

'Yes,' I said. 'Um, no one you know. It's actually an old schoolfriend who moved to Australia and who just sort of showed up. He's really tired. Jet lag.'

240

Yossi looked at me, and then at Amanda. Neither of them was buying.

'Well, okay,' said Yossi, 'if your friend is tired, I suppose we can give it a miss today, but I'd like Amanda to see the room soon, Alex. You two will have to work that out between you.'

Yossi turned and walked down the hallway. Amanda stood for a moment shaking her head very slightly so that only I could see. She wanted to let me know that she didn't believe a word I'd said.

'Come on, Amanda,' said Yossi, who was now halfway down the stairs. 'Let's take a look at the contract.'

Amanda's stare haunted me throughout the rest of that day. I worked on autopilot – despite the fact that Java Jamboree had reopened, Caitlin and Ollie's antics had significantly increased our business, but I was now so familiar with the needs and rhythms of the café that I was able to sleepwalk through even the most complicated orders. After work I went home, made dinner and put Caitlin to bed. I cleaned the kitchen. I put out the recycling. I made soup for the following night's dinner. I knew that this activity meant just one thing: I was avoiding. I could find no further domestic duties or chores to prevent me from calling Amanda. I dialled her number before putting the phone down and rehearsing my lines again.

'Hi, Amanda, I'm just calling to ...'

To what, exactly? To talk? To ask her out?

We were married, for Christ's sake, and I was too anxious to call her and ask if we could smoke the pipe of peace. It wasn't like I wanted to move back in with her pronto; I just wanted to re-establish contact, to let her know that I was interested in us as a couple.

I wanted to move on from our secrets, to prevent our

relationship from being just a series of misunderstandings and sort-of truths.

I dialled her number again, and slammed the receiver down before even hearing her phone ring. This was ridiculous. I practised my greeting again:

'Hello, Amanda.' Too formal.

'Hey, it's me.' Given the circumstances this seemed too familiar.

'Hi there.' Oddly wimp-like.

'Whassup, dawg?' Nope.

For fuck's sake. If Caitlin could see me she'd probably give me a severe talking-to. I needed to take control of the situation. I needed to save my marriage, for goodness' sake. Wasn't that enough motivation? I dialled again. The ringing of the phone felt like the sound of an EKG machine that was monitoring my heart.

'Hello?' I guessed she was holding the phone in trademark Amanda fashion, cradled under her chin with a cigarette in one hand and a drink in another.

'Oh, hi, it's Alex,' I said. Not a good start. There was zero authority or charm.

Silence.

'So, Alex,' said Amanda, after a couple of beats. 'To what do I owe the pleasure?'

'Just, you know, calling to see how you're doing,' I said.

'I'm doing just fine, thank you,' replied Amanda, drily. 'And yourself?'

'Fine. Yeah, look, I was wondering if you wanted to meet up at some point. Go for a drink or something.'

'Really?'

'Yes, you know, just to talk.'

There was another pause.

'Well, I'm sort of busy this week,' she said.

'Well, how about—'

'How about you tell me who was in the house today?' Her voice was firm, to the point.

'Just an old mate.'

'An old mate,' Amanda repeated, flatly.

'Yeah,' I replied, trying to tough it out.

'Really?' said Amanda. 'Well, you know what I think? I think that you had a special friend up there. A friend whom you didn't want to have me meet.'

'A *special* friend?' I asked. 'What are you talking about?'

'Look, if you want to start seeing other people, that's okay,' said Amanda. 'It's been long enough.'

'Amanda, you've totally got the wrong end of the stick—'

'And, for your information,' continued Amanda, 'you're not the only one with options.'

'What the fuck does that mean?' I was angry now. Angry at her for threatening me, but most of all I was angry at myself for screwing up the conversation so royally. I couldn't have handled it much worse.

'You've got an active imagination, Alex – try using it.'

'Amanda, listen to me,' I said. 'There is no one else.'

'Then why was there a fucking box of tampons in your bathroom?'

I didn't even have a chance to answer that one. Amanda put the phone down.

I had begun the conversation hoping that we might start to repair our relationship. I ended it by discovering that not only was she seeing someone else, she thought that I was too.

A really terrific night's work.

The following afternoon, as I approached the offices of Dyer & Liphoff, I pulled my jacket around me just a little tighter. It wasn't just the weather that was making me feel a chill. This would not be fun.

The receptionist was doing her nails when I walked in. She looked up with a welcoming look; when she saw who it was she put down the scarlet bottle of nail polish and kept a nervous eye on me.

'Amanda,' she said, 'someone for you.'

Caitlin was sitting at a desk next to Amanda's. There was no overhead light. Both of them were bathed in a glow from desk lamps. Caitlin waved to me.

'There in a minute,' she said.

Amanda continued to type away on her keyboard while Caitlin tidied the desk she'd been working on.

'I'll see you Wednesday,' she said to Amanda.

'All right sweetheart,' Amanda answered, smiling. 'Thanks.'

Caitlin put her bag on her shoulder and walked towards me. I pretended to look at her while all the time looking at my wife.

Amanda looked up from her computer for a moment, her gaze settling on me before returning to her screen. The message was simple: you're not even worth the effort. And I couldn't help thinking, Well, maybe she's right – maybe I'm not.

Caitlin chattered on in the car. I tried to engage, but my mind was elsewhere. I made a quick dinner and then she went upstairs to do her homework. I called Mike.

'You okay?' he asked. 'You don't sound right.'

'I'm fine,' I said. 'I just need your help with something.'

'And that would be?' he asked.

'Revenge,' I said.

'Belagio?' he asked with a hint of excitement in his voice.

'Yes,' I replied.

'About fucking time,' Mike said. 'Count me in.'

Chapter 26

Two days later Mike and I were standing at the bar in the rugby club sipping our pints. It was the annual meeting of the management committee, which Mike was chairing this year. The group was made up of local bigwigs and blowhards who liked to use the club as a means of advertising their success in the world. Making it onto the supervisory body of the club was like getting onto the State Council of the People's Republic of China: it was secretive and impenetrable, offering its members power and influence that was respected and never questioned by those beyond its hallowed confines. I had no idea how I'd ended up anointed, but I suspect it was something to do with my access to discount travel packages while I was at TicketBusters. Travel packages were always very popular items at charity auctions.

'What time are we expecting our friend?' I asked Mike.

'What time is it now?' he replied.

'Ten to eight,' I said, checking my watch.

'I told him quarter past eight,' said Mike. 'To make sure that everyone is here before he arrives.'

'Wicked,' I said, taking a sip of my lager. I could barely contain my excitement. Looking round the room I could see most of the local movers and shakers, people whose opinion mattered in the pubs, schools and shops of the town and on the commuter trains into London. I tried to imagine where Belagio was at this very moment, what was going through his head. There was no way he could be prepared for what was to come.

'Just make sure that you nip outside once the meeting starts and put the sign up,' Mike said.

'Affirmative,' I replied in an American military voice. I was enjoying this. 'It's in the boot of the car.'

'I called him earlier,' said Mike with a smirk. 'He's raring to go.'

I tried not to choke on my drink. This was going to be good.

'Thanks, Mike,' I said. 'I owe you one.'

'That prick has had it coming for a while,' Mike said. 'Can't believe that we've only just got around to sticking it to him.'

The pair of us circulated the room, making small talk with the twenty other committee members. As much as I was able to glad-hand and do a little PR for the Bean & Gone, my mind was never far from what was to come.

Mike let everyone know that the meeting was about to start. Someone asked where Nick was and Mike explained that Belagio had called to let him know that he was running late and that we should proceed without him. I waited until everyone had passed into the meeting room before stepping out into the chilly evening and pulling a large home-made sign from the boot of my car. I carried it across the car park and placed it under a light outside the entrance to the meeting room. I stepped back to review my handiwork. The sign read: Pimps and Hos Party. I had spent some time looking up seventies typefaces on the internet and then carefully copying them onto a large piece of fibreboard.

The committee meeting was well under way by the time I got back, although I could barely register what they were discussing: donating part of the proceeds of our annual charity ball to Christ Church to help with their appeal for a new roof. Mike was doing a pretty good job, though: he was focused and appeared to be utterly oblivious to anything other than the matter in hand. I crossed my arms and savoured the moment. Just when Keith the treasurer was running through the accounts the door opened and in walked Nick Belagio.

Well, at least Mike and I knew that it was Belagio.

'What the hell . . .?' someone said before all heads swivelled to look in Nick's direction.

A split second later the laughter started.

Belagio stood in the committee room dressed like a Times Square streetwalker from the 1970s. He was wearing a huge blonde wig, a bra that he had stuffed with something to give himself two misshapen boobs, a tight satin dress with a slit up the side, fishnet tights and vertiginous high heels. He looked like the least successful transvestite hooker of all time.

The room was engulfed with hoots of laughter.

'How much, darling?' someone shouted.

'Don't fancy yours much,' yelled someone else.

'I didn't realise there was cabaret,' called another.

The laughter hung there, not abating, like a torrent of water from a fire hose aimed at Belagio. There were tears running down my cheeks; my stomach hurt so much that I thought I was going to puke. Belagio tried to tough it out, shifting from side to side in his stilettos, trying to think of something clever to say to deflect the laughter. He wasn't used to not being in control, to not being able to make the calls. Even though he was wearing thick make-up I could see that he was trying to fight back, to turn the tables, but such was the force of the hilarity that he was overwhelmed. All he could see was a room of his friends and peers purple-faced and pointing at him. Eventually he just muttered 'you bastards', turned round and stormed out of the door.

After a few minutes the meeting was called to order and we tried to get through the agenda, but there were still occasional outbursts of hilarity at just the memory of Belagio in all his party finery. His entrance was referred to almost constantly throughout the rest of the evening, and into the night beyond.

The man would never live it down.

I was thrilled. Of course, I couldn't have done it without Mike, who was the person who really sold Belagio the lie, but it was my concept. I had remembered that Belagio loved to dress up. I'd asked Mike to tell Nick that he was hosting a Pimps and Hos party at the rugby club (for charity, of course) and – in a hilarious twist – it had been decided that both the men and the women were to dress as hos. We'd been able to bet that Belagio's vanity and desire to be the centre of attention would lead him to try to push taste and decency to the limits.

For the rest of the night I left my sorry situation behind and revelled in the sweet smell of victory.

I awoke the next morning feeling like I'd slept with a rugby player's foot in my mouth. I slogged my way into work. In the cold light of day my trick on Belagio rang a little hollow. Maybe it was booze-gloom, but all I could think about was my calamitous conversation with Amanda a couple of days before. Mel must have noticed the change in my mood, but she remained quiet. I assumed that her malaise was Kenny-related, but I couldn't be sure – it may very well have been to do with me. I felt like my ability to read people was diminished. The energy that I had put into my relationship with Caitlin, the never-ending battle of the Bean & Gone and now the Amanda fiasco, had pretty much drained me. Just when Caitlin and I had got onto a decent footing everything else was turning rotten.

Mel went out for an early lunch and came back clutching a couple of shopping bags.

'What did you get?' I asked her. It was the first time I'd asked her a personal question for days. Our recent conversation had been all business.

Mel looked sheepish. 'A dress,' she replied.

'Why are you looking so guilty then?' I said it playfully, but I was hoping to get a serious response. Mel didn't look right.

'Oh, you know ...'

'Kenny?'

'It's pretty bloody pathetic,' said Mel, taking a swig from a bottle of water. 'Not like me at all. But I can't help feeling guilty. It's the money, you know.'

'Was it worth it, though?'

Mel laughed. 'Course it bloody was.'

'Good,' I said. 'You deserve it. You work hard. You should be able to treat yourself now and again.'

Mel nodded and looked down at her feet. She leaned back against the counter. 'Thanks,' she said. She reached forward and patted my forearm. It was a small gesture, but was loaded with intimacy. We're friends again, was my first thought. But then it occurred to me: maybe she likes me. She must have realised that sometimes I'd watch as she manoeuvred her way around the café, her slim hips never catching the edge of a table or a counter. I'd noticed several male customers hit on her, but ...

And I wasn't even sure where the gesture came from, but I reached up with my right hand and cupped her cheek. She held my gaze and leaned ever so gently into me. We were frozen there for a moment. I should lean in and kiss her. If Amanda thought that I was running around behind her back, then I should at least get something out of it other than suspicion and punishment.

Do it.

I started to close in on her.

Ring, ring.

A young mum walked into the shop, scolding her toddler. Mel and I both reacted with a start, as if we had been roused by thunder from a deep sleep. We scuttled off to different parts of the shop and from our distant orbs furiously attempted to ignore each other for the rest of the day.

I locked up early and walked over to Dyer & Liphoff to collect Caitlin. The lights were on, but the door was locked. Amanda pulled it open without greeting me.

'I'm collecting Caitlin,' I said.

'Really,' Amanda replied.

'Your mum said I should pick you up,' I called to Caitlin, who looked to be stuffing sheets of paper into envelopes,

'OK,' Caitlin said. 'There in a minute.'

I leaned awkwardly on the reception desk. Amanda drummed her nails on her forearms.

'It's not what you think,' I said.

'How do you know what I'm thinking?' she snapped back.

The situation with Caitlin working for Amanda was a double-edged sword. It meant that I could see my ex-wife, that I could try to repair things, but also meant that I was subject to the full force of her dissatisfaction. She thought that I was banging someone; actually, not someone, she thought that I was banging Mel.

'Look, Amanda—' I started.

'Save it,' she snapped, before conjuring a smile for Caitlin, who was approaching us while pulling on her coat.

'Thank you so much, sweetheart,' she said to the girl.

'I haven't quite finished,' Caitlin replied. 'I'll do the rest next time.'

'That's fine,' said Amanda, stroking the girl's head.

'Thanks, Amanda,' I said.

'Say hi to your mum,' Amanda instructed Caitlin.

I turned to give her a 'what the fuck?' look, but she had already closed the door.

*

The following day I volunteered to pick up Ollie and Caitlin from school while Mel watched the shop. Both of them had after-school activities and the nights were drawing in, so I'd got into the habit of seeing them home safely. Usually I made an effort to tune out the white noise of worry about Social Services, Amanda and the café and fully engage with their conversation. But the afternoon after Mel and I had had our awkward moment, before Amanda and I locked horns, I was oblivious to Caitlin's concerns about the casting for the school play and her questions about the migration of the Mongolians to China. Nor did I express concern when Ollie fretted that he had left his gym kit in the changing room. My mind chugged on in its particular furrow: in every aspect of my life, I was in a state of bewilderment.

I sucked cool air into my lungs and looked over at Caitlin and something extraordinary happened: she smiled at me. I melted. It was as if I'd just leapt on one of those water slides at an amusement park: I was powerless to do anything but go with it. And I knew that I had been wrong about so much in life, including my daughter. Yes, things were pretty bloody confounding, but her simple act of warmth had made me realise that there was one circumstance that I now knew I could cling on to, it was the one that I had struggled with most over the preceding months,

I wanted to keep Caitlin.

My head needed examining. Why hadn't I worked this out sooner, for God's sake? I'd shot myself in the foot so many times that I wondered if it was even possible to fuck things up any worse than I already had. My conversation with Amanda the previous night meant that trying to enrol her to be part of the next visit by Social Services was as likely as my bumping into Lord Lucan and Shergar having a pint with the Loch Ness monster. And, despite the upturn, the café was still not out of the woods. Oh, and let's not forget that I had just made a pass at my sole employee. Did I really want to get involved with Mel? I wasn't even sure. I knew that I wanted to sleep with her, but doubted that even I had the self-destructive flair to complicate my life even further.

When I got back with the kids I told Mel that she should leave early – things at the café had wound down to manageable levels. She seemed a little downcast as she went to gather her things. 'Shame that you can't find an excuse to wear that dress tomorrow,' I said. I was trying to cheer her up but, in my role as Mr Foot-in-the-mouth, I managed to make it suggestive as well. 'That would brighten up the place.'

'I'll think about it,' Mel replied. 'Not quite sure that it's right for making cappuccinos.'

'I'll wear a suit in return,' I said.

'We'll see,' replied Mel. 'Come on, Ollie, we're off.'

'Are we going too?' Caitlin asked.

'Have you finished your homework?' I replied.

'Almost.'

'Well, almost isn't finished,' I said. 'Once you've done that we'll get out of here.'

'Jawohl, Commandant!' replied Caitlin, snapping a salute.

Something about her delivery and manner made this even funnier than it already was. I laughed long and hard. I had a funny daughter. Forget that: I had a daughter. And nobody – not Mel or Amanda or Social Services – was going to take her away from me. I was a dad and – even though it had taken me far longer than it should have to understand this simple truth – I was just as capable of making it up as I went along as all the others.

*

Caitlin went over to a friend's house for a couple of hours before dinner. I was tidying the place when the doorbell rang. I wondered why she hadn't used her keys. Must have forgotten them, I supposed. I pulled open the door to see Amanda leaning against one of the posts that supported the veranda.

'Are you going to invite me in, then?' she asked, after a pause.

'Yeah, of course,' I said, stepping aside and closing the door behind her. One part of my mind was running calculations – was there anything of Caitlin's lying around? What time was she due back? The other part of me no longer cared. Let the cards fall where they may. I had Caitlin and, as much as the spectre of Joan Kennedy lurked in the background, I would deal with the Social Services headache as and when I needed to. We'd flee to Rio if we needed to. I would spend my life having plastic surgery to alter my identity and Caitlin could sit reading on the beach all day.

'Yossi emailed me,' Amanda said. He wanted me to check that bit of damp you mentioned hadn't got any worse.'

This is the first time I've seen a surveyor looking red-carpet ready, I thought to myself.

'I think it's fine,' I said, moving in to the living room. 'It's just here.'

The pair of us bent down to examine the patch of wall that I'd falsely told Yossi was problematic. I felt her hair brush against my shoulder and turned to talk to her. Before I could even focus on her her lips were on mine. We stood and I reached behind her to pull her close while she held my face in her pale hands. Our breathing intensified. And then we were on the floor and I was wondering if we had enough time for this ahead of Caitlin getting home before I let my parental standards slip; I pushed the living-room door closed with my foot without breaking my kiss with Amanda.

*

I was in no mood to cook that night. Amanda hadn't lingered, promising to call me. Her parting line had been, 'Let's sort this out', which I mulled over. I hoped that we could. The idea of Amanda, Caitlin and myself all under one roof was quite delicious to me. When she got in, Caitlin went upstairs and I cracked open a cold one and flicked through a newspaper that I'd salvaged from the café. By the time Caitlin came downstairs to see what was for dinner I was fairly refreshed, courtesy of the Heineken brewery.

'Sorry, sweetheart,' I apologised, getting up from the kitchen table. 'I totally forgot to put it on. No worries though; I froze some soup the other night. It won't take five minutes.'

'Can we warm some baguette up as well?' asked Caitlin, picking up the bread from the kitchen counter. 'I love it when it's hot.'

'Of course,' I said, turning on the oven. I poured her an apple juice and sat back down at the table.

'Want to watch a film while we eat? We can take trays in the living room if you want.'

'Oh, can we watch *Titanic*?' asked Caitlin excitedly. 'I haven't watched that for ages.'

'No problem,' I said. 'Why don't you go and put it in the DVD? I'll bring the food.'

We sat watching the film eating soup. And something quite amazing happened: for the first time in months I began to relax. Being able to sit at home with my daughter watching a film was all I wanted. I would work out the situation with Social Services. I would work it out with Amanda. I would keep my relationship with Mel strictly professional. Things would get better, I was sure of it.

The film came to an end. Caitlin stretched. I was settled. Calm. I didn't want her to leave the room, for this to be the end of the evening.

'Caitlin, have you ever played golf?' I asked.

Mystified, the girl looked at me and shook her head.

'Would you like to try?'

'What? Now?'

'Why not?'

Caitlin gave me a look that suggested: *you've had a couple too many beers*. But then she relented.

'Okay,' she said, shrugging her shoulders a little.

'That's the spirit,' I said, rousing myself from the sofa. 'Go and fetch your coat and I'll meet you on the patio.'

By the time Caitlin arrived wearing her boots and coat over her pyjamas I had hauled my golf clubs from the garage and planted a ball on the ground.

'So we're just going to start off with some of the basics,' I said. 'Come over here.'

I gave her a one iron.

'You see the reason we have all these different clubs is that they all do different jobs according to their heads. Some of them are for hitting the ball a long way' – I showed her a driver – 'and some are for just tapping the ball a short distance, like this one.'

I produced a putter. She was humouring me (God knows that before Ratgate there was no way I would have got her out here) but I was losing her. She was cold and tired and wasn't interested in learning the subtleties of the game. She might, however, be interested in hitting things.

'Here,' I said. I stood behind Caitlin, reached over her shoulders, held her hands and addressed the ball. I helped her arc the club back and hit it crisply. It connected and went skipping across the lawn, thumping into the fence at the end of the garden. I placed another ball before her and we repeated the motion: this time she giggled.

'See,' I said. 'That wasn't so hard, was it?'

'No,' Caitlin said. We did it several more times before I thought she was ready to try on her own. The club was too big for her, but she was strong enough to be able to wield it. And I was wise enough – for the sake of my teeth – to stand well back. She swung wildly at first. She then calmed herself for a second swipe, and connected on her third attempt. It was a good, clean strike of the ball.

'Wow,' I said. 'That was good.'

'Ha!' said Caitlin. 'This is fun.'

I placed another ball in front of her. She swung at it a few times before sending the ball all the way down the garden. Caitlin stuck with it, improving somewhat until she was too tired to hit the ball at all.

'I think I'll watch now,' she said, handing me the club.

I wanted to show her how it was done. I was a pretty good player and I had a sudden urge to hit the ball hard and far. I looked at the houses surrounding the garden. They were largely the same, except for Belagio's grand, detached house at the end of the lane. The playground-bully scale of the place was such that it dwarfed the surrounding properties. Like a cuckoo in the nest of a family of sparrows it sat corpulent and ascendant even in this cul-de-sac of providence. The house, much like its owner, appeared to communicate only one message: *I have prevailed*. Not when you're dressed like a ten-quid Kings Cross brass, I thought to myself with a chuckle.

I took a swig of my lager. I had not considered the distance of my garden from Nick Belagio's patio before, but now that I turned my mind to it I imagined that it was no more than three hundred metres. There were lights on throughout the house, the conservatory radiant in the face of global warming. I reached into my bag and pulled out my driver.

'I reckon that I can get it into the garden of that house over there,' I said, my breath steaming in the cold night air.

'Which one?'

'That one.' I nodded at the Belagio house.

'What, the big one?'

I nodded. 'Yup.'

'No way.'

'Way.'

'Want to bet?' asked Caitlin, pulling her coat tighter over her shoulders.

'Yeah,' I said, continuing to eye up my target.

'All right then,' said Caitlin. 'I bet you the washing-up.'

'You're on,' I said. 'Heads I win, tails you lose, OK?'

'What?' Caitlin said, confused.

'It's a joke. Think about it.'

'Heads I win, tails you lose,' Caitlin repeated to herself. 'Oh, I get it.'

At that moment I rotated my hips and shoulders, swung the club high over my head. I brought it down in a perfect arc that powered the ball into the night. The pair of us peered into the darkness.

'Looks like I'm doing the washing-up,' I said.

'What do you mean?' asked Caitlin.

'I don't think I made it.'

'How do you know?'

'You just know,' I said. I thought it was likely I'd come close, but Belagio's garden was so big that it was hard to tell if my ball had landed in the right vicinity. No cigar, Alex.

'That's all right,' said Caitlin. 'It's my turn. I'll take care of it.'

'No, no ...' I said. 'You won fair and square.'

'It's just two soup bowls,' Caitlin replied. 'How about this: I'll swap you. I'll do tonight and you do the next two nights.'

'Deal.'

'Anyway, I want to go in,' she added. 'I'm getting cold.'

'That's fine,' I said. 'I'll be in in a couple of minutes.'

I looked up at the sky. It was clear. It would be a cold night. I started packing away my clubs but the Belagio house caught my attention again. I wasn't going out like this. I had business to take care of.

I addressed the ball before swinging and connecting with it sweetly. It sailed off into the night. That one probably made it, I thought to myself.

Still, no harm in having another go. I swung again. And after that I did it again and again. All in all I must have hit more than a dozen balls at Nick Belagio's house.

Eventually I grew bored of hitting. As much as it had seemed fun when I'd started, it now appeared fairly futile. I returned my clubs to the garage and went back inside the house. Caitlin had left the dishes to dry. I called upstairs.

'You OK, love?'

'Yeah,' she called downstairs. 'Just brushing my teeth.'

Ah … Suburban family bliss.

I started walking upstairs but was interrupted by the sound of the doorbell.

Bloody hell, I thought. Who the hell is that at this time?

I trudged back down and opened the door.

Two police officers were standing on the porch.

'Good evening, sir,' one of them said.

'Hi,' I replied, as brightly as I could. My tactic with the police was always to play the 'I'm a pillar of the community and will do anything to uphold law and order' card.

'Any chance we can come inside, sir?' asked one. His tone was friendly, his face youthful and polite.

'Of course,' I said, doing my best Mr Upstanding Citizen impression.

'We're investigating a complaint,' said the officer after brushing his feet thoroughly on the doormat. His colleague

– older, pallid, hanging on for his full pension – stepped inside
the house without even acknowledging me, and proceeded to
fiddle with his radio until it crackled into life. For some reason I
found it easier to focus on the older bloke than on his colleague,
who was addressing me.

'Would you mind taking us out to the back of the house, sir?'
the copper asked.

His over-reliance on the word 'sir' was beginning to grate. It
reeked of training courses and community initiatives. The three
of us passed through to the back of the house.

'We'll need to get out there, please, sir,' said the policeman.
I opened the door to the patio. A cold wind blew in. I had
begun to sober up. We all walked out on to the herringbone
brickwork. I hugged myself to keep warm and looked up at
a plane passing overhead to show the police how completely
unconcerned I was.

And then it dawned upon me.

My head spun with terrible scenarios.

The policemen looked around, as if gathering their bearings,
before registering Nick Belagio's house. I began to feel nauseous.
A sharp pain appeared above my groin and I wondered whether
fear had caused my appendix to burst. My heartbeat rose and I
started to run my hands through my hair.

'Have you got any golf clubs?' asked the older one.

Oh, God.

'Um, yes,' I said, praying for an end to the interrogation.

'Can you show me where they are, please?' said the older
cop. He was gruff, no-nonsense. He just wanted to get this over
with, get back to the station and file the paperwork with a nice
cup of hot chocolate and a Marlboro Light.

I led them into the garage and handed over my clubs.

The older cop pulled each of them out and examined them.

When he came to the one iron he noted that it was slightly damp and had fresh grass cuttings on it.

'Where are the balls then?' asked the older policeman. I squatted down to unzip the bag. When I looked up I saw the silhouette of the younger cop talking into his radio.

This was not going well.

'Do you mind if I take one?' he asked.

'That's fine,' I said, in one last moment of 'I'm cooperating because I have nothing to hide' bonhomie, despite the fact that I knew I was sunk.

'Look,' said the older policeman, 'we're investigating a complaint from a neighbour who says that someone has been hitting golf balls at his property. He's had a couple of windows smashed. He's very distressed.'

Not as distressed as me when I found out he had screwed my wife, I thought.

The three of us stood in the cold air waiting for something else to happen.

'Is there anything you'd like to tell us, Mr Taylor?' enquired the younger one.

I pretended to think hard before shaking my head. 'Nope,' I said.

The older cop sagged a little and groaned.

'Sir, I'm afraid we're going to have to ask you to accompany us to the station,' said the younger policeman, seemingly back in charge as his colleague returned to fiddling with his crackling radio.

Was this really happening?

'Can't we sort this out some other way?' I asked, trying not to allow the desperation that was flooding my system to creep into my voice. 'It's just that my daughter is asleep upstairs.'

The policemen exchanged a look. The younger one was

gauging how intransigent his colleague was on the matter. I felt a small surge of hope.

The younger one spoke. 'I'm really sorry, sir, but the man who made the complaint has damage to his property. We need to make further inquiries. Is there anyone who could look after your daughter until we sort it out?'

'No, no . . .' I said. There was a feverish tone to my voice. 'I'm a single dad, you see. Her mum is dead.'

'I'm sorry to hear that, sir.'

There was a gloomy silence. The older one sighed, annoyed.

'Mr Taylor,' started the younger one, looking at me with a newfound intensity, 'is there anyone else you can think of who might be able to assist you?'

I wanted to sit down badly. I just needed to try to absorb what was happening. I was no longer sure that my legs were capable of holding my weight. I looked up at Caitlin's window. Her curtains, with their cheerful, graphic print, were drawn tight. I would find a way out of this that didn't involve waking her.

'Look,' I said, trying to sound reasonable, 'is there any way we can work this out differently? I really don't think that it's necessary that we—'

'Sir, I don't think you understand,' said the younger officer impatiently. 'You can either come down to the station voluntarily to assist us with our inquiries or we can place you under arrest. Now which is it to be?'

'I'll come down to the station,' I mumbled quickly.

'Then we need to work out what we're going to do with your daughter, and quickly.'

'I'll make a call,' I said. I stepped through the patio doors into the living room. I couldn't quite believe I was thinking of trivial domestic matters, but I found myself hoping that the cops' boots weren't too dirty. I didn't want them to stain the carpet. Yossi would be annoyed and Amanda wouldn't give me my security deposit back.

I needed someone I could rely on. I didn't want to bother Mike. The bloke had enough on his plate, and I was fairly certain that his wife wouldn't appreciate a late-night trouble-with-the-law call.

I started to dial Amanda. I'd explain everything and she'd be sure to help.

I pressed the 'end call' button on the phone and placed it back in the cradle. This wasn't the way to introduce Caitlin as my daughter.

'I just remembered,' I said to the police officers by way of explanation. 'She's away on holiday. Canaries.'

'Nice,' said the older policeman.

I phoned Mel.

'Hello?'

Jesus, it was Kenny.

'Hi, Kenny,' I said. 'Is Mel there please?'

Silence.

'Hello?' It was Mel.

'Mel, it's me,' I said. 'Look, I've got a favour to ask you. It's a long story, but is there any chance I could drop Caitlin off at your house? It would probably be for the night, so I'd need you to make sure she gets to school tomorrow morning, if that's all right.'

'Um, sure, sure,' said Mel. Her words were slightly slurred with sleep. 'What's going on? Are you all right?'

I looked at the policemen waiting solemnly in my living room.

'I really have no idea,' I said eventually.

Then I went upstairs, woke my daughter up, got her into the

262

back of the squad car and took her to Mel's before being taken to the police station.

I thought that I had reached rock bottom. Sadly, I turned out to be wrong.

Chapter 27

The streets were slick with rain when I came out of the police station. Having neither a coat nor an umbrella I dashed to the taxi rank in the town centre, holding an *Evening Standard* above my head. I just wanted to collect Caitlin from Mel's and pretend that the evening had never happened.

The paper grew soggy, so I chucked it in a bin and left myself at the mercy of the elements. After a while I began to enjoy the rain. It felt good on my face, reviving me after the stuffy, overheated rooms of the police station.

After considerable toing and froing I had been released with a caution. I got the feeling that the cops had just got fed up with the whole business – a storm in a teacup that didn't help the way their crime statistics looked to those upstairs.

If Belagio was going to retaliate he would have to do it through the civil courts. Off the record, the cops had told me it was unlikely that anything would happen beyond this point – Belagio would find it impossible to prove on the 'balance of probabilities' that it had been me. I had a motive, of course, but the police weren't to know that and I intended to keep it that way.

There were no cabs in the centre of town. I pulled out my mobile and dialled Mel, hoping she might give me a lift, but she wasn't picking up. I didn't have her home number on me. I would walk. It would do me some good, clear my head and stretch my back after hours spent hunched in a moulded plastic chair suffering cups of powdery vending-machine coffee (I wanted to recommend that they came and sampled my espresso at the Bean & Gone).

I arrived on Mel's doorstep and registered the utter silence of the street. I wondered whether it might be better if I left Caitlin there for the night. Maybe so, but I was anxious to get her back. She had last seen me being driven away in a police car. This was not how I wanted her to think of her father.

I rang the doorbell. I wanted to press it again – to rouse the house and get my daughter back – but I waited until a light went on upstairs. A couple of minutes later Mel opened the door.

'Hi, Alex,' she said. Her face was puffy with sleep. Maybe I should have waited till the morning after all; I should have let Caitlin sleep through.

'When did you get out?' Mel asked.

'Not too long ago,' I said, shifting my feet. I wondered why she didn't step aside and allow me into the house. I supposed that she was half asleep.

'So, did you get the message?' she asked.

I pulled my mobile out of my pocket. 'Sometimes this thing can be slow,' I said, examining it.

'Maybe they didn't tell you,' said Mel quietly, almost to her-self. 'The woman said that the police had told her where Caitlin was. They said they'd tell you.'

'Who'd tell me?' I asked. I was smiling at her, still slightly giddy after escaping the stifling grind of the police station. Jesus, was I happy to be out of there. The prospect of being reunited with Caitlin made me feel buoyant. For the first time in hours my stomach had unclenched.

Mel sighed, aggravated. 'I just, you know, it's surprising that ...' she blurted. She closed her eyes momentarily to com-pose herself.

'Hang on,' I said. 'Hang on.' I wiped a film of sweaty rain from my upper lip. 'Say that again.'

Mel sighed again.

'Where's Caitlin?' I demanded.

'She's ... She's ...' Mel fumbled. 'Look, do you want to come in?'

'No,' I said impatiently. 'I don't want to come in.'

'I thought they would have told you,' she said. She ran her hand through her hair where it was matted from resting on a pillow. 'She's not here, Alex. A woman took her.'

'Shit!' I shouted, my voice cutting right through the still, silent night. A couple of lights went on up the street. Curtains were lifted to see what was unfolding outside number 342.

I crouched down, holding my head in my hands. It was as if I wanted to be as close to the earth as I could be. Things were less likely to hurt me that way. I was a smaller target.

'Alex,' said Mel quietly, 'I really think you should come inside. We can sort it out, have a cup of tea, warm up.'

'I don't want a fucking cup of tea,' I said moodily.

'The lady gave me this,' Mel said, handing me a scrap of paper. 'Her name was Joan something.'

'Kennedy,' I said impatiently. 'I know who she is.'

'But I thought you said you ...'

I was hunched on the floor, rocking on the balls of my feet.

'I can't explain right now,' I said, springing to my feet. I inhaled deeply, pulling damp air inside myself. 'Okay, I need to ... I need to call. I need to sort it out.'

I paced up and down Mel's garden path, my wet trainers squelching on the concrete. I walked out into the street, watched by several weary but inquisitive residents of Acacia Avenue. I used a street light to read the number written on the scrap of paper that Mel had given me. I angrily punched the digits into my mobile. Mel watched as I had a brief conversation. I snapped the phone shut. I looked over at Mel, who was still standing on the chilly doorstep, her dressing gown pulled tightly about her.

I could tell that she was eager to know how it had gone.

She would have known the answer to that question when she saw me hurl the mobile down the street with all my might. The device broke into several pieces, which rattled across the glistening Tarmac in the hushed night.

Chapter 28

A little over three months after I had first met my daughter curled up in a care-centre bedroom I walked into the same room to find her sitting in the same chair.

Outwardly, it was as if nothing had changed. Caitlin's body language – her legs tucked under her, the tilt of her torso away from me – was the same impassive form that had stirred my heart that first time. Now it was happening all over again.

'Hi,' I said quietly. Caitlin glanced over at me but didn't hold my gaze. I was aware how I must look to her: unkempt, un-shaven and with dark circles under my eyes. I made to embrace her, holding her impassive body against mine, her shoulders rising into a shrug as I squeezed her.

'Hi,' she said eventually. I cupped my hand on her cheek and noticed a redness to her eyes that matched my own.

'I am so sorry about this,' I said. 'I am so, so sorry.'

I watched as she took a deep breath.

'Are they going to let me come home?' she asked.

Home. Just hearing her say the word distressed me.

There was nothing that I wanted more than to be able to answer this question in the affirmative. Nothing. However, after just a brief conversation with Joan Kennedy before com-ing upstairs to see Caitlin it was clear that the situation was grave. After months of my failing to offer Joan tangible evidence of Amanda's presence it was hard to imagine that I would be able to persuade her of anything unless I could get Amanda to cooperate.

'I'm going to talk to Joan now,' I said, injecting my voice with confidence. This wasn't enough for Caitlin.

'What *happened*?' Her tone was exasperated, but also angry.

'It was just, you know, a misunderstanding,' I said. 'The police were just going through the motions.'

'But they took you away.'

Her eyes were full of tears, but she didn't cry. I was her sole protector, all that she had left, and I had failed her.

'When can I get out of here?'

There was a pause, during which I released a small, exasperated gasp. I wanted to correct this unholy shift in the world's axis. I wanted to tell her what she wanted to hear.

But I didn't. As much as I wanted to be Dad again I just couldn't tell another lie.

'I don't know,' I said, squatting next to her and putting my hand on her shoulder. 'I'm sorry, but I don't know.'

Caitlin bit her bottom lip before shaking off the sadness and straightening herself.

'Caitlin,' I said, focusing everything I had on the girl. 'I will get you out of here. This is your dad talking. They can't do this to us, okay? I will get you out.'

I meant it, of course. I would do everything in my power to help her. But, as I walked home through the dank night, I was ashamed that I could let Caitlin down in this way. I prayed that I wasn't just another in a growing pile of disappointments for her, although I suspected that might already be the case.

Chapter 29

'Come in, come in,' said Joan Kennedy, ushering me into her office.

Her desk, which had seen better days, was covered in wire baskets containing manila files with names printed on them. I wondered whereabouts Caitlin's dossier was on her priority list. Kennedy gestured to an easy chair. I sat down and realised that, if I sat back, my nose would be at the same level as the desk. I moved forward and perched on the front edge of the chair. I found the situation – my legs were pressed tightly together in order to maintain my position – oddly feminine.

'So …' said Kennedy, breezily. She took a sip of what looked like tea from a mug that had a Windsor Castle logo on it. 'Do you want to tell me what happened last night?'

I nodded. 'Absolutely,' I said. I wasn't sure how to present myself: should I be contrite and apologetic, or should I be blasé, as if the whole situation was clearly a terrible (but easily rectified) misunderstanding? I decided to try the latter.

'Well,' I said with a shake of my head, 'I'm still trying to process it myself.'

Kennedy took another sip of tea and stared at me through her wire-rimmed glasses. Clearly she was not interested by my commentary. I repositioned myself on the chair, sickness flowering in my stomach.

'It was all a misunderstanding,' I said, a little defensively. 'Honestly. You can call the police and ask them. I haven't been charged.'

'I know,' said Kennedy. 'But Child Protection has to get involved when any child in whom we have an interest finds themselves in a position where their legal guardian fails to live up to the agreement we have with them.'

Her use of the word 'fails' reverberated around the room. Another small pebble lodged itself in my gut. It sounded legal, harsh, absolute. It sounded like something that I would not recover from. I thought back to Caitlin in her lonely room in the foster home. I had promised to get her out. I would be true to my word, but it was time that I started to tell the truth. Starting with Kennedy.

'I was teaching Caitlin to play golf,' I told her.

'What time was this?' asked Kennedy. She traced a small arc across the table with her finger.

'Probably about nine o'clock.'

'That seems late for a golf lesson.'

Don't say anything, I thought. There's trouble here. I shifted my position on the chair.

'What was it like outside?'

'Well, you know, it's November.'

'That's what I mean,' said Kennedy, widening her eyes slightly. 'I imagine that it was cold and damp. And dark.'

'She had her coat on,' I said defensively. I didn't want to engage with the woman, but it was clear that stonewalling would not get me anywhere.

'So what happened when she was outside with her coat on?'

'We were just messing about,' I said, exasperated. 'It was just a father and daughter having some fun.'

'Having some fun by making a nuisance of themselves—'

'I don't think it's fair to characterise it in that way,' I interrupted. 'Anyway, there's no evidence to suggest that anything occurred in the way that Mr Belagio is alleging.'

'Well, there is evidence,' said Kennedy. 'There are broken windows.'

'But there's no proof that I had anything to do with that,' I said. My toes curled with annoyance – did she think she was in an episode of *The Bill*? 'Anyway, what has that got to do with Caitlin? I'd like it if we could focus on her welfare.'

'Oh,' said Kennedy ominously, 'we're on the same page there. I have nothing but Caitlin's welfare in mind.'

I nodded, attempting to mollify her.

'I feel that there are major question marks over your future as Caitlin's guardian,' said Kennedy.

'What are you talking about?' I said, my brow knitted together darkly. 'I'm her father not her guardian.'

'When Caitlin was first put into your care we had an agreement that, because of her vulnerable situation, she would enter a stable family environment,' Kennedy said.

'Absolutely,' I agreed.

'But Alex,' Kennedy continued, 'despite my best efforts I have yet to meet your wife.'

'I'm sorry,' I said, my anxiety building. Maybe apologising, showing how very, very sorry I was might work with Kennedy. I was prepared to be as sorry as I needed to be. I was prepared to grovel. I would kiss her feet if it would help. 'I really don't know how that happened. Amanda travels a lot for work.'

'I understand,' Kennedy said reproachfully. 'People are busy, but what we're doing has to take precedence over everything else.'

'Yes, yes,' I said. 'I totally agree.'

Kennedy pulled a file from the pile and opened it. She made a note in the margin of a piece of paper. I couldn't wait any longer.

'So when can I take her home?' I smiled slightly as if we had reached an accord.

Kennedy leaned back in her chair and performed some kind of back stretch.

'I really don't know,' she said, closing the folder. 'I'm sorry to tell you that, but I really don't know. I have to recommend whatever I feel is in Caitlin's best interests.'

'Her best interests are served by being returned home,' I said firmly.

'Here's where we are, Alex,' Kennedy said. 'The events of last night mean that your case is under review. Because of this it's very hard for me to give you any kind of timeframe.'

'So what are you saying?' I demanded with a small, nervous laugh.

'I'm sorry to say that Caitlin won't be going home with you today,' said Kennedy firmly. 'A guardian under arrest—'

'I wasn't under arrest and I'm not her guardian,' I said.

'Okay,' said Kennedy a little impatiently. 'But you were asked to go in for questioning and when that happens the police are obliged to inform us as soon as your name pops up in their system. That means that your case is under review. It's the way it works, Alex.'

I reached up and held my head in my hands.

'I understand that this is difficult for you to hear,' Kennedy said, 'but we have procedures to follow. I'm sure that you appreciate that ...' She continued to talk for a while but I wasn't listening any longer. All I could think about was Caitlin alone in her room. I had made her a solemn promise, and I had failed her twice. I had been absent when she was an infant and now, as she was on the verge of womanhood, I had proved myself a brutal letdown. I couldn't help wondering if she might just be better off without me.

Chapter 30

I left Joan Kennedy's office and wandered the streets aimlessly. There was nowhere I wanted to be. Although I was in no state to go to work, I couldn't face the silence that would greet me at home. So I just walked through town and zigzagged my way through roads that I'd never trodden before I wasted a half-hour in the Carphone Warehouse sorting out a new phone, seeing as my old one was in bits on Mel's street. Moments after leaving the shop I got my first call. I looked at the caller ID. It was Mel. I wondered if she'd opened up the shop.

'Hi, Mel.'

'Hi,' the voice was small, clipped. 'Where are you?'

'I'm on my way,' I lied. 'I'll be there in a while. How's it going?'

'It's fine, it's fine,' Mel replied. 'Nothing to report really.'

So, if there was nothing to report, why was she calling?

'Look, Alex,' she said with a sigh, 'I was going to wait until you came in, but ...'

'All right ...'

'It's just that I've been thinking a lot about things and obviously I've got Ollie to think about and—'

'What are you telling me?' I interrupted her. First the arrest, then Caitlin being taken away, now this – if it played out the way it sounded – parting of the ways.

'I've been offered another job,' said Mel.

'Oh, I see,' I said.

Of course.

'I'm sorry, Alex.'

I was so mentally overloaded I could barely absorb what she was saying.

'I ... er ... where?'

'Java Jamboree.'

'*Java Jamboree?*'

'Yes.'

This was treachery of the highest order. I sat down on the edge of the kerb.

'What? Did they find you at the Bean & Gone?'

'No, no,' she said. 'Nothing like that.'

'I don't understand,' I said. 'Did you apply for a job there?'

'No,' said Mel, her voice becoming quieter.

'Well, how did it come about then?'

'Does it matter?'

'Actually, it does to me,' I said urgently.

'It was Kenny,' said Mel quickly, as if she was taking little responsibility for it herself.

'Kenny?'

'Yes,' she said. 'He started going there after you two fell out. I suppose I told him that I was worried about the way things were going. There didn't seem to be enough customers. I must have said something to him. He got talking to the manager at Java Jamboree one day and he called me because there was a job going and ...'

I closed my eyes.

'I'm sorry, Alex,' Mel said. 'I really am. You know that it isn't personal.'

I covered the mouthpiece. *Not personal.* What the fuck did she think I had at stake with a new business and inheriting a daughter?

'I think today should be your last day.'

'Okay,' replied Mel despondently.

'Do me a favour,' I said. 'After you finish, close the place up and put your keys through the letterbox.'

'Of course,' said Mel, regaining her composure before adding, 'if that's what you want.'

I didn't tell her, but it was only a tiny part of what I wanted. Finally, after months of stumbling and confusion, I was clear about what I had chosen. My desires were simple and tangible. After walking around in a fog for months I was now close enough to Caitlin to know that what we shared was permanent, powerful and irrevocable. But, just as I had struggled to reconcile myself to my daughter, I had come to realise that, despite what had happened between Amanda and Belagio, I really didn't want to be with anyone else.

My wife had apologised, sworn that it was a one-off and pleaded with me not to leave. And what had I done? I'd seen Caitlin as a way of not only exploring a new, intoxicating life, but also punishing Amanda. Fair enough, she probably deserved it, but I was now in the position where I was cutting off my nose to spite my face. She had come to tell me about Caitlin and the rats and, to my surprise, kept the matter between the two of us. More than that, I could tell that she wanted to make things right between us – and not just because she came round the house yesterday and made love to me. I'd sort of known it when she'd come to the house with Yossi and thought that I had a woman upstairs. The kind of rage she went into was the kind that only a lover might be overcome by. It was clear to me now – finally! – that I was meant to be with Caitlin and Amanda. If only I had the capacity to make it happen.

The café remained closed the following day. I was in no state to work. I hadn't slept or eaten for two days. My mind lurched from one dire scenario to another. I sat and looked at my mobile, which I placed on the kitchen table in the exact spot where

Caitlin ate her cereal in the morning. Occasionally I would pick it up and examine the device for signs of a missed message. Maybe Joan Kennedy had called with good news and I'd just not heard the phone ring? Maybe there was something wrong with the ringer? Maybe there was a problem with the network? And I'd not heard from Amanda following our, um, reunion, which seemed strange to me.

I picked the mobile up and shook it – maybe I could dislodge the good news. I even dialled Joan's number before quickly turning the phone off. I had already left her two messages to ask what was happening. Any more and she'd think I was a crank.

I had been told that I would be allowed to see Caitlin that afternoon, after she had finished school. Joan had warned me that any contact other than this was unacceptable and would result in severe but unspecified punishments. So I sat at home and waited through the gloomy morning and the prematurely dark afternoon until I was allowed to visit my daughter, who sat in her chair, feet placed wide apart, her knees pressed together, staring at me with a mixture of fear and resentment.

'I'm going to get you out of here,' I said, horribly unsure as to how I might deliver on this bold promise.

'Really?' she said flatly. And the fact that it was a question, that her words were rooted in disbelief, made me go cold. I was her father: If I wasn't able to do this then, well, what the hell kind of person was I?

'Yes,' I said, boldly. I wanted her to believe in me. 'Really.'

Amanda had barely opened the front door before her features hardened.

'What's the matter?' she asked before I had had a chance to open my mouth.

'Can I come in?' I asked.

She nodded and stepped back from the doorway.

'You look terrible,' Amanda said.

I nodded. Couldn't argue with that. I could feel the tension – a dull rigidity – in my face. I tried to shake it out. I didn't want my decision-making to overwhelm my mood. I needed to be clear about what I was trying to do. There must be no mistakes.

'You want a tea or coffee or something?'

I could tell that my unannounced appearance had her rattled. Strange. This wasn't like Amanda.

'I need to talk to you,' I said.

'That sounds ominous.' She laughed hollowly. 'Look, if it's about the other day, we don't need to talk, if that's what you'd prefer. Shall I put the kettle on?'

As much as I had no interest in having a cup of tea or coffee I told her to go ahead. It was the way that things were done.

She went into the kitchen and started rummaging around in the cupboards, pulling out mugs and teabags. I wandered around the living room, examining the ornaments and photos as though they were foreign to me. Moments later Amanda was walking into the room with a tray stacked with drinks and biscuits when her mobile rang.

'Who the feck is that?' she said rhetorically. She put down the tray on the coffee table and pulled her phone out of her handbag, checking the number.

'Oh, I have to take this . . .' she said and walked back into the kitchen. Although she had retreated a discreet distance, I heard her say: 'Hello, Nick.' It was unmistakable.

And it wasn't any old 'Hello, Nick'. There was a flirty tone to her voice, a musicality to it that told me only one thing: she was fucking whoever was on the other end of the line. I listened as she kept her voice lowered, the register undulating warmly. I looked at the tray of tea and biscuits. What the hell was I doing here asking my estranged wife to pretend to Social Services that

278

she would provide maternal guidance to a girl who she had no idea was my daughter?

No, this wouldn't do, despite our recent tumble. I opened a packet of digestives, pulled one out and stood up. Amanda was lost in conversation in the kitchen. I heard a torrent of laughter for a moment and then I closed the front door behind me.

It was cold outside. I turned my collar up and started walking. I saw Amanda's number come up on my mobile, but she didn't leave a message. I headed across town and stood in a suburban street that looked just dissimilar enough from the other streets for its residents not to worry that there might be a bar code installed beneath their skin. I skulked in the shadows, aware that the last thing I needed was further acquaintance with the Surrey Constabulary. From a vantage point next to a laurel bush I spied the house where my daughter was, to my mind, being held captive. Her bedroom light was on. She would, of course, be reading. She had a taste for elaborate fantasies, stories set in eccentric, magical kingdoms where children found themselves challenged to accomplish seemingly impossible tasks.

I hoped that she was buried in one of these whimsical worlds rather than fretting over the fearsome one in which she now found herself. Her situation was entirely my fault: had I managed to maintain a successful relationship with Cathy then she would not have been raised by a single parent. Had I been a better father then she would not have found herself returned to the state for her own wellbeing. Had I not been a moron I wouldn't be in this position.

Her light went off and I was overcome with an urge to wish her goodnight. I picked up a pebble and tossed it gently up at the glass. The stone arced upwards before peeling off in the wrong direction and hitting the window frame. I searched for another missile, eventually settling on something heavier. I had cocked my arm backwards and was just about to let it fly when I heard a sudden, creaking noise. To my ears it might as well have been the creaking of a coffin lid: terrified that I had been spotted, I disappeared back into a laurel bush.

'Dad!' the voice was whispering, but there was a force to it that caused me to freeze.

'Caitlin?' I said her name even before I had looked up. Her face was wedged in between the window and its frame. There were probably bureaucratic reasons – health and safety – why she wasn't able to open it fully.

'What are you doing here?'

I actually didn't know how to answer this. Hanging around hoping to catch a glimpse of you? Moping around feeling like the world's most disastrous adult? Thinking of burgling that posh house over the way? None of them seemed adequate, so I decided to go for an option that Caitlin, as a teenager, might herself employ.

'I don't know.'

'Oh.'

I stood there staring at her. 'Are you okay?' I asked.

'I can't really sleep,' she replied.

I offered a small smile of recognition. 'Me neither.'

The biting wind picked up. I was worried about her standing at an open window with just her pyjamas on.

'You should get inside,' I said. 'It's freezing.'

Caitlin didn't move. 'You should go, Dad,' she said. 'You'll get in trouble if they see you.'

I wanted to shrug it off, like it was no big deal that I was skulking late at night outside the house where my daughter was living. But, maddeningly, she was right. There would indeed be 'trouble' if I was discovered. There would be further questions regarding my fitness to parent, additional disquieting scepticism from Joan Kennedy, who loomed in my mind with unhealthy frequency.

'You're right, kiddo,' I said. 'I should have thought of that. You go back inside now. You're going to catch your death.'

She gave me a thumbs-up, which I returned, thankful that she didn't ask me when I was going to get her out of there.

'Night, Dad.'

'Night.'

'Don't let the bedbugs bite.'

'You neither.'

And then – magically! – she blew me a kiss and closed the window and, I hoped, found her way to a deep, peaceful sleep.

I rose early the next morning, having long since abandoned the notion that I might sleep. I needed to open the café. Another day without a cheery sign explaining that I was either on holiday or redecorating would surely be calamitous for the business. I showered, drank a glass of water (again I had no appetite) and walked to the store. I needed some air. The roads were busy with mums ferrying their precious offspring to school. From the way that some of the kids looked at me it seemed that they could no sooner understand why someone would voluntarily walk somewhere than they could grasp the mechanics of their parents' mammoth vehicles.

I arrived at the café and reached in my pocket . . .

Jesus Christ. I had forgotten the keys. I was so used to Mel opening up that I had totally forgotten to bring my own set. I looked through the glass door and there, exasperatingly close, were the keys that Mel had put through the letterbox.

I sat down on the step. It was okay, I told myself. Everything was fine. I would go home and pick up the other set and—

Shit. Fuck. Bollocks. How could I have been so *idiotic*? Was I incapable of even remembering simple details any longer?

I rested my head on my knees for a moment. I needed to gather my thoughts. Sitting there like a drunk, I heard a car stop at the kerb. I looked up and saw Amanda idling in her 3-Series.

'What are you doing?' she asked.

'I can't get in,' I said. 'I forgot my keys.'

'It's going to rain again, Alex,' Amanda said.

This news seemed utterly irrelevant. I sat on the step glumly.

'I need to talk to you,' I said eventually. I looked at my wife. I didn't want there to be any artifice in what followed. Amanda switched off the engine, opened the car door and folded herself out of the vehicle. She closed the door and – seemingly reflexively – locked it. I saw her coming towards me and then, suddenly, stumble. She threw her arms out to steady herself.

'Shit,' said Amanda, regaining her balance.

'Shit,' I agreed, emerging from my haze of self-commiseration.

'Bloody heel snapped,' she revealed, removing one shoe and examining the sole of it. 'I lost my mobile yesterday as well. I'm sure I had it in the office when I was with Caitlin, but I went back and it wasn't there. I suppose it'll turn up.'

She stood, lop-sided for a moment, before realising that this was not practical. She bent down, lifted her leg and removed her remaining shoe.

I reached up and touched my head. There was a layer of moisture on my hair. I realised that it was already raining ever so slightly. I stood and, to my surprise, wondered whether it was true that cows lay down before it rained. Why was I so damned distracted?

'So what happened last night?' Amanda asked.

'I just ...' I fumbled. 'I just had to go.'

'Hmmm. I'm not sure I believe that.'

Amanda stuck her hand out. 'It's starting to rain,' she said.

I nodded. *Ask her if she'll see Social Services*, I thought to myself.

'Amanda ...'

Do it.

'I just wanted ...'

Tell her that you miss her.

The rain began to fall with a hiss. There was no escalation. It just arrived, as if someone had turned a tap on to full strength. Neither of us moved. I could see the water gathering on my wife's face.

'Are you trying to tell me something?' Amanda said eventually. Her eyelids flickered from the raindrops falling on her lashes.

'Yes, I am,' I said, wiping the wetness from my forehead. 'I have a daughter.'

The rain continued to fall on us. Amanda wiped a drop that had gathered at the end of her nose.

'Caitlin,' she said.

I nodded.

She turned and walked back to her car, her tights turning darker where she was walking on the rain-soaked pavement.

There. It was done. I had no more secrets, nothing left to hide. I left Amanda to her own thoughts as I headed towards the high street, my hair matted to my forehead.

I had no idea that I'd see my daughter ten minutes later, lying in the street, her eyes firmly shut.

Chapter 31

Breathless and panicked I rushed into the hospital. My chest heaved just to supply me with the oxygen to keep myself functioning. My limbs felt slow and indolent; it was as if my body was in shock and had begun to shut down. I had not been allowed to travel in the ambulance with Caitlin, so I'd had to run home to get the car.

A harried woman at reception, who appeared to be on three unrelated phone calls as well as having several different folders of paperwork tucked under her arm, pointed me to the A&E where I was unable to find anyone who could offer me immediate assistance. I was told that they would be with me 'in a minute' by three different members of staff. Unwilling to wait a minute, I walked into the treatment area, peering between curtains and interrupting consultations to try to glean information as to Caitlin's whereabouts.

'Caitlin Meades?' I asked randomly, wishing that I had had the foresight to instruct Mr Singh to change Caitlin's name, with the girl's blessing, to my own. I received only blank stares and the shaking of heads despite my increasingly agitated questioning. Eventually I located a nurse who actually engaged with me.

'The girl?' she asked. 'Road accident?' She guided me back to a desk and looked at a chart. 'She's under the care of Dr Koya. You need to go to the ICU.'

'ICU?'

'The Intensive Care Unit.'

I had heard the expression that people's 'knees buckled', but

I had never experienced it until then. I really tried not to collapse as I processed the information, reaching out and steadying myself on the desk.

'She's under observation,' the nurse added. 'Do you need anything?'

I had no idea how to answer that question. An honest reply would not be helpful.

'Second floor,' said the nurse. 'The lifts are at the end of the corridor. I'll call them to let them know that you're coming.'

I ran up the corridor with a dark buzzing in my head. It was as if everything had narrowed to one thought: *Please let her be okay*. Later I'd be unable to recall any of the trips I had made between A&E and the ICU. My world had contracted to a single desire, and I would trade anything – anything at all – for it to become real.

I arrived at the desk. There was an atmosphere of calm in this part of the hospital, an intensity that suggested deliberation, that important matters were being determined at that very moment. A nurse paged the doctor, who came striding towards me purposefully moments later. I was struck by how young she looked, another reminder for me of how, while I'd been in the pub, other people were getting on with their lives.

'Mr ... ?' she asked.

'Taylor,' I replied. 'How is she?'

'Taylor?' she said, confused.

'Sorry,' I explained. 'She's my daughter; we just don't have the same surname.'

'I see. Let's take a seat, shall we?' Her features were fine, almost feline, and her hands thin and willowy. I couldn't believe that this was the person who was going to tell me that my daughter was ...

'Caitlin was involved in a collision with a motor vehicle this afternoon,' she started. She was confident, had done this kind of thing before. I concentrated on preventing myself from blurting out the only question that I cared about: *Is she going to be all right?*

'She was brought here, where we examined her. The good news is that there are no signs of any major trauma injuries that we would associate with this kind of incident: there are no broken bones and no internal injuries of any kind ...'

'Thank God ...' I said. I wiped a tear that had formed in the corner of my eye. The doctor paused and her tone changed. She continued to speak carefully, but the clarity of her initial words was lacking.

'However, we've brought her here because we're concerned that she might have sustained an injury to her head.'

I moved my hand to my stomach reflexively. It contracted into a tiny ball.

'She has not regained consciousness since the accident. We are monitoring her and waiting for results of tests.' She looked at her watch. 'They should be here within the hour. Once we've got those we'll have a clearer understanding of the prognosis.'

'Oh, God ...' I said. 'What, you know ...? How ...?' I couldn't think clearly enough to ask an appropriate question.

'It's too early to tell,' replied the doctor. 'I understand how difficult this is for you but we just have to wait.'

At that moment the nurse's phone rang and she beckoned the doctor over. I wondered if it might be Caitlin's test results. The doctor glanced over at me and I assumed that this was the case. She replaced the phone and muttered something to the nurse before returning to talk to me. This time she didn't sit down.

'This is a little tricky ...' she said, exhaling. 'I've just had a call from Social Services. Apparently Caitlin is in foster care, meaning that I have to clear it with the appropriate agencies before you can see her.' She paused, clearly not comfortable with delivering this kind of news.

'But I'm her father. I …' I couldn't find any words. I stopped trying to speak and lay back on the benches where we'd been talking.

'I'm really sorry about this,' said the doctor. 'I will, of course, keep you informed and will recommend to Social Services that you are allowed to see her as soon as possible.'

I held onto a chair leg just to have contact with something tangible, something that wasn't melting at my touch, but as hard as I gripped it my world continued to fade to black.

I was given a cup of sour tea and told to wait. I paced the reception area, agitated and desperate to be with Caitlin. I felt utterly ineffectual. At one point I began to sneak looks up the corridor that lead to the rooms, only to be politely reminded by an Eastern European security guard that I wasn't allowed access to that area.

I then sat with my arms wrapped around myself wishing that time would pass, hating that I had made such a mess of everything. I heard footsteps coming along the corridor from the main building and, hoping that it was Dr Koya, stood up. I was frustrated to see that the shuffling feet belonged to Joan Kennedy, who was sipping from a Costa Coffee cup. I was thrilled to know that she'd had time to go and pick up a delicious beverage on her way to the hospital. She acknowledged me, but first went to see the receptionist with whom she had a whispered conversation.

I would have been willing to chew off one of my fingers if she had allowed me to see Caitlin.

'Alex,' said Joan, hitching her bag up on her shoulder. I noticed that the upper reaches of her coat were flecked with dandruff. 'I'm very sorry to meet you here under these circumstances.'

I wanted to remain calm, to prove what fine parent material

I was, but the anger rose in my gut and I couldn't help jabbing a finger in her face.

'Nice job of taking care of her,' I said.

She looked at me severely and started to unbutton her coat.

'She was in your care when this occurred,' I said. 'Not mine.'

Kennedy folded her coat and put it on one of the chairs.

'I understand that emotions are running high,' she said. 'And there will be a full investigation as to how something as awful as this happened, but there's nothing to be gained by recrimination.'

I realised that I was still holding my finger up.

'I think today should be about ensuring the best possible care for Caitlin,' Kennedy continued.

'You're unbelievable!' I said in a louder voice than I intended. 'Unbelievable. You phone the hospital to give them instructions that I can't see her and then talk about getting Caitlin the best possible care? Do you understand, even for a minute, how absurd that sounds? I'm her father, for Christ's sake. I'm not Fred West or Denis Nielsen, or Ronald fucking McDonald for that matter. I'm the flesh and blood of a girl who's lying through there with God knows what wrong with her, and you're playing games?'

'It's not games,' said Kennedy. 'It's procedure. And while I understand why you're frustrated you have to understand that these rules have been put in place for very good reasons.'

I rolled my eyes. This was lunacy.

'Do you really think I care about that?' I asked her.

Joan took a sip of coffee.

I peeled away from her, walking in a small circle and went to kick a chair leg, restraining myself at the last minute.

'I've put a call in to my boss,' Kennedy said coolly. 'It's likely that, because of the exceptional circumstances, we'll be able to get you in to see Caitlin. You'll just have to wait until I hear back.'

'Great,' I said. I realised that I had laced my fingers together and placed them on the top of my head. At the moment, the only thing that was keeping me calm was moving around. 'That's just fucking awesome.'

Joan sat down and checked her mobile while I continued to pace. The security guard eyed me cautiously and moved nearer the entrance to the ward, as if worried that I might bolt up the corridor.

'You know,' Joan said, 'we really wouldn't be in this position if there hadn't been so much confusion at our meetings over the past few months.'

What the fuck was she talking about?

'Confusion?' I said, an incredulous stare on my face.

'Well, if we'd managed to meet your wife and confirm that Caitlin was being placed in a stable family environment then life would have been easier for all of us.'

'Oh, that's exactly what I was thinking about,' I said. 'Making your life easier. It's my top priority from morning to night.'

'There's no need to be facetious,' said Joan. 'Where is your wife today, as a matter of fact? Is she on a business trip?'

I ignored the question, wheeling around the room again. I had absolutely no idea why Joan should want to pour scorn on me in this way. The situation was intractable. How on earth was I going to persuade her that Caitlin and I were playing happy families with Amanda when there was no sign of my wife on an occasion as grave as this?

I calmed a little and considered how I might manage the situation better. Eventually I sat down near Joan, who was making a show of leaving a message for her boss explaining the situation. I ran through worst-case scenarios for Caitlin, and had begun planning a life of caring for a daughter with a traumatic brain injury when I heard a familiar noise coming from the corridor.

There was only one person whose heels clicked in that way, only one person whose hair and nails and clothes resonated in that manner. I saw her, still bedraggled from the rain, but wearing shoes now. She must have gone home and picked up a pair before collecting her car and coming directly to the hospital.

'Hello, Alex,' she said, enveloping me in hair and perfume. She hugged me close, our hip bones touching. 'How is she?'

I was so shocked to see her that I didn't answer the question. I gestured to Joan with an upturned palm.

'This is Joan,' I explained, realising immediately that I should have explained Joan's role.

'Amanda,' said Amanda boldly, reaching towards Kennedy. The social worker remained seated, offering up a dry, small hand.

'Oh,' she said, with an arched eyebrow.

'I'm Alex's wife,' Amanda said.

And while I had very little but trouble on my mind, at that moment it was a wonderful thing to hear. Now I knew how a dehydrated man crawling through the desert felt like when he saw a beer truck coming over the horizon.

Chapter 32

Dr Koya led us down a linoleum corridor that had been buffed so intensely that the ceiling lights glimmered on its surface. Amanda took my hand. I could feel the metal from two rings – one for our engagement, one a wedding ring. They were the only pieces of jewellery that I had ever bought.

We were shown into a large room. There was a bathroom on the left, a seating area, a window looking over the park next to the hospital. In the middle was an institutional bed, surrounded by machinery that made me literally gasp. And there she was, one side of her face red and scratched, her hair pulled back severely and tape where a saline drip was inserted in her arm.

'There's good news,' Dr Koya announced. 'The CAT scans and other tests we've done have revealed that there's no damage to the cerebral cortex. She has suffered a fairly severe concussion, and is probably in shock, but we're confident that there are no causes for concern even in the short term.'

'Thank you, Doctor, thank you, thank you,' I said. 'That's ... That's just wonderful to hear.'

The doctor nodded. Amanda squeezed my hand so tightly I thought something might snap.

'She's beautiful,' Koya said, before returning to her professional self. 'We'll want to keep her under observation for a few days, so we'll have to see how long it is before you can take her home.'

She paused for a moment and looked down at her notes. I offered her a half smile, acknowledging the honest mistake.

'I'm sorry,' Koya said.

'No apology needed,' I said, waving her off. I reached out and touched Caitlin's uninjured cheek with the back of my hand and saw her eye flicker.

'I'll be back in a few minutes,' Koya said. 'If you need anything press the button over there and a nurse will come.'

'Thank you,' I replied, distracted: I was sure that I had seen Caitlin's eyes flicker. A moment later her lids opened slightly.

'It's all right, sweetheart,' I said. 'Dad's here. You're absolutely fine.'

I looked for recognition in her eyes, but Caitlin wasn't registering anything yet. It was as if she was still submerged in sleep.

'You're all right, darling,' said Amanda, sweetly. 'You're in a hospital, but you're all right.'

Caitlin suddenly took a deep breath and sat up slightly, as if she had just arrived from somewhere else. She looked at both of us before settling back on her pillows.

'Hello, miss,' I said.

Caitlin swallowed and took several shallow breaths. I offered her a glass of water and she took a sip. She seemed to be fully conscious now.

'Am I in trouble?' she asked.

Taken aback, I looked to Amanda for interpretation.

'In trouble for what?' I asked.

Caitlin was silent for a moment. I wondered whether she'd heard me.

'For what, sweetheart?' I repeated.

'For, you know …'

'No,' I said quickly. 'You're not in any trouble at all.'

This seemed to calm her.

'I was just coming to see you,' she said to me after a few moments.

Amanda smiled as I attempted to swallow the lump in my

throat. I didn't want Caitlin to see her father losing it.

'We'll get you home,' I said. 'Very soon. Very soon indeed.' I squeezed Caitlin's hand and my damaged, delicate daughter grasped mine in return, before closing her eyes and falling back asleep.

After a while Dr Koya came in to examine Caitlin and asked us to return later. Amanda and I left the room and hung around the crappy 'hospitality' area. I leaned against the coffee machine, my face pressed against it.

'What are you trying to do?' Amanda asked. 'Listen to its heartbeat?'

I laughed.

'Wow, look at that,' said Amanda.

'What?'

'That's the first time I've seen you smile since that bloke at La Famiglia forgot to charge us for a second bottle of Chianti,' said Amanda. 'You want anything?'

'Not really,' I said.

'Me neither,' Amanda said, looking at the machine forlornly. 'I'd rather drink piss than something out of here.'

It was the kind of comment that Amanda tossed off not even looking for a laugh. I remembered how much I liked the way that she could deliver lines in this dry, straightforward way. The way she said it, you'd believe that she actually *would* rather drink piss than a cup of coffee from the machine.

'I've a favour to ask,' I said, my cheek still flat against the glowing plastic rectangle. 'And I want you to know that you have a choice.'

'Hmmm ... Don't know if I like the sound of this,' Amanda said. 'Are you sure I don't need one of these crappy coffees to soften whatever it is that you're about to ask me?'

'Would you come to the Social Services interview with me?'

I asked. 'I just need you to pretend that we're together.' In the time between her meeting Joan and the social worker getting the call from her boss that allowed us to see Caitlin, I had delicately explained the agency's scepticism.

'No,' she replied firmly.

My heart sank. It was not what I had expected. Nevertheless, I could understand the way she felt. She had just discovered that her husband of five years had a daughter.

'No, I won't pretend that we're together. I want it for real. I've finished with Nick. I want to be with you again. I want us to be a family.'

I pushed myself off the vending machine wearily, stepped forward and embraced her, feeling her weight against mine.

'Thank you,' I said. 'Thank you, thank you, thank you ...'

We walked outside to the car park. There was a parking ticket on my windscreen. Amanda removed it and ripped it up.

'They can fuck right off,' she said.

I didn't respond. Despite the relief I felt that she was going to help with Caitlin, I needed to know something else. There was still unfinished business.

'What about Nick?' I asked.

'Nick?' She pulled a quizzical face.

'Last night, on the phone,' I said. 'You were talking to Nick.'

'Oh? *Nick*,' said Amanda, making the connection. 'Nicky. Yeah, she's one of the new girls in the office. Started a few weeks ago. Nice kid. We've been going out a bit.'

'Oh,' I said.

'I see,' Amanda said smiling. 'That's why you left without so much as a goodbye.'

She laughed at me and hitched her bag up on her shoulder.

'She's going to be fine,' Amanda said in due course, cupping my face in her hands. 'We'll work that grumpy old Social

Services woman over. It'll be okay. There's just one thing we need to work out.'

'What's that?' I asked.

'Us,' said Amanda, putting a lollipop in her mouth. 'Sorry,' she apologised, pulling it out and waving it in the air. 'Trying to give up smoking.'

'It's about time,' I said.

She nodded.

'And there are plenty of other things that are overdue as well,' I said.

'Like what?' she asked.

'Why don't we have dinner tonight?' I said.

'I'll see if I can fit you in,' she replied, winking at me.

Chapter 33

I sat on a metal chair in Caitlin's room in the ICU, bemused and amazed: it was still mind-blowing that this girl asleep in the bed before me, the one with the IV drip and heart monitor attached to her, was my oh-so-vulnerable flesh and blood.

It hardly seemed possible. What was equally extraordinary was that Amanda and I would find ourselves, after years of failed attempts at pregnancy, in the role of parents. I reasoned that Caitlin's appearance in our lives was exactly the focus that our fractured marriage needed: instead of being remote satellites propelling ourselves randomly through the universe, we would connect by means of a common being around which to orbit. Watching over her that afternoon I was convinced that Caitlin could sustain and mesmerise us in equal measure.

I watched her chest rise and fall; listened to her small, nasal breaths. I could not imagine life without her. (Maybe it was possible, but it would be no life at all.) It was beyond me that I could ever have considered rejecting her in favour of freewheeling bachelordom.

I had no real sense of what her life had been like before we met at the foster home. I'd known Cathy, of course (or thought that I'd known Cathy, at least), but people change when they become parents – they become more concentrated versions of themselves – and I found it impossible to get a fix on their daily lives: the look and smell of their home, the daily routine, the toing and froing of friends. I sensed that it would be chaotic and busy and full.

By comparison my life had been so … what, exactly? Embryonic, maybe? Not fully formed? It had taken Caitlin to make me realise that I was cruising along not noticing very much on my journey. I heard a woman laugh outside the room and the tone of it reminded me of Cathy. I wondered how different things might have been had we stayed together. I couldn't help mourning the years of Caitlin's life that I'd missed. Neither of us would ever know what it's like to be part of a young family. Of course, I'd had other experiences in the meantime, but they added up to something very different, something far less precious.

I thought back to the last time that Cathy and I had slept with each other, during a frigid night on that messy weekend away with Liz and Barney. The entire two days had been a nightmare from beginning to end. That had put me off the countryside for ever, and with good fucking reason.

I wondered what had happened to Liz and Barney. I hadn't seen them since their wedding up in Liverpool. It was a strange quirk of your late thirties that you can stumble across photos of yourself from only a decade earlier and find that you can barely remember the names of half the people you're hugging at your twenty-ninth birthday party. Even the ones you can recall you haven't seen for years. How can you be a part of someone's nuptials, yet drift out of their life so absolutely while your stomach is still full of their wedding cake?

I looked at Caitlin, who continued to sleep. Part of me wanted to wake her. After the urgent hours waiting for my child to regain consciousness I ached for her eyes to remain open. I just wanted for us to be able to look at each other.

A nurse walked into the room. I couldn't figure out her accent – South African, maybe? Who knew? I was so confused that I could barely work the vending machines in the hallway. She asked me something about Caitlin's blood type. I said I didn't know. She told me that she would go and check and returned to the room with a clipboard.

'So she's B,' she said, leafing through a couple of sheets of paper.

'B,' I said to myself. 'Group B ... Okay, thanks. I'll remember that.'

Then it occurred to me that I had absolutely no idea of Cathy's blood group. If I was going to parent Caitlin wasn't this the kind of thing I should know?

'Is there any record of her mum's blood group?'

The nurse turned a couple of pages. 'I'm not sure that we ...' She picked up the clipboard again and flipped through several more sheets of paper.

'Oh, yes, we got it faxed over from her GP, sorry, former GP, and ... she was ... Type A.'

Type A? Now my memory of Mr Higson's biology class was pretty foggy, but this didn't make sense to me.

'So the father would be what group?' I asked.

'Hmm ...' said the nurse thoughtfully. 'He would have to be either B or AB.'

'You're sure about that?' I asked.

'Yes,' she said. 'There are only two groups that he could be in.'

I stood up, accidentally knocking over the chair that I'd been sitting in. Caitlin continued to sleep despite our conversation. Caitlin was blood type B. It was just one letter – a seemingly insignificant detail. But it could not have been more momentous.

'I need to go and take care of something,' I said, pulling on my coat.

'Okay,' said the nurse, bemused as she watched me leave the room and stride down the corridor.

*

I drove straight to my doctor's surgery and camped in the waiting room until I was able to wedge myself into his back-to-back appointment schedule.

'What can I do for you, Alex?' Dr Baker asked. His office was cluttered and disorganised: stacks of paperwork and books teetered precariously on almost every surface. Baker himself was dishevelled and overweight but his manner – authoritative, patrician – made up for his physical appearance.

I was silent for a moment.

'I haven't seen you for a while. How's everything going?' asked Baker. 'If you don't mind me saying, you look a little tired.'

'I need to know my blood type,' I said.

Baker looked surprised. 'Goodness,' he said. 'A man in his late thirties ...'

'*Mid* to late thirties,' I corrected him. It wasn't over yet.

'A man in his mid thirties,' Baker repeated, 'who doesn't know his own blood group ...'

He leaned over, tutting to himself, joking, picked up my medical file and pulled out a clutch of shabby notes.

'I know my blood group,' I said quietly. I was slumped back in my chair, holding both hands awkwardly in my lap. I crossed my legs, agitated. 'I just need you to confirm it, that's all.'

Baker examined his notes, before pulling off his glasses. He inserted one of the plastic arms in his mouth and chewed on it gently.

'Which group do you think you're in?'

'O,' I said firmly.

Baker nodded.

I stood up impulsively and pinched the bridge of my nose with my right hand as if trying to shake a headache.

'Okay,' I said. 'There we have it.'

'You don't seem too happy about this,' Baker said, leaning forward on his desk and resting his chin in his palm.

'So ...' I said, gesturing with my hands in tight, small move-ments. 'If I'm blood type O and I was with a woman who was a type A, what are the chances that we'd have a child with blood group B?'

'Oh,' Dr Baker said. He carefully re-folded the pieces of paper he'd taken out of my file, pressing his index finger along the edges. 'It's like that, is it?'

I nodded and picked my coat off the back of the chair.

'I see,' Dr Baker said. 'I'm sorry about that.'

'Don't be,' I replied.

Caitlin was still asleep when I got back to the hospital. I sat on the edge of the bed and listened to her deep, calm breathing, her body moving yet so still. Arms pressed against her sides as rigidly as a Coldstream Guard, her hair was spread out on the pillow around her head like a spillage of black paint on the white hospital pillowcase. It seemed to me that if I kept looking at her, if I ensured that she was in my line of sight, then nothing bad could happen to her. Asleep there was a softness to her that I rarely noticed when she was animated, when her features appeared more angular and defined. I thought back to the first time we had met, two strangers in a room neither of us wanted to be in, trying to make a connection that neither of us could yet feel, searching for common ground. Caitlin stirred and turned her head to the side so that I was now looking at her in profile and ...

I suddenly knew.

My God, I could see who she looked like ...

The hairline, the curve of the nose, the way her chin had a pronounced angularity ...

Barney.

I stood up, but continued to stare at her, overpowered by my realisation. The blood tests couldn't lie, but having this sudden glimpse of something – or someone – tangible was somehow more powerful than the scientific proof. Electricity was flowing through me. Was I just imagining things? I had, after all, had a fairly intense few days and it was possible that the combination of lack of sleep and stress had driven me to delusion. I looked at Caitlin again, wondering whether I might have made a mistake.

But no, it was unmistakable: I was staring at Barney's *doppelgänger*.

Chapter 34

Caitlin slept and slept. Dr Koya gently told me that this was perfectly normal, nothing to be concerned about. The girl had had a significant shock, and for many people the physiological response to this was slumber.

'We're moving her to a non-critical ward this evening once she wakes up,' Dr Koya said. 'There's no reason to keep her in here.'

'I'm glad to hear that,' I said. 'Thank you so much for everything you've done.'

'Of course,' said the doctor with a courteous smile. 'She's going to be fine. Just tell her to remember her Green Cross Code.'

'I will,' I said, nodding.

Dr Koya left the room and I settled into the chair next to the bed. So Caitlin wasn't my daughter: she was the love child of Cathy and Barney. Not only that, she was conceived when Cathy and I were still together. I was – how I loved the sound if not the implication of this word – a cuckold. I could walk away. A DNA test would absolve me of all legal responsibility. *Nothing to do with me, mate.* I could sell the café and have my old life, such as it was, back tomorrow. There would be no obligations, no complications, no kid. Just me and, it looked likely, Amanda. The two of us back together again.

Just one call to Social Services would do it. *Hello, Joan. It's Alex Taylor. Guess what? There's been a big mix-up and I've just discovered that I'm not actually Caitlin's dad. Sorry for the confusion and do let me know how she gets on in foster care.*

But that wasn't what I wanted. Not any more.

The biological origins of the child, while important to the state, were of no interest to me. Clearly they were of little concern to Cathy either, who could easily have handed Caitlin over to her natural dad.

But she didn't: she handed the most precious thing in her abruptly curtailed life over to me, a man whom she hadn't even seen for close to ten years. I wanted to be worthy of that kind of trust.

As she continued to sleep, I took Caitlin's left hand and examined it. Very faintly, as if she had washed her hands several times but the mark had still to come off, I saw that she had drawn a heart and inside it were three faint letters: 'MUM'.

Unexpectedly I felt the hand pull away. Caitlin was waking up. She stretched her long, willowy body, clasping her hands together and raising them above her head. The stretching went on for a minute until she rolled over onto her side and looked at me.

'Hi,' I said.

'Hi.'

'How you feeling?'

'Fine.'

Fine! Caitlin's default answer for everything from describing her day at school to her physical state after a road accident.

'Good.'

We both listened to a bed being wheeled along the corridor outside. Another life in the balance, the daily routine of the ICU continuing during our small moment of engagement.

'That's strange,' Caitlin said. 'For a moment I thought I was in my room.'

'Really?' I said.

'I suppose it must have been a dream.'

'Maybe,' I said. 'Maybe not.'

303

She smiled, but I could see doubt in her expression.

'I guarantee it.'

She laughed.

'I'm serious,' I said.

Caitlin nodded. 'I believe you,' she said after a while. 'If you can't believe your dad who can you believe?'

I laughed and then noticed that her face had taken on a serious cast.

'Can you pass me my bag please?' she asked.

I leaned over and retrieved it from a chair. Caitlin sat up a little straighter in bed and reached inside. She pulled out a mobile and handed it to me.

'What's this?' I asked.

'It's Amanda's,' Caitlin said.

'Oh,' I replied, a little confused. 'She mentioned that she'd lost it.'

'She didn't lose it,' Caitlin said quietly. 'I took it.'

I looked at her. As relieved as I was to have Caitlin healthy again it was a reminder of the antisocial behaviour that I was going to have to address once she'd fully recovered.

'You're going to need to return it to her,' I said sternly.

Caitlin shook her head. 'I took it for a reason,' she said. 'She thought I couldn't hear her when I was doing my work, but I could.'

I was still confused.

'When I was working with her . . .' she started. 'She was always on the phone to this bloke. You know, Nick.'

'Yeah, I know,' I said.

'She'd go away from her desk and her phone would keep ringing with texts. And I'd look and they were all from Nick.'

I nodded.

'It just made me think,' she said.

The two of us sat in silence for a moment.

'I'm sorry,' she said eventually. 'I thought that I should tell you. I know that you like her still.'

'Thank you,' I told her, patting her on the hand. 'Let's just keep this between us.'

'Okay,' Caitlin agreed. 'What about the phone?'

'Oh, I'll take care of it,' I promised before kissing her and letting her know that I'd be back that evening.

Outside the hospital, I called the offices of Dyer & Liphoff. I asked to speak to Nicky.

'Who?' asked the receptionist.

'Nicky,' I repeated.

'There's no Nicky here.'

'That's strange,' I said, 'I'm sure that I had a woman over to value my place from your office and she was called Nicky.'

'No,' the receptionist insisted. 'We don't have anyone of that name.'

'And no one who used to work there called Nicky?'

'Definitely not,' she said. 'And I should remember, that's my sister's name.'

'So, are you feeling all right?' Amanda asked two days later. We were standing outside the Social Services office next to the town hall, a gloomy box built in a Dijon-mustard shade of brick.

'I'm fighting fit,' I replied.

Amanda crushed her cigarette under her shoe before straightening my tie.

'That was my last cigarette,' she said, adding dramatically, 'ever.'

I nodded.

'You look nice,' she said with a lop-sided smile. She pecked me on the cheek.

'Thanks,' I said.

'Well, I tried to tone it down for that lot in there,' Amanda said. 'Don't want to come across as the slutty mum.'

We walked inside to face Joan Kennedy who, it appeared, had become a very different, more understanding, person since Caitlin's accident. Half an hour later we were outside. Case closed and paperwork signed – I was Caitlin's official legal guardian. No ifs, no buts, no maybes.

Amanda hugged me.

'Thanks for that,' I said.

'Of course,' she replied. 'What now?'

'That's a pretty big question,' I said. I looked away from her.

'What's the matter?' she asked.

I pulled her mobile from my pocket.

'You found it,' she said, taking it from me. And, as that exchange occurred, something else happened between us. She looked at me and I could tell by her face that she knew what I knew.

'That's it then,' she said, after a while. 'I suppose it was inevitable really.'

I nodded.

'It was Caitlin, then,' Amanda said, holding up the phone. She gave a wry chuckle. 'Funny that. I still think she's a great kid, though.'

'I know she is,' I agreed. We stood there, both of us shuffling a little on the gritty surface of the car park.

'Fuck it,' Amanda said, pulling a packet of cigarettes from her bag and lighting one. 'Maybe this isn't the best time to try to give up.'

We walked towards our cars. I watched Amanda get in hers and give me a half-hearted wave before driving off. I looked over towards a playground where a beaming father was pushing his son on a swing. The boy, who was probably five years old, was whooping.

'This is the best day ever!' the boy shouted.

And, perversely, his bright, shiny words suddenly made me feel overwhelmingly sad. Maybe it was the implicit low expectations that the boy appeared to have. Maybe it was the fact that the best day ever should occur so early in his life and that everything else would fail to live up to the day his dad pushed him on the swing. Maybe it was a sense of what I had missed with Caitlin, but I was suddenly overcome by thoughts of the transience of relationships. How those we love inevitably leave us. How life is brief and baffling and we should just take whatever love we can find and cling to it with hard determination because we might never find its like again. How love comes upon us in the most unexpected places and in the strangest ways and often at the worst times. But when it seizes us, my God, its power is transformative, can light up the world, can affect your every waking thought. How just a simple dinner in a garden under the stars with nothing but fish and chips and a few jokes can remain with you for ever if the person sitting opposite you is someone you adore.

I got in the car and headed along the service road away from the town hall. I was going to collect my daughter. Before we got to the turning onto the main road I snatched one last look at the father and son in the rear-view mirror.

Maybe it really was the best day ever.